LUST

A SINFUL EMPIRE TRILOGY (BOOK 2)

EVA CHARLES

QUARRY ROAD PUBLISHING

Copyright © 2022 by Eva Charles

ALL RIGHTS RESERVED

No part of this book may be used or reproduced in any form whatsoever without express written permission from the author or publisher, except in the case of brief quotations embedded in critical articles and reviews.

This book is a work of fiction. Any references to historical events, real people, or real places are used fictitiously. All other names, characters, places, and incidents are products of the author's imagination. Any resemblance to actual events, places, organizations, or persons living or dead is entirely coincidental.

Murphy Rae, Cover Design

Dawn Alexander, Evident Ink, Content Editor

Nancy Smay, Evident Ink, Copy Editor

Faith Williams, The Atwater Group, Proofreader

Virginia Tesi Carey, Proofreader

❀ Created with Vellum

"Of the fruit of the tree which is in the midst of the garden, God has said, 'You shall not eat it, nor shall you touch it, lest you die.'"

— GENESIS 3:3

NOTE TO READERS

Dear Reader,

Welcome back to Porto! I trust you are here because you have read Greed. Lust is the second book in A Sinful Empire Trilogy. It is not a standalone.

If you hate spoilers, skip to the last paragraph.

For those who experience emotional triggers, please know that **this is not a safe story.** In addition to the dark elements one would expect to find in a novel featuring a dangerous anti-hero, please recall that at the end of Greed, Daniela was about to divulge a long-held secret. In Lust, we learn what she's been hiding. As a survivor, I took great pains to tell her story with the utmost care and respect, sweating every small detail, even still, it will be more difficult to read than you imagine. Proceed cautiously, and feel free to contact me with any questions or concerns.

I hope you love Lust, with all its twists and turns. Buckle up and enjoy the ride!

xoxo
Eva

PROLOGUE

Antonio

"Valentina isn't Isabel's daughter."
What the hell?

1
ANTONIO

"What do you mean she's not Isabel's daughter?" I probe cautiously, keeping my voice low and well-modulated so as not to frighten her. But despite my efforts to remain calm, the last fleck of color evaporates from Daniela's cheeks.

"Valentina"—she draws one ragged breath after another, averting my gaze while she chokes out the words—"is my daughter."

Valentina is my daughter.

Jesus Christ.

I study her carefully, trying to wrap my head around what she's telling me. There was always something about her relationship with Isabel that didn't add up. But this? It never crossed my mind. Not once.

Daniela winds her arms around her body, glazed eyes focused on the Persian rug under her feet.

The stillness of the room is ominous. The longer it goes on, the louder and more clawing it becomes, rousing my worst instincts until I spiral into the familiar darkness.

Trust no one.

Question everything.

It's how I survive. *How I've always survived.*

Even if I wanted to, I can't abandon my base instincts for a beautiful face—not even hers.

It's a lie, a voice inside my head cautions. *She's manipulating. She wants to go to the girl. This is nothing more than a clever ploy.* I could ignore the warning, but I won't. "Your daughter? Bullshit."

"It's true," she mouths, barely a whisper.

"Stop lying," I demand, without a shred of civility. She shudders at the harsh, unforgiving tone. *Good.*

"Didn't you learn your lesson the day you ran?" I step closer, looming over her hunched frame. Waiting for her to cower or tremble again—but she doesn't.

"Manipulating won't end well for you this time either. If anything, your punishment will be far worse." She doesn't blink at the threat. "But you don't care. You'll say anything to go to the girl. Or maybe it's Josh you want to see?"

I pause, looking for some reaction. There's none, but I'm not done. "My dick isn't enough? Because you seemed plenty satisfied when I fucked you raw last night."

She lifts her head in a tentative movement. Her brow furrows while she gapes at me, the lines etching deeply. For a long moment, she studies me as though I'm some peculiar creature she's never encountered before. "Isabel's dead. You know how much I loved her. Why are you doing this?"

There's an innocence in her voice, an incredulity that challenges my humanity. My decency. But I don't have an answer for her. Not a single one.

She deserves empathy and compassion. Part of me knows it.

Somewhere inside, I know what she said is true. Somewhere inside, I know my uncle and Tomas are responsible for her pain. *That's why she's afraid of them. My family did this to her.* Somewhere inside, I'm certain she's telling the truth. I taste it in the acid on my tongue. But I refuse to accept it. *I can't.*

Instead, I choose to believe she's a liar, and I'll cling to that belief until she proves otherwise. I didn't get where I am by being some chump who caves at the first sign of tears. And I'm not starting now—not even for her. I don't give a fuck what kind of bastard it makes me.

"Why am I questioning your story? Why don't I take you at your word? Because you've already shown yourself to be a little manipulator. And manipulators use *anything* and *everything* to their advantage. Let me give you a small dose of reality. I don't care how good your pussy feels around my cock. There's plenty of pussy in the world—some of it right here in Porto—more than enough to keep me entertained during our marriage."

She glares at me. I see the pain in her eyes. The grief. But I don't stop.

"Fabricating a story isn't going to get me to change my mind about letting you travel to the US. I'm not a fool." The words are sharp and the delivery searing, but she doesn't show any sign of backing down.

"It's the truth. I swear on my mother's soul."

She's as earnest as I've ever seen her. But it's impossible. *She's just shy of twenty-five, and from what we know, Valentina's twelve.* That would have made Daniela—too damn young. Plus, we would have known if the kid was hers. We might be wrong about Valentina's age, but how far off can we be?

Seven people are dead and a piece of iconic history destroyed. While I'm skeptical, this bombshell requires a ruthless pursuit of the truth—wherever it leads. If she's lying, she'll never lay eyes on that kid again. I'll keep them separated forever, regardless of the cost. That'll be her punishment. It's harsh, but she'll have earned it.

Daniela's eyes are trained on the rug, again. She can't even look at me. *Because she's guilty as fuck.*

I lift her chin, forcing her to look me in the eye. "How old is Valentina?"

2

ANTONIO

"Twelve." She doesn't blink, and she doesn't hesitate or stammer. There's not a hitch in her voice, or anything else to suggest she's lying.

"Twelve," I mutter aloud, my gut gnawing like a sonofabitch. That would have made Daniela twelve when—

"She's just a few months younger than I was when she was born."

Her features soften, but the anguish lingers in her eyes. Her pain hits me hard, and I release my hold on her, so that I don't do something stupid like pull her against my chest.

I remember her as a young girl atop a feisty horse, brave and spirited, eyes sparkling with light. No sorrow anywhere to be found. She was so young. So innocent.

The bile tickles my throat as the pieces form a vile picture. Abel and Tomas are up to their eyeballs in this. *I'm sure of it.*

That's not the only possibility, Antonio. Don't let a sentimental moment from more than a decade ago cloud your thinking. She's neither young nor innocent.

While she certainly didn't kill Isabel, Daniela would do

anything for the girl. If she can convince me Valentina's her daughter, I might let the kid come live with us. This could be another lie. Just a few weeks ago, she took a huge risk to get to the US. She's capable of anything in that regard.

"We need to talk, *Princesa*." I take her elbow and lead her to the edge of the bed. She sits, while I stand, positioning myself to assess her veracity as she speaks, like she's a criminal I'm waiting to trap. *It's monstrous under these circumstances, but I can't afford to be taken in by her again.*

Besides, even if this new admission is true, she lied to me about Valentina. Even after several warnings and punishment that left her skin welted, she lied. She had plenty of opportunity to come clean, but she never did.

"You're a liar," I growl. "And you're not going anywhere until I know the truth—every disgusting detail."

A muffled cry twists from her lips. It lands squarely in my chest. But despite my warring emotions, I'm not prepared to grant clemency at this point. Although, the longer I watch her, the softer I'm becoming. She's mired in grief and uncertainty, with a fragileness about her I haven't seen since the funeral home after her father died.

I step back to put her at arms' length and bolster my resolve.

The bed is high, and Daniela's feet dangle well above the floor. Pale, and naked, except for a wrinkled sheet wrapped around her, she eyes me like a broken bird waiting to be eaten alive.

This is how I prefer to run interrogations. Where there's no doubt about who holds the power.

Normally I strip away every creature comfort, leaving a prisoner better incentivized to speak truthfully. *But Daniela's not a prisoner. She's my wife.* In the end, I don't have the stomach to question her while she's so vulnerable.

I glance at my T-shirt on the floor. It's exactly where I dropped it last night before dragging her to bed, and burying a myriad of tortured feelings inside her, along with my dick. *She welcomed you. She embraced your pain. Offered her body as a vessel for your anguish, right on this very bed. For that alone, you owe her some decency.*

I snatch the shirt from the rug. "Put this on."

She takes it from me without balking and slips her arms through the soft cotton. It's a simple act, not meant to provoke, but even under these conditions, everything about her is arousing. My cock twitches when she raises her arms above her head, fully exposing her breasts. All I can think about is how she looked last night as her pussy squeezed my throbbing shaft, until I gave it up for her.

The room still reeks of sex. The kind of sex that sends seasoned men to their graves with a smile. She has little experience, but the passion burns hot inside her. And nothing, *nothing* has ever given me more pleasure than coaxing that passion from her, teasing her until she begs shamelessly, whimpering my name into the thick air. I could spend a lifetime worshipping her luscious body. *And up until a few moments ago, I thought I would.*

Stop, Antonio. Stop. You have responsibilities that are bigger than yourself. Bigger than her. If I say it enough, maybe it'll knock some sense into me, because right now I'm having trouble focusing on what's important—on what's expected of me as a leader. I need to stay strong. Tough. It's the only road to the truth.

Daniela fidgets with the T-shirt hem, her nipples beaded and her limbs covered in gooseflesh. It takes everything I have not to use my mouth and hands to warm her supple skin. But I don't bow to those desires. Instead, I quietly offer her a velvet throw from the foot of the bed.

The color is still absent from her cheeks, as she arranges

the cover over her bare legs. When she's finished, she gazes up at me through the thick, inky lashes that fluttered against my skin as we fell asleep last night. I quickly shove away the memory before it weakens my resolve.

"I want every detail. Leave nothing out if you hope to ever see Valentina again."

3

DANIELA

Isabel's dead—Valentina's alone—She could be next—I'm an ocean away—What if I can't get to her in time—What if I can't get there at all—Isabel's dead—Valentina's alone—They're coming for her—I can't save her—Isabel's dead—

It's too much!

Too much.

The paralyzing thoughts chase each other, screeching louder and louder, tripping over one another as they drag me around the track.

I can't take the noise for another second. I press the heels of my hands into my temples to lessen the roar.

My brain is about to explode. No matter how hard I try, it's impossible to concentrate on any one thing for more than a fleeting moment. *You must.* I know. *But how? How?*

Desperate to make the crazy stop, I slide my fingers through my hair, tugging until I feel the burn on my scalp. I learned many years ago that pain—physical pain—can be a warm embrace, calming and soothing when all else fails.

I pull and pull until there is only the throb of pain. *It hurts so good.* Who sings that? *Focus, Daniela, focus.*

My screaming scalp grounds me enough to slow the racing thoughts so that I can catch a few.

"I want every detail. Leave nothing out if you hope to ever see Valentina again."

I'm not sure I can, Antonio. I'm not sure I have the words—or the courage to go back there. It was awful. But the worst of it wasn't what they did to me, but what they did to my mother. They forced her to watch as they violated me. I shudder. That must have been worse than death itself. I'd rather die a thousand painful deaths than to be there, helpless, as monsters raped Valentina.

I glance at him. His body is tight. Angry. Mean. The hostility vibrates off him in giant waves that echo in the vast silence. It's terrifying. And I am deathly afraid. Not for myself. But for Valentina.

When he learns the truth, will he order his men to kill her? She poses a threat to him—to the power he's amassed in the region. It's a challenge I can't wave away. I can't do a damn thing about it.

A numbing cold engulfs me, filtering through my porous flesh and finding a home in my soul. I don't take a single life-saving breath before retreating inside myself, where I'm small and invisible. Where nothing can touch me. There's a high cost to this type of security, but I don't fight it. I let it happen. *I pray for it.* Soon I'll be safe, watching my life unfold around me.

You're almost there. Almost.

It's been so long since I've been here. I'd forgotten how slow everything moves. How dreamlike it feels to float.

You need to snap out of it! Right now, Daniela, before you can't!

I don't want to, Mamai. There's nothing I can do. It's better this way.

Better for who? Valentina needs you!

Valentina needs me. Valentina needs me. Valentina needs me.

The words are more than a mantra. They're a spark of electricity that races through me. I shiver as the jolt surges, shoving me out of the cocoon where I desperately want to hide forever.

You're not twelve. The Huntsmans can't hurt you. But they can hurt Valentina.

I won't allow it. Not while I have a single breath left in me. They will not harm her.

I gaze at the man who stands between me and my daughter. He wants the truth. *Every detail.* Like it's so easy.

I don't know even know where to begin. I've relived the events of that day, but only in my head. And I haven't allowed myself to dwell on most of it for over a decade. I've never shared *every* detail with anyone. *No one.*

Yes, I talked with Isabel after it happened, but I couldn't remember everything at first, and later, as it started to come back in fits and spurts, she urged me to put it out of my head. She helped me cope in the best way she knew. I'm sure it's how she dealt with the assaults from her past too. "*When a memory from that day intrudes, don't let it stay. Push it away immediately. Focus on something else. Ride your horse, think of beautiful things, anything that fills your heart with joy. Don't ruminate about what happened because it will slowly kill you if you do.*"

For a long time, I took her advice literally, and because I didn't want to die, I never allowed myself to think about it—not too much, anyway. As I got older, I knew that dying inside was a figure of speech, but still, a small part of me is always afraid to tempt fate.

My father and I never spoke of the details. When we discussed it at all, we talked around *the tragedy*, as he called it. He would have preferred never to speak of it, but my pregnancy made that a challenge.

Antonio isn't like them. He doesn't want me to think of rainbows and unicorns to forget what happened. He wants me to remember *everything*. He's not the type of man who shies away from *tragedy,* skirting the edges politely. He marches straight into the center, eyes open, and grabs it by the throat until he learns every detail. Every *disgusting* detail. Those were his words.

There's nothing to do but to tell him. At least I don't see another way around it. Not if I want to see Valentina. *Maybe it's time, anyway—to tell someone.*

A twelve-year-old girl held down and brutally raped. *Brutally raped. Is there any other kind?*

I ward off the swell of emotion and gather my courage.

"Daniela," he calls impatiently.

"Give me a moment, please. This isn't easy."

"I'll give you a moment. But time isn't going to make it any easier."

It did. Time eased some of it. It blurred the sharpest edges, making it easier for the pain to live inside me without slicing too deep a gash. There have been nicks and scrapes over the years, but I managed never to bleed out. *I'm a survivor.*

Now, this man, *my husband*, who has turned on me as though he's the one who was stripped naked and held down while savages violated him, expects me to bare my soul. To use words to express an evil that can't be described—only experienced. Words will never do it justice.

I curl my toes around the bedframe, reaching for the carved wooden post for support.

You can do this. You can do this. For Valentina, you can do it. The voice inside my head is my mother's, woven through mine. Propping me up. Making my own voice stronger. Infusing me with strength. With her last breath, *Mamai* didn't beg for mercy for herself. She pleaded for my life. Compared to what she endured that day—what I endured—this is nothing.

They can't hurt you. Oh, but they can.

I gaze up at Antonio. He doesn't seem as volatile now. After drawing a large breath, I make the decision to trust him—with all of it. He might prove himself unworthy of that trust, but I'm out of options, and something inside whispers that it's safe to trust him—or maybe that's just the sound of surrender.

"My mother and I were picnicking in the meadow beside our house. Just outside the gates."

His body is rigid, as though he's bracing for what's to come.

"Abel Huntsman," I continue in a hollow voice, devoid of emotion. It's almost as though I've retreated inside myself, but I haven't. I give my toes a little squeeze around the sideboard, just to be sure. *I'm here.* "Tomas. And your father," I add in a whisper.

"No!" he hisses. "No!" His voice booms, as he says it again, and again.

"No!

"No!

"No!"

The word bounces off the ornate plaster walls. Heavy and tormented. The mournful sound of a dying beast. It's as though I stuck a knife into his chest and twisted, delivering a deadly blow.

Startled by his reaction, I clench the bedpost tighter.

I expected something from him, although I'm not sure exactly what—but it wasn't this.

Antonio jerks to the edge of the room, clutching the back of his neck with both hands, gasping for a breath that seems to evade him.

I've just started. I haven't even gotten to the worst part of the story, yet. *But he's guessed what's coming.*

4

DANIELA

As the seconds tick on, I'm so focused on Antonio's reaction that my own fears bleed into the background. He doesn't look at me. Not even a glance in my direction. *He can't.* It was my father's reaction when he learned what happened, too.

Empathy is what one might expect in this situation, but in my father's world, Antonio's world, where everything is a commodity, empathy is in short supply. A man believes he has a pretty little jewel to admire, to pet, to barter with, unblemished and pure. Then he learns she's been soiled in the most revolting way. *Damaged. Worthless.* But still, he's stuck with her. It can cut a man to the quick—especially a powerful man.

My first instinct is to make Antonio feel better. To think about how I might cajole myself back into his good graces, like I did with my father. A few charming words and a shy smile to win back his love and affection. But I groveled once, and I don't have the energy or the desire to do it for Antonio—unlike my father, Antonio never loved me.

I dig my heels into the bedframe and lift my chin. "I realize this is unsettling, and not at all what you expected when you agreed to marry me, but none of it was my doing. Or Valentina's. I expect you to ensure her safety until I get to the US." I don't hedge or act as though he might not allow me to go, even though it's a real concern. And I don't fucking apologize.

"I need to know what happened," he says quietly, from the window, a safe distance away.

"I'll answer all your questions. But first, I need to know where Valentina is and who's with her. She's too young to be left alone—especially under these circumstances. I want to talk to her." I pause to push away the memories—the horror—of me alone in the meadow with my mother after they killed her and left us. *Oh God.* The panic begins to rise, again. "Is Valentina at the apartment with Isabel?"

He shakes his head. "She's still at the school event."

Thank God. I don't want her to see Isabel—not like that. "I want your word she'll be safe."

"She's safe. There are guards stationed outside the school building. We have a few hours before the students are released. It's enough time to come up with a solid plan."

She's safe and guarded. Then why is my heart still hammering? The ups and downs make me feel like I'm in an aged theme park on a never-ending roller coaster with rickety tracks.

Although, right now, the ground seems less shaky, and I'm starting to feel less numb. Having a conversation with him about Valentina's safety gives me purpose, and it makes me feel less alone.

"I need to go to the US. Now." My voice is low, but firm. "You can come with me, or send me alone, but I need to go, and it can't wait." Despite my confidence, there's no telling what he'll decide. I doubt I'm going anywhere just yet. At least not until I've laid out every *disgusting* detail.

Antonio swivels and stalks toward the bed, stopping a few feet away. "You're not leaving here until I know more." He might be battered around the edges, but he's fully in charge again. His tone makes it clear he's not negotiating this point. "This could be a setup. Some kind of ruse to lure you out into the open. Someone tried to kill you yesterday."

Someone tried to kill you yesterday. My stomach knots. It's not exactly a surprise, but I'm still struggling to come to terms with it. It's especially troubling now that Isabel is dead, and if I die, Valentina will be left alone, or worse—given to her father.

"I need more information to assess and manage the risk," he continues. "It's a dangerous situation for all of us, but especially for you."

You have that wrong—Valentina is in a far more perilous situation.

There's no pity in his gaze—at least not more than a brief flash. Although there's sorrow behind those chiseled features, and real concern. I hang on to the rare glimpse of humanity, not saying a word that might cause it to evaporate.

"If you expect to get on a plane anytime soon, I need more." His voice is challenging now, and whatever compassion was there has vanished. The cool, calculating businessman is back. He holds all the cards. We both know it.

My stomach begins to protest, raising anger and resentment as it roils.

You want to know what happened? You really want to know? Because from your reaction a few minutes ago, I'm not sure you can handle the truth—but you're about to get it.

I glare at him with a fury that propels the words from the depths of my soul, where I've squirreled it all away. *The horror. The shame. The terror. The pain.*

"Your father raped my mother while your uncle forced me to watch, and when he was finished with her, he tried to rape me, but he couldn't—*perform*." My insides tremble as I spit out the bitter words—words that I can never take back. My relationship with Antonio never had a chance. Whether we'll remain married is another matter. One I can't worry about, because my daughter needs me.

The numbness is back. But it's okay, because I need it right now. It's the only thing standing between me and a complete meltdown.

"Your father hovered over me with his spent cock, slapping me in the face, and demanding that I scream and fight him. I didn't understand at the time, but I'm sure he thought my struggle would arouse him. But I didn't fight or scream. I didn't utter a word. I was in shock, and my brain took me somewhere safe to protect me."

Antonio hisses, and even from several feet away, I feel his rage. But I can't see it—not really, because the more I talk, the fuzzier he becomes.

"When Hugo moved off me, Abel started to take his place. There were some angry words between them, then your father shoved him away, and made Tomas get on top of me. Your father knelt behind me and pinned my shoulders to the ground. 'Use her well,' he sneered. 'Be as rough as you can with the little virgin so that she never forgets her place. Don't hold back, boy.'"

I don't look at Antonio, not because I'm ashamed, but because the story, with all its ugly details, has taken on a life of its own. It wants out. Even if he begged me to stop talking, I couldn't. I don't weigh the words or form the sounds. I'm just a conduit.

"My mother begged for my safety. For my life. Quiet tears slid down her cheeks while they made her watch my torture. I kept my eyes latched to hers while Tomas violated me—until your father held my head firm and forced me to look at Tomas's red face. He was sweating like a pig. He grunted when he finished and collapsed on top of me until they pulled him off to admire the spoils.

"After they cheered the blood on my thighs, your father

went to my mother and held her up by the hair. He called her a whore and said this was her punishment for sticking her nose in his business. Then he slit her throat with a long blade while I watched."

I gasp as the memory rushes back. For a moment, the world fades away, and I'm back in the meadow, surrounded by freshly mowed grass and honeysuckle, the sweet scent a staggering contrast to Hugo Huntsman's viciousness.

"'Tell your father how I took everything he holds dear, soiled everything he loves most,' Hugo taunted. 'Tell him that the last thing his precious Rosa saw before she took her last breath was my dick.'

"Then they left through the woods without another word."

A salty droplet lands on my lips while I finish the story. I bring my fingers to my face. It's wet. *Tears.* But I don't know where they came from. I don't remember crying. Even as I wonder about the tears, the words continue to fall from my mouth. There's no holding them back now.

"When I was sure they were gone, I went to my mother. Her eyes were open, but she was limp. The gash in her neck was so deep, her head was partially severed. There was so much blood. *So much blood.* I used the picnic blanket to cover her, because she would be embarrassed to be naked in the meadow. Then I crawled under the blanket and curled my body around hers, and slept until Isabel found us. It was months later when we learned I was pregnant."

I pull in jagged breath after jagged breath, blinking a few times. For a few seconds, I can't remember where I am.

Antonio is on his haunches, in front of me, massaging my fingers with his. *How long has he been here, like this? I don't know.*

His hands are warm, but his eyes are icy, and the energy surrounding him is thrumming—a drumbeat signaling war.

"That's everything. Pretty much. I'll clarify whatever you

want, but it's getting late. I need to go to Valentina. I've already wasted too much time."

He uses his thumbs to wipe the tears from my face. "Who else knows about this?" The lines in his forehead are etched deep, and his voice is low.

"Isabel and my father. Jorge knew bits and pieces. I don't know who the Huntsmans told."

He winces at *Huntsmans*. "Does Tomas know about Valentina?"

My stomach does a somersault, like I'm back on the roller coaster. "You won't give her to him, will you?"

"Don't be ridiculous. But I need to know if he's aware he has a daughter. The information will help ensure her long-term safety."

I nod and take a breath. "I don't think so. But I can't be sure. He asked about Isabel and Valentina at the funeral home when my father died, and then again at the Camelia Ball. But mostly I felt like he was fishing for information."

He wets his lips and nods. "It'll take some time to assemble the crew and get the plane ready. Why don't you get dressed and put a bag together for the flight."

He's letting me go to Valentina. *He's letting me go.*

"Or better yet," he adds, "lie down for a little while. I'll wake you with plenty of time if you fall asleep." He smooths my hair and stands.

"How long before I can leave?" I still can't believe I'm going.

"I'll know more after I make some calls," he says, striding toward the door, his gait uncharacteristically halting. Antonio Huntsman isn't a tentative man. Not his words, or his actions. What if he's giving a second thought to turning her over? Or using her as a pawn in some power play?

"Antonio."

He stops and turns to face me.

"I need your word that she'll be safe."

"Lucas and Cristiano are on it. There's no one better. Nothing's going to happen to her. You have my word."

If I know anything about him, it's that his word is gold. He doesn't ever feel compelled to promise anything, but when he has in the past, he's never gone back on it. Not with me—at least not yet.

"Let me make the arrangements so we can leave."

We? I assumed he'd send me with guards, and maybe Cristiano. I never expected he'd make the trip with me. "You're coming?"

"Of course I'm coming. I'm your husband. Nothing's changed."

I don't challenge him, but I don't believe nothing's changed. He doesn't believe it, either.

5

ANTONIO

Your father. Your father. Your father. The words are still echoing inside my throbbing head. I don't know if they'll ever stop.

Abel and Tomas I was prepared for, but my father? *Sonofabitch.* Even from the fires of hell, his reign of terror continues.

"Your father is somewhere right now, delighted to see her at your side. I can almost see his big grin. God bless his soul." That's what Tomas said to me the night of the Camelia Ball. *I'm going to murder that fucking monster.* It's going to be long and agonizing, and I'm going to enjoy every damn second.

My father.

I can barely breathe. She was an innocent little girl, caught in a power struggle between adults. My father used her to exact vengeance.

The list of people I'd like to raise from the dead and murder is growing. Why the fuck didn't Manuel D'Sousa tell me? Why?

Because he didn't think you'd have the balls to go anywhere near Daniela after your father had been so close.

He was right. Had I known it, I wouldn't have agreed to marry her. Not because she was raped, but because *my* father, *my* family was responsible. And Valentina? She's just a reminder of what they did to Daniela. I owed D'Sousa, and I wanted those vineyards, but I wouldn't have been willing to put either Daniela or myself through the kind of hell that our future together holds. *That's bullshit.* I would have done whatever he asked, consequences be damned.

When I leave the bedroom, I keep the door ajar. She probably shouldn't be alone right now, but I need to think clearly and I can't do it near her. When I look at her, all I see is the young girl atop her stallion. Courageous and in charge, glittering eyes full of life. They tried to take it all away—and in some ways, they succeeded.

I stop to pour a whiskey on the way to my study. One drink. That's it, until Valentina is safely back with her mother.

I sit behind my desk and call the villa where Cristiano and Lucas are gathering intel and putting out fires.

"Any news on the girl?"

"She's still at school," Lucas replies. "We have eyes surrounding the place, and one of our own inside."

Lucas and Cristiano are well compensated, but at times like these, it never seems like they're paid enough.

"Have you told Daniela about Isabel?" Cristiano asks.

"Yeah."

"How is she?"

For a moment, I hesitate. It's hard to know. I forced her to dredge up memories that were nowhere near the surface. At least they didn't seem to be. "Honestly, I'm not sure."

But I can't leave it at that, as much as I'd prefer to. I suck some air into my lungs and blow it out. It's not my story to tell, but there's no way around it. Cristiano and Lucas need to know. We can't plan appropriately if they're in the dark.

"The girl—Valentina—isn't Isabel's child." There's dead silence on the other end of the line. "She's Daniela's daughter. Hugo raped and murdered Maria Rosa. Tomas raped

Daniela." I can barely choke out the words. "Abel was a cheerleader."

A vein in my neck throbs relentlessly. If I don't stroke out before the day is over, it'll be a fucking miracle.

"Sonsofbitches," Cristiano hisses through gritted teeth. "Let me pick up Tomas."

"I'll deal with Tomas. But not yet. This fucking mess might be in our house, but we operate the same as always. Everything's well-thought-out and calculated. We stay under the radar until we know exactly what we're dealing with. The explosion at Santa Ana's and Isabel's murder are related—likely ordered by the same person.

"Tomas is involved," I continue. "But I'm not convinced he's pulling the strings. He doesn't have the aptitude or the guts for it. I want this over for Daniela. But it doesn't end until we take down the man issuing orders. We still don't know who that is. The second, the *very* second we have the answers we need, Tomas is mine."

"Given the gravity of this news, you sound awfully calm," Cristiano observes, carefully. "You okay?"

Okay? No, I'm not fucking *okay*. I'm so pissed off I could roam the streets for a month strangling assholes with my bare hands, and it still wouldn't take the edge off.

"I can't afford to indulge my rage right now. But when we have what we need, I'll burn down the entire region, if necessary, to destroy anyone and everyone who played a role."

"Sign me up," Cristiano mutters.

"What about the girl?" Lucas is ruthlessly practical, never venturing too far from the job at hand. He holds every thread in an organized fashion that allows the rest of us to breathe periodically. "That dance-a-thon is going to end soon, and they're going to feed those kids breakfast and let them loose."

"Our first order of business is to get the girl out of the US safely. I promised Daniela, and I intend on keeping that promise. She's eager to go to the US and get Valentina herself, but I'd like to avoid that. This could be a trap. No one knows that I made the arrangement with her father. And even if they did, that arrangement is gospel in our world, but I'd rather not take my chances before some judge in Lisbon—or worse, in the US—who we can't control. If Daniela dies, a court could decide Valentina is the rightful heir to the vineyards."

"And her father would get custody of her and take control."

Over my dead body. That will *never* happen, but it's a fight I'd prefer to avoid.

"Anyone who's willing to murder is willing to kidnap." To a casual observer, it would seem that Lucas is just stating the obvious, but I know better. He's laying out the consequences so that they're fresh on my mind as I make decisions. "They're going to try to grab that kid."

"We should expect it."

"Getting an uncooperative kid out of the US on such short notice is going to be a challenge," Lucas mutters. "I assume we're not going to drug her to smuggle her out without a scene."

"Don't assume anything. But before we go down that road, let me make a call. In the meantime, contact Luis to get the plane ready—tell him to file a flight plan to London. We'll change it at the last minute so we don't tip off anyone. And book a charter flight under a dummy corporation to carry an advance team. I'm going to reach out to a contact in the US, and I'll get back to you within fifteen minutes with more particulars."

I disconnect the call and place another.

6

ANTONIO

"What the hell do you want at this hour?" Gray Wilder deadpans from across the Atlantic. "You're lucky I run a club and I'm still awake."

I swallow my pride and do something I hate. "I need your help."

He's quiet for a moment. "Must be a big problem for you to be asking for help. I know how much it pains you to admit you're human."

He's not wrong. "Can you put me in touch with your brother's buddy, Smith Sinclair?"

It's not that I don't know how to reach Sinclair, but he doesn't really know me, and I'm going to ask him to move a kid across international borders. He's more likely to be amenable if Gray makes the initial call.

"That depends," Gray drawls. "What do you need?"

The silence looms between us. It doesn't feel suspicious, but he wants me to come clean. Bare my soul. Something else he knows I hate.

"It's probably better if you don't get involved in the particulars."

"Already involved. If you don't tell me what's going on, I'm not lifting a finger to connect you to Smith."

"It's a long story."

"We just closed up shop and I'm pretty wired. Got some time on my hands."

Fucker. "Don't say I didn't warn you."

"I'm all ears."

It takes me a minute to pull together a few sentences that don't divulge too much of Daniela's story but are enough to satisfy Gray.

"My wife left a twelve-year-old daughter in the US when she returned to Porto. The child's guardian died a few hours ago, and we need to get the girl out of the US quickly. We're concerned about her being abducted."

"I still can't believe you're fucking married," Gray mutters. "By 'her guardian died'—you mean she was murdered."

"That's what I mean."

"What aren't you telling me?"

There's a long list. While I don't want Gray in the middle of this, even more, I don't want to expose Daniela. She kept this secret for more than twelve years, and it seems *wrong*—just plain wrong—for me to share it unless there's no choice. *I'm not at that point yet.* "There are complicated custody issues."

"Complicated custody issues. I don't like where this is going."

"I need the kid back here where I can protect her."

"And you want, what? Smith to smuggle a twelve-year-old out of the country?"

I'm losing my patience quickly, but I rein it in. Sinclair is our best hope to get Valentina back without compromising Daniela's safety, and Gray has appointed himself the gatekeeper. "She's in the US alone. What part of 'someone might abduct her' don't you understand?"

"That's all fine and dandy, but you expect me to traffic a child?"

"I don't expect you to do anything. I'm hoping to hire Sinclair."

"I trust you, man. But you've said it yourself: your world is different than mine. I need some assurances that we're reuniting a mother and child. I want to talk to Daniela. I need to hear it from her mouth."

This is not going as expected. If anything, I thought the issues would arise with Sinclair.

Gray isn't the bastard I am, but he won't handle Daniela with kid gloves either—not with so much at stake. Not unless he has a heads-up.

"She's been through a lot—especially in the last twenty-four hours. She was very close to the woman who was killed. And if you consult Google, you'll find that a room in the church, the room where Daniela was supposed to be waiting, exploded right before we took our vows. There were no survivors. I'm trying to save her from any more heartache."

"Jesus."

He doesn't say anything else for a moment, but I'm already on my way to find Daniela, because I doubt he'll change his mind about speaking to her. I would want the same assurances if I were him. But at least he's aware of her state of mind.

"I get it," he says, finally, with some conviction, "but I'm not lifting a finger to help without more information—from her."

"Hold on a second. I'm on my way to give her the phone." As I go to the bedroom, I pass the table where I took her hard last night. *I've made her whole damn life hard.* "Go easy, Gray. She just finished with one asshole demanding answers."

"Put it on video. I want to see for myself that this isn't a hostage situation."

"Your confidence in me is heartwarming."

"I've been burned before."
"Never by me."
"I'll give you that."

7

ANTONIO

When I get to the bedroom, Daniela's dressed in leggings and a tunic that falls mid-thigh. With her hair braided, she looks like a teenager.

"Any news on Valentina?" she asks, eyes wide and wary.

I shake my head. "I have a friend in the US on the phone. He might be able to help us get Valentina back safely. He'd like to talk to you."

She nods.

"I trust him. You can trust him too." I switch to a video call and hand the phone to Daniela.

"Hi," she says softly.

"This is Gray Wilder. Who am I speaking with?"

"Daniela D'Sousa. Huntsman," she adds quickly.

Daniela D'Sousa Huntsman. I wonder if she threw up a little in her mouth when she gave him her name. The same name my father, Abel, and Tomas share.

"Daniela, I have a friend with me who is a former federal agent. She works for a private security firm now, and happens to be highly experienced in human extractions. If what

Antonio told me checks out, today's your lucky day. But first I have some questions."

Questions. I'll end it at the first sign of her distress.

"Hey Daniela," a woman's voice calls from off screen. "I'm Delilah Porter. What Gray means by human extractions is that I rescue people who are in trouble. Tell me what you need from us."

Daniela's head bobs up and down, as she wets her lips.

"My daughter—Valentina—is in a small city in the US. Fall River, Massachusetts. She's been with my friend Isabel, who was killed earlier. Valentina is at school, participating in a lockdown charity event. She doesn't know about Isabel."

Her voice is starting to wobble a bit, but she's doing fine. I've known powerful men who have shown less strength and dignity under these circumstances.

"Give me the phone," Delilah tells Gray. "That's better."

The blonde on the screen looks more like a Southern belle than a federal agent, but I trust Gray's judgment. He likes to come off like a dumb pretty boy, but he's a shrewd businessman who knows how to get shit done.

"Okay," Delilah murmurs. "Where were we? How old is Valentina?"

"She's twelve."

"Does she have a passport?"

"Yes. All her documents are at the apartment in the bottom drawer of the desk in the living room. The key is normally in a jewelry box on a tall chest in my room. It's the room with twin beds. But I don't know if Isabel moved it while I've been away," Daniela adds, cupping her hand in a tight fist.

"If it's anywhere in the house, we'll find it," Delilah assures her. "We can also break into the desk, if we need to. It's a small thing."

Daniela's body visibly relaxes. "Inside that desk drawer,

there's also a notarized document giving me custody of Valentina if something should happen to Isabel."

"Giving you custody?" Gray asks, the apprehension wound tight in his voice. "I thought she was your daughter?"

"Let me explain." I reach for the phone because I'm not going to let him put her through this, but Daniela shakes her head, and pushes my hand away.

"Valentina is my daughter," she responds candidly before I can intervene.

"You don't need to do this," I murmur. "We can find another way."

She ignores me, and I allow it. Because even as I said it, I knew it was wishful thinking. Sure, we could find another way, but this is still our best chance to get the kid without adding to the trauma, and without endangering Daniela.

"I—I was very young when she was born. Isabel worked for us, and really, she was one of the family. She and her husband raised Valentina, but I've always been a big part of their lives—of my daughter's life. Please don't let anything happen to her. For the last twelve years, she's been my entire reason for being. I don't think I could go on if I lost her too."

She chokes back a sob, and I lay my hand on her shoulder for support.

It's very quiet on the other end, and Gray has moved behind Delilah.

"Who's Valentina's father?"

Fucking Gray. But we've come this far, I can't end it now.

"Tomas Huntsman," Daniela replies, just above a whisper.

It lands like a spear in my chest.

"Antonio's cousin?" Gray's voice is gentle, without a hint of judgment.

"Yes. I don't think he knows about Valentina. And Valentina only knows Isabel and Jorge as her parents. She would be shocked to hear differently."

"Where is Jorge?" my friend asks, eyes fixed on the screen.

"Dead. It happened several months ago," I add. Gray shoots me daggers. Complicated custody arrangements, and now another dead body—I'm quite certain he wants to kill me about now.

"Don't you worry," Delilah coos into the phone. "We're going to bring Valentina back to you, and no one is telling her anything."

Gray moves out of the picture, but not before his fiancée throws him a look over her shoulder.

"Thank you," Daniela gushes, her voice filled with emotion.

"You don't need to thank me. Compared to some of the extractions I've done, this is a walk in the park. Send us the apartment address, and a list of anything you want us to pack. Valentina's at school?"

"Yes. Until eight o'clock."

"Send us the name and address of the school too. Also, call them and have them hold Valentina until I get there. Give them permission to release her to me."

"You'll go, yourself?" Daniela asks, her voice wobbling again. "Will you stay with her until I get there?"

"Daniela," Delilah purrs. "I promise you that I'll be the one who goes to pick her up. Tell the school her mama had an accident, you're out of the country, and you're sending friends for Valentina. I'll take Gray with me. His daddy was kind of a big deal and people tend to do whatever he asks."

"Except for you," Gray mutters in the background.

"We have you covered," Delilah continues, ignoring him. "We'll be in touch every step of the way. No one, I mean *no one*, is going to harm a hair on your baby's head. That's a promise."

She's so adamant, I almost believe it myself.

"When you see Valentina," Daniela explains, "say something—it can be anything—about brown M&Ms, and she'll know it's safe to go with you. It's our emergency code."

An emergency code. My *Princesa* is full of surprises. I have an emergency code too, as do my top men, in case we're ever in a hostage situation.

"Brown M&Ms it is." Delilah nods. "Now let's get off, so we can make the necessary travel arrangements. We'll pick a rendezvous point, and we'll be in touch. Work it out with the school, and then take a big breath and try to relax. She'll be in your arms before you know it."

"Antonio," Gray drawls. "I'd like a private word with you once the ladies are done."

Sure you would. More like you want to shove your boot up my ass.

"We're done," Delilah chirps, passing him the phone. "But don't spend all day gossiping, darlin'. We've got work to do."

8

ANTONIO

"Are we off speaker?" Gray asks.

"Yeah."

"Before I send my fiancée into a shitstorm, I'd like to know who you think might be killing people."

"Is she up for this?" I ask, gauging his reaction.

"Delilah? Is she up for it? *Pfft.* She's up to kicking your ass all over town without breaking a sweat. Don't let the angelic face and sexy drawl fool you. She was a deadly covert agent for the CIA, and now she's the shining star of Sinclair's team. So yeah, she's up for it. That's not a concern. What I'm worried about is that there's no time to gather our own intel, because the rescue can't wait. I'm relying on you to give us everything you have. Even if it's a hunch. I don't want to be blindsided."

"I'll tell you what I know. It's not much, but my best people are on it, and we'll pass information along in real time. If Tomas knows about Valentina, he'll do anything to get his clutches into her. But as Daniela told you, it's unclear whether he knows she's his child. And even if he does, he's barely capable of tying his shoelaces without help."

"But you think he has help."

"There's valuable property at stake—with the potential for a foreign entity to gain a foothold in the region. I'm concerned about the Eastern Europeans. Mainly the Russians, who've been dying to expand their operations in Porto."

"Are we talking state sponsored, or something else?"

"It's all state sponsored as far as I'm concerned."

"Isn't that the truth," he groans.

"There are two oligarchs living in the valley, and the *Pakhan* of the Elite Division of the European Bratva has made Porto his home. I don't think there's any love lost between them, and I would be surprised if they saw Tomas as anything more than a useful idiot. But any one of them is capable of using him to gain ground in the region. My biggest concern is that Valentina might become a pawn in a property battle."

That's not actually my biggest concern. Daniela would have to be dead for Valentina's rights to fully vest. That's what makes my blood run cold.

"Let's meet in a remote location outside the US."

"Agreed. Wheels down to make the exchange, and then we're out of there. Give me a half an hour to figure it out."

9

DANIELA

When their noses weren't buried in tablets, Antonio and Cristiano exchanged concerned looks all the way to the airport.

We're meeting Gray and Delilah on a private island in the Atlantic. From what little I've been able to gather, it's owned by a college friend of Antonio and Gray's, named Jake, who is some kind of bourbon king.

No surprise that Antonio and Cristiano were tight-lipped and refused to answer questions with more than a yes, no, we don't know, or an impatient grunt left for me to decipher. It's also no surprise that as soon as we boarded the plane, Antonio pawned me off on Monica, the flight attendant, with instructions for me to rest, before holing up in a conference room to work.

One minute I'm numb, and the next I'm jumping out of my skin, anxious for news about Valentina. About thirty minutes after takeoff, I've had enough.

I pass Monica on my way to the front of the plane. "Can I help you with something?" she asks.

"I need a word with Antonio."

She's still smiling, but it's forced now. "*Senhor* Huntsman said he doesn't want to be disturbed. His instructions were clear. It's been my experience that he means what he says. But I can get a message to him."

"Thank you. But this can't wait." I'm off before she can say anything else.

It's a good-sized plane, but I go in the direction that he headed when he left me with Monica. As I turn the corner, there are a few rooms along the hall, but only one has a closed door.

I press my ear against the cool door. For several minutes, I listen, but until the boss raises his voice, it's little more than a din. Once that happens, the chatter gets louder.

"No," Antonio barks. "She's been through enough. You need to know something, I'll ask her. But unless it's critical, it'll have to wait."

"At this stage, we don't know what's critical. She might have information that could be helpful," Lucas chimes in. "She might not even realize she has it."

"No." Antonio's voice booms, as I turn the handle and open the door.

"I'll answer whatever questions you have," I say coolly from the doorway.

All eyes are on me. Even Lucas, who's on the large screen, is gawking.

"Daniela."

Antonio's tone holds a warning that I don't miss. I doubt anyone else missed it, either. A smart woman would hightail it back to her seat, flip through a magazine, and pretend this never happened.

I look straight at him. "I appreciate your concern. But I'll do anything to keep Valentina safe, and to find whoever killed Isabel. I understand this is a flagrant act of disobedience. You can punish me when we're done."

10

DANIELA

"That's not how it works." Antonio glares at me, his eyes flaring with anger—or maybe it's defeat.

Cristiano is busy studying his fingernails, and Lucas is shuffling papers in the background.

"Is there any word on Valentina?" I ask, ignoring Antonio's glower.

"They're close. They'll contact us as soon as they have her."

"Ask me whatever you need to know. Don't hold back."

Secrets are heavy. Some heavier than others. They burden the mind, body, and soul. But once they're out, courage settles in, with its partner, strength. After baring my soul to Antonio, and then sharing some of the details with Delilah and Gray, I feel braver and stronger. *And more determined.* "I'm not a fragile flower."

The room falls silent while I pull out a chair and sit down.

Antonio gets up and brings me a bottle of water from a rolling cart. He unscrews the cap before leaning over to place it on the table in front of me. "You don't need to do this," he murmurs above my ear.

He's going to allow me to make the decision to answer questions.

It's a small empowerment from a man who likes to hold all the power, and it strengthens my resolve.

"I do." My reply is only for him.

I turn to Lucas, since he was the one who originally asked to speak to me. He's on a screen so large, it feels almost as though he's in the room with us. "How can I help?"

Antonio emits a low growl and takes the seat perpendicular to mine.

Lucas doesn't hesitate. "The records say Valentina was born at Santo Vicente's hospital on February 14. Isabel's name is on the birth certificate as her mother. Is that correct?"

"Yes. I was scheduled to deliver at the convent where Isabel and I lived while I was pregnant. But because I was so young and small, Isabel was worried about my health. She convinced my father to arrange a hospital birth. We told everyone that my name was Isabel."

"What's the name of the convent?"

"Santa Clara's. It's a home for unwed mothers, up north, almost to the border with Spain."

"Did you make friends with any of the other women at the convent?"

"No. We stayed to ourselves."

"Who delivered the baby?"

"Dr. Flores." *I said I'd answer whatever questions they have, but why is this important? We're wasting time. Dr. Flores and the nuns at Santa Clara's are not a danger to Valentina.* "I'm happy to tell you whatever you need to know, but I don't see how these questions are relevant to getting Valentina out of the US safely."

"Enough," Antonio shouts, slamming his fist on the table.

His jaw is tight, and I know he's trying to protect me, but I can't let him put an end to the questions. I glare at him, dismissing his concerns without addressing them head-on. "Lucas can ask what he needs to know. I just want to be sure we're not wasting precious time."

"We're trying to narrow the list of suspects," Cristiano explains, "and knowing who might have known, or suspected, that you were Manuel and Maria Rosa's daughter would save us a lot of time."

I nod. "That makes sense. I would be surprised if my father told anyone. It wasn't one of those proud papa moments. Isabel would have never breathed a word. Jorge knew, but he was paid handsomely to keep his mouth shut, although before he disappeared his behavior was erratic and out of character. He was drinking and prone to outbursts. But I suspect you know more about that time than I do."

The room quiets again. Although if they have any misgivings about Jorge's death or spying on me in the US, they don't let on.

"What about your father's guards?"

"I don't think so. No one knew my mother and I were at the meadow, except for Isabel. Although—as I've gotten older, I've wondered if my mother's guard might have known we were up to something and let it go. He was fiercely loyal to my mother. He committed suicide shortly after it happened."

"It's not likely he killed himself before there was justice for your mother. Your father probably killed him for allowing her to leave the property alone," Antonio says matter-of-factly. "It's what I would have done."

A chill runs up my spine at his callousness. It never occurred to me—but there's a lot about my father that I'm just learning.

"What about the convent? Aside from the women, was there anyone there who would have known you?"

"No. No one. The nuns who ran it asked no questions. They took in any pregnant woman who found herself alone. My father donated money so I wouldn't have to do chores that would put me around the others, and so that I could have additional food. I was the youngest girl there, by several years, and I wasn't there because my family put me on the street, but to keep the secret of my pregnancy. Isabel didn't let anyone near me."

I was alone, cloistered away, miserable without my girlfriends, and missing my mother. As it turned out, it was good practice for what was to come. After we learned about the pregnancy, I never saw my little friends again. I had my father, Isabel, Valentina, and my horses, but parts of my life ended when I was twelve. My mother, my friends, my childhood—they were all vital limbs severed. But girls, like young trees, can sustain a lot of damage and survive. Although they're never the same.

"Your family was prominent, especially in the north," Lucas prods. "You don't think anyone recognized you? Nothing happened while you were there that made you wonder, not even now?"

"She was twelve," Antonio says with a sharp glare. If looks could kill, Lucas would be on his way to the morgue right now.

"Nothing happened while you were there that made you wonder, not even now?"

Father Ferreira. A shiver runs through me, and I rub my arms to warm myself. "There was a priest who visited once a month or so. I only talked with him once. He might have known something. My father paid someone, and it surely wasn't the nuns."

"Do you remember his name?" Cristiano asks gently. His manner is never as brusque as Lucas's.

"Father Ferreira. He asked a lot of questions. And when Isabel tried to intervene, he sent her out of the room so he could hear my confession. At least that's what he told her." I rub my palms over my arms, trying to warm myself. Father Ferreira was a memory that I would have preferred to keep buried.

For several seconds, you could hear a pin drop.

"What kinds of questions did he ask?"

"He wanted to know if I pushed away the man who *did this* to me—or if I invited him to lay on top of me with my silence. He asked if I enjoyed it. 'It's not rape unless you fight and say no.'" The vomit tickles my throat.

Antonio's hands are clasped tightly and pressed to his mouth. His eyes are black as coal.

"What did you tell him?" Lucas asks.

"Bits and pieces. I never gave him my name, and he never asked. I never mentioned who raped me, or that my mother was there too. There was something about him I didn't trust. I can't explain it. My mother used to say that priests were just men in robes, with the same failings as other men—they weren't God. So I lied to him. I remember crossing my fingers and apologizing to God before I told Father Ferreira that I didn't remember what happened."

What I should have done was kick him in the balls, but I was twelve and pregnant. I'm proud that I even had the nerve to lie to him.

"He just let it go?"

I nod. "Even if he knew something, he was old. He's probably dead by now."

"Father Ferreira is still alive," Lucas responds dryly.

Pity. "Do you think he would have had anything to do with Isabel's murder?" That seems far-fetched.

"We need to turn over every stone," Cristiano explains, his voice tight.

"Did you ever confide in a doctor or therapist?"

I glance at Lucas. "Not until recently. I was a child, and Valentina was born early. She weighed two pounds. I didn't have the body of a woman when I gave birth. Not really. And as I continued to develop and grow, I healed fully. My doctor in the US is the only person who ever asked if I'd had a baby. She suspected because of the way my cervix looks. I told her the baby was born early and didn't survive." *God forgive me.*

There's a low rumble to my left, where Antonio is seated, but Lucas isn't deterred. "What about a therapist?"

A therapist? You've got to be kidding. Despite the seriousness of the moment, I snicker. "Girls like me don't get to talk to therapists. We protect our families by taking our secrets to the grave. Otherwise, how could we ever make a good marriage?" My words are laced with bitterness. But it's true. Every word. And the men in this room? They know it.

I don't look at Antonio, who was sold a bag of goods. *Not my problem.*

11

DANIELA

"If we have any more questions, we'll pass them through Antonio," Lucas says, in effect dismissing me.

"You can ask me anything, any of you, at any time. It's a little late now for secrets or modesty."

They don't say a word.

"Have we heard anything more from the school?" I ask, hoping that my honesty has bought me some leverage. I told the principal that Isabel had a heart attack and is unresponsive, and she seemed to believe it, but I don't know how long the lie will hold up.

There have been so many lies. I can't even keep track of them all.

Cristiano shakes his head. "It's a good sign that we haven't heard back from the principal."

I stand, and then sit back down, my knees wobbling. "I was going to talk to Antonio about this, but it's probably a conversation that the four of us should have." I look each man in the eyes, one at a time. Antonio has been mostly silent, up until now. Although his rage was palpable the entire time Lucas was questioning me. The anger is still there, but now he appears somewhat guarded. He needs to hear this before we get to Valentina. They all do.

"The discussion about whether a twelve-year-old should carry a baby to term and deliver was never had with me," I admit freely. "Putting the baby up for adoption was something that was never a consideration. Valentina's bloodline leads to Quinta Rosa do Vale, and that gives her life a certain kind of value, especially to people who don't care about her. It also puts her at considerable risk. But besides that, my father didn't want an adoptive parent coming forward to claim ownership of the family vineyards. As it turned out, that rather selfish attitude was a blessing. It meant I could watch my daughter grow up, even if she would never call me *mamai*."

The air in the room is thick and chewy as grown men grapple with a tsunami of emotion. Their *modus operandi* is to destroy everything that makes them uncomfortable. But they will not destroy my daughter.

"The circumstances surrounding my pregnancy are not what we'd want for any girl, or any woman, not even our worst enemy. But no one, not even my father, who was distressed over my mother's death, ever treated Valentina as anything but a cherished blessing. This was important to Isabel, who grew up feeling unwanted, and it's been vitally important to me since I was old enough to understand." I pause for a breath.

While I've managed to remain outwardly composed, my emotions are seconds from getting the best of me. These are not men who respect the word of a distraught woman. These are men who respond to strength. *You will stay strong.*

"My innocence was not the most important thing they took from me that day. It was my mother, who surely would have had an opinion about how the circumstances of my life turned out. But hear this," I say, with more authority than I have, and more confidence than I feel. "I love that little girl with every cell of my being. And I expect each of you to treat Valentina, not like the byproduct of a monstrous act, but like the precious child she is. No exceptions."

With the words still hanging in the air, I grip the edge of the table and stand with as much dignity as I can muster.

Antonio takes hold of my wrist as I walk past him. "That's not something you need to spend one second worrying about. You're my wife. Valentina is your daughter, and she's under my protection. Anyone who treats her as anything less will answer directly to me."

He's deadly serious—his words, his tone, his expression—all of it.

A sense of relief courses through me. No one will go against him. They wouldn't dare.

I nod, and he releases me.

With one hand on the door, I pause for a moment. "I want Isabel's body sent home so she can have a proper burial. Please let me know the moment you hear any news about Valentina."

No one responds, but they heard me.

I shut the door behind me, and put one foot in front of the other, until I reach the sofa in the main cabin and collapse against the cool leather.

12

ANTONIO

After Daniela leaves the room, no one says a word for a few moments. Not because she might be listening outside the door, but out of respect for her. And admiration. She's tough. Tougher than she looks. Tougher than she should have to be.

I can't think. I treated her—fuck—there are no words to describe it. Letting her get on that boat. Letting her think she was going to be raped. *Jesus Christ.* I'm going to burn in hell. And I deserve it.

"You didn't know," Cristiano says quietly, like he can read my mind.

Why didn't I know? It's consuming me, and as we sit here without a word, I'm sure it's eating at Cristiano and Lucas too.

Cristiano breaks the grating silence. "I don't think we can get the body back. I believe it's been disposed of."

"You heard her. Do whatever it takes to get it back, and for some reason you're not successful, figure something out. But I don't want to hear a word about it. I'm not going to lie to her about the identity of the body.

"How the fuck did we not know this?" I slam my fist on the table. "How?" I glower at Lucas through the screen.

"It was buried deep," he says, his voice conveying all of our frustration. "Even knowing what we do, I can't find a thing. D'Sousa did not want it uncovered."

"Why would he do this?" I have my theories, but I'm too close to this. It's too personal. "Why didn't he just tell me?"

Cristiano shrugs. "Maybe it's exactly what she said. That the knowledge would make her unmarriageable to someone like you."

That's what I thought initially. But there's no way.

I shake my head. I owed him big. He knew I'd do whatever he asked regarding his daughter, especially if her safety was at risk. "Too simple. And not remotely within the possibilities. He knew I couldn't refuse him."

Cristiano shrugs. "Then why did he feel the need to sweeten the deal with the vineyards?"

"He gave me the vineyards to protect her. D'Sousa knew I was the best person to take on my uncle." It's clear now. "If I owned the vineyards, his daughter and granddaughter would be safe. At least that's what he thought. But I didn't marry Daniela right away, like he probably expected, and for six years, I did everything in my power to keep the betrothal contract under wraps."

That was a major fuck-up. But she was too young—and I wasn't ready. I had an empire to build. In hindsight, both are piss-poor excuses, especially the latter.

"Are we underestimating Tomas?" I have strong opinions about my cousin, but I can't let my lifelong disdain for him throw me off track. "Is it possible that he could pull all this off himself?"

"No," they reply in unison.

"What's next?" Cristiano asks.

"Getting Valentina to Porto without any more casualties. Securing Isabel's body and sending it back."

"I contacted the person in charge on the ground in the US. He's on it."

"I want Tomas. Tell me why I can't kill him as soon as this goddamn plane lands back in Porto with Daniela and Valentina." I know why. But I'm looking for a way around it, and these guys are my best hope.

"Because he's a fucking incompetent bastard and there's no way he could have done this alone. If we pick him up now, whoever is the mastermind will go underground before we know their identity, and they'll strike when we least expect it." Cristiano has changed his tune about this. When he first heard, he was ready to bring in Tomas.

"Let's go through this methodically," Lucas mutters. "Someone wanted to stop the wedding. That explains the explosion in the church. But Isabel was killed after you were already married. Her death couldn't stop the wedding."

"Once the plan was put in motion, it might have been impossible to stop," Cristiano offers.

It's a possibility, but unlikely. Her life wasn't that valuable—not to whoever is behind this.

"I don't believe Isabel was the target. They want Valentina. But they don't want her dead."

"Other than for blackmail purposes, no one besides Tomas benefits from having Valentina under their control. And he might not even know about her."

"He knows something. I guarantee that Jorge, Isabel's husband, went to my uncle to sell information while he was trying to sell it to us." Now we know the big secret he was trying to peddle before he was murdered. "He talked, and then they killed him to stay one step ahead of us."

"Everything points to that."

"I want inside my uncle's house. It's the only way we're going to know what Tomas is up to."

"It's swept regularly. Anything we plant, they'll find. Even if they can't trace it back to us, it's not likely to bear fruit."

Cristiano's right.

"We need someone on the ground. Can we activate our plant?"

"We can," Lucas replies, with some hesitancy. "But we get one shot. If he's discovered, he's a dead man, and we risk all-out war. And we'll never get anyone in there again—not for a long time. We might want to hold tight a bit longer."

Fuck. He's right too.

"Daniela seems to be holding up okay," Cristiano says, trying to steer me away from activating our asset inside my uncle's house.

Holding up okay? Really? That's not how I see it. "I'm not sure about that. She's been through hell." *I put her through hell, on top of everything else.*

After she told me what happened, she went into full operational mode, shutting down all emotion. Her friend is dead, and her daughter is in danger. She's too even-keeled. Too dispassionate. She's just moving through the paces. It's not like her, and it's making me edgy.

"She's tough."

"She doesn't need to be tough. That's my job."

"We've got this for now," Cristiano says, "if you want to keep her company. We'll come get you, if we have anything."

I really don't want to be around her when she's so vulnerable. It makes me soft. And that makes me feel things I don't want to feel—things I can't afford to feel. But it'll be hours before we land. She shouldn't spend the entire trip alone. I'm going to have to suck it up.

"Come get me if there's anything new. *Anything.*"

13

ANTONIO

On my way to the cabin, I stick my head in the galley where Monica is puttering around. "Would you bring us some tea and coffee in the cabin?"

"Of course. Are you ready for breakfast?"

Breakfast? What time is it? I glance at my watch. *Earlier than I thought.* "That would be good. Something very light," I add. "We'll have a heavier meal on the return flight."

I leave Monica and go find the woman whose life my father tried to destroy. Just like Tomas isn't a ringleader, Abel wasn't the mastermind behind what happened. He was certainly capable, at one time anyway, but he always deferred to his big brother. My father was the genius behind the murder and rape. I'd stake my life on it.

When I reach the cabin, Daniela's sitting on the sofa, staring out the window into the bleak sky.

Unlike this morning, I take a seat near her and push aside a book on the coffee table. "It's going to be another long day. Why don't you put your feet up and try to rest?"

She nods but doesn't move.

"Monica's preparing breakfast."

"Have you heard anything from Gray or Delilah?"

"Nothing new. It'll be a bit before they get to the school."

We sit in silence that's so goddamn uncomfortable my skin is crawling. Daniela's somewhere else, somewhere far away, and I'm not even sure she notices the disquiet.

My father was dead. But why didn't Manuel kill Abel and Tomas after what they did? Even if he didn't crave retribution, it would have ensured Daniela's safety, and ultimately, Valentina's too. I don't get it. I glance at Daniela. *Maybe she knows.* As much as I'd love to shield her from reliving the events over and over, we're shooting into the dark. We need all the background we can get.

"Why didn't your father have Abel and Tomas killed?"

She sniffs, still staring straight ahead. "He believed it was your father's plan, and that it was executed on his order."

That's definitely true.

"And he thought that avenging my mother's death would turn the region on its head. Maybe start a war that would destroy everything. He wasn't willing to take that risk."

He wasn't willing to avenge his wife's death or the evil that was done to his daughter? *Fuck that.* Manuel D'Sousa might not have been willing to take the risk, but I sure as hell am. My uncle has one foot in the grave, but Tomas? He won't live to see his next birthday.

Monica enters the cabin with a large tray and a big smile.

"Just leave it there," I tell her, pointing to the coffee table.

"Is there anything else I can get you?" she asks.

Daniela doesn't respond.

"We're all set for now. I'll let you know if we need anything." That's her cue to leave us the fuck alone.

"Of course," she says politely.

There's a plate of pastries and some fruit on the tray. Ordinarily, Daniela would be eyeing the chocolate croissant, but she shakes her head when I offer it.

I pour her some tea and add a breakfast biscuit to the saucer before handing it to her.

She shakes her head, again. "I don't want anything. Thank you."

"It's just tea and a dry cookie. You need to put something in your stomach."

She accepts it reluctantly, but I doubt she'll eat a morsel.

I desperately want a whiskey, but I pour myself a coffee. The caffeine won't dull my senses like booze.

We've been careful to cover our tracks, even filing multiple flight plans. The island where we're meeting Gray is about as private as one could hope for, but we don't know what we're up against. When the advance team lands, we'll have more information.

The events of the last few days could have been avoided if D'Sousa had just told me about the rape and murder. I look at Daniela, but there are no answers on her face. *Find your balls and ask. She's not going to wither.*

"I'm still having trouble understanding why your father wouldn't have shared any of this with me."

She gazes at me, her wary eyes fixed on mine. "Would you have wanted me if you'd known?"

14

ANTONIO

Daniela's chin is turned up, defiantly, but she's holding her breath, waiting, and watching for my response.

"Don't be ridiculous. Of course I would have married you." I don't hesitate. But it would have been hard to marry her, not because she was damaged—I don't believe that for a second—but because of how my family was involved. "Your father knew I would do anything he asked."

"Why is that?" She's still gauging my reaction carefully.

"He was my mentor." It's only part of the equation, but she doesn't need to know more—not right now. *Not ever.*

"And you're such a loyal minion that you would have been willing to take a tarnished daughter off his hands. How noble of you."

"Anyone would have married you, under any circumstances. It was hardly a chore."

Daniela places the saucer with the biscuit on the table and sits back, grasping the teacup between her hands.

"My father was ashamed. I'm sure a part of him was grateful to send me away while I was pregnant. It must have made it easier for him. For a long time after it happened, he could barely look at me. His precious jewel, sullied. It was a lot like earlier this morning, when you couldn't even spare me a glance after you learned about the rape."

"That's not true." I feel the anger rising. Although I'm not sure if I'm more pissed off at her for believing that shit, or at myself for the way I behaved. This morning is a perfect example of what happens when you let your emotions control you. I should have done better.

She shrugs. "I know what I saw."

"You have no idea what was going through my mind while you were talking. There were lots of things. The overwhelming desire to dig up my father so I could murder him was chief among them." *I'd make his death long and torturous this time.* "Don't you dare tell me that I see you as a sullied jewel. That's never entered my mind. Not once."

Daniela sips her tea while I stew beside her. She can believe whatever she wants about her father, and maybe she really does feel that he saw her as ruined, but he never, *never*, talked about her with anything but love and affection. He adored her. If he was ashamed, it was because they tortured his wife and child under his watch.

As for me, I won't allow her to fill her head with the idea that I see her as some tarnished treasure. Nothing could be further from the truth.

My respect for her grew immeasurably as I listened to her describe every loathsome thing the Huntsmans did to her. *That includes my own behavior, which she never once brought up.* I'm not capable of the kind of romantic love she deserves. But Daniela's my wife, and she's far better than anything I deserve. *That's for damn sure.* I'll keep her, and Valentina, safe. Even if I die tomorrow, they'll want for nothing. *It's the best I can do.*

"You're my wife. Nothing you've told me changes that. And nothing will."

She tips her head up and peers into my eyes. "I'm not a child. Things will never be the same between us. Not that it was so great to begin with. But there were moments." Her voice trails off. "Moments when I had started to believe that maybe our mutual love of the valley, the vineyards, the history, the Port —that maybe we could build a decent life together. But that was a pipe dream of the little girl who once believed you were the brightest star in the sky."

It's the first time she's ever come close to admitting having a girlish crush on me. There's something terribly poignant about it. Even an asshole like me can appreciate it.

"We can still build a decent life together. Our love of the region is more than most people who enter into a betrothal contract share."

I don't promise her love. It would be an empty promise, and she'd see right through it. I've never told any woman that lie, and I have too much respect for her to say it now.

"He was right, you know," she says, just above a whisper.

"Who was right?"

"The priest. Father Ferreira. I never said no. I didn't fight. Maybe Tomas saw it as my acquiescence."

The blood pounds in my ears. *Acquiescence? You're fucking kidding me.* The anger, lying in wait inside, has turned to rage. "Tell me you don't believe that bullshit."

She shakes her head slowly. "No, not really. But it's a lie I told myself over the years—mainly as a teenager. In a strange way, it made what happened easier to fathom. It's hard for a kid to understand how people you know—could do something so heinous."

"Twelve-year-old girls don't have the capacity to consent to sex with men. Under any circumstances. End of story."

She takes hold of my hand and squeezes. "Promise me, that regardless of how you feel about me, you'll keep Valentina safe. That no one will hurt her. In exchange for her safety, I'll—I'll close my eyes to whatever you do outside the marriage."

"Valentina will be safe, and no one, not a fucking soul, will lay a finger on her. But so you know, I don't feel the same way you do. If you step out on the vows you took before God, you better make sure it's with someone you love. Because I will bring you his heart in a box, set under glass, and affix it to your nightstand for you to look at forever. You. Are. Mine."

She doesn't believe I'll be faithful, or even that she deserves my faithfulness. I see the apprehension in her face. "Come here." I pull her onto my lap.

"What are you doing?"

"I want you here. I want you to know that not only is Valentina safe, but so are you."

"I don't need to sit on your lap to know it." She starts to pull away.

"You're not going anywhere, *Princesa*. This is where you belong." I tighten my grip, so she can't climb off. She doesn't fight me, and after a few moments, I feel her body relax against mine. Her breathing is shallow, and I can almost hear her thoughts running wild.

"I never told anyone everything I told you today."

"Not even Josh before you were intimate?" I ask, like a needy motherfucker.

"No one. I couldn't risk anyone knowing about Valentina. If Tomas knew, he'd try to take her away."

I tip her head back until our eyes meet. The terror there is startling. *This is what she's been walking around with since her father died—maybe before.* "He's not going to take her away. You have my word." I mean it. He'll have to kill me first.

She searches my face, looking for evidence of my veracity. "I believe you," she murmurs, the lines easing on her brow.

"I want you. More than I should. You can believe that too." I lower my mouth to hers. It's not gentle. It's possessive and demanding. The kind of kiss that makes my dick hard, and elicits small gasps and moans from her.

She responds just like I knew she would, before catching herself and pulling back. "No. I can't. Isabel's dead. I need to stay focused on Valentina."

That's not what I want for her. It's not what she needs. It's simply what her conscience dictates. "You can wring your hands all you want about Isabel and Valentina. It won't make you feel any better, and it won't change a damn thing for them. You need to turn your focus to me for the next few hours. I want you naked and needy."

"Why are you doing this?"

She tries to wriggle off my lap, but I don't let her. I wrap my arms around her, holding her in place while I speak softly into her hair. "Last night, I was hurting, raw and angry, feeling helpless. My world had spun out of control. You let me find comfort in your body. You used sex as a vehicle to bring me solace—although it was much more than that. You helped me find the control I desperately needed, and you gave me some peace. I want to do that for you. Let me."

She's thinking about it, but her conscience is loud and judgmental. I doubt I've convinced her of anything—not yet.

"This isn't the time or the place. Sex isn't the answer to everything."

No, but it's the answer now. At least, it's the best I have to offer. "Don't fight me on this."

"My daughter is in danger. My closest friend is dead. This isn't a time for pleasure."

I take her hand and bring it to my mouth, pressing a small kiss to each knuckle. "I'm not talking about pleasure, per se. I'm talking about comfort, about release, about letting me carry your pain for a little while. I want to take care of you. Let me."

Her breath hitches, and her eyelids flutter closed.

"Sex might not be the answer to everything. But it's the best way I know to make you forget for a little while." *God help me if I fuck this up.*

Daniela doesn't say anything more. She doesn't resist or struggle. I use the reprieve to scoop her into my arms and carry her to the bedroom.

15

DANIELA

Last night I was hurting, raw and angry, feeling helpless. My world had spun out of control. You let me find comfort in your body. You used sex as a vehicle to bring me solace—although it was much more than that. You helped me find the control I desperately needed, and you gave me some peace. I want to do that for you. Let me.

How do I say no to that? I want comfort. And I want peace, too.

Sex might not be the answer to everything. But it's the best way I know to make you forget for a little while.

I let him lose himself in passion last night. In his passion, and mine. It was the only way I knew to comfort him. But we're different people. I can find solace in a million ways, none of them having a thing to do with sex.

As he strides toward the back of the plane, I bury my face in his neck, my mind whirling. Am I doing this for him—to let him feel he has the ability to make me feel better? Or am I doing this for myself—surrendering to the moment, and letting him take care of me?

It's been a long time since someone took care of me. Isabel

still fussed over me, right until the end, but it was mostly out of her pent-up anxiety. I was responsible for putting a roof over our heads and food on the table—even while Jorge was alive. The hard decisions—and even the easy ones—were mine to make.

Does it make me weak to want the comfort of Antonio's body, to crave his warm skin against mine? Or is it just human? Would it be so bad if I handed him control of my body—of my mind—and let him make the decisions? Not forever, but for a few hours.

But if I relinquish all control, will he break me? Will that be my punishment for having sex while Valentina is in danger?

"Stop overthinking. There's nothing about what we're doing that's wrong, or immoral. None of it makes you a bad mother or a bad friend. I could take the responsibility from you—force you to comply. I've done that before, but I won't. Not today," he adds, under his breath.

My body shifts in his arms as he opens the door and kicks it shut behind us. He doesn't toss me on the bed, but sets me on my feet, cradling my face in his hands. "Trust me to give you what you need." It's not a question, but a command.

"How did you know?"

He tips his head to the side, and I see the confusion in his eyes.

"How did you know that I feel guilty about being here with you—while . . ."

He kisses me gently. He's careful and restrained, but I feel the hunger throbbing inside him. "You're a good person, Daniela, with a good heart and a highly calibrated moral compass—too well-calibrated. You don't have a selfish bone in your body. It wasn't difficult to figure out."

He lowers his mouth, and I'm not sure how much time passes before our tongues are tangling and my body is pressed against his, seeking *anything* and *everything* he's willing to give.

"The door," I gasp. "Lock the door."

Antonio shakes his head. "I'm not locking the door. No one will enter without knocking. If you want it locked, you'll have to do it yourself."

It hits me like a giant swell, leaving me drenched and confused. He wants me to know I'm free to leave. I control the exit. I'm not a prisoner to his whims. Some part of me is taken off guard. This isn't the man I've come to know. *Is it?*

But despite being off-kilter, a part of me—a big part—is beyond grateful that he cares enough about my state of mind to alter his behavior.

"Thank you."

He raises a single eyebrow. "For what?"

"For wanting me to feel safe."

"Don't thank me, Daniela. I'm no angel. I'm going to push you—hard. I'm going to take you farther than you think you can go. And you're going to let me." His voice is hypnotic, but it's laced with danger. "Can you do that?"

I lift one shoulder, because I'm not sure. He's pushed me so much since I arrived in Porto. Especially with regard to sex. I can't imagine what more he wants from me.

"Have you ever had a safeword?"

I sink my teeth into my bottom lip and shake my head.

"I'm going to give you one. It's how you'll stop me if your emotions are taking you somewhere that's too scary."

"I thought safewords were to prevent physical harm?"

The edge of his mouth curls. "They can be. But I'm going to watch you carefully, and that shouldn't be an issue. You've revisited some awful moments today, and we haven't been lovers for all that long. It's easy to know when a body is at the breaking point, but the psyche is something else entirely. That's what the safeword is for. Red," he says clearly, enunciating each letter. "That's what you'll say if it gets to be too much."

Antonio Huntsman controlled by a three-letter word. That's

difficult to believe. "If I say it, you'll stop whatever you're doing?" I don't hide the skepticism.

"Immediately." He doesn't hesitate. "But I don't want you to use it unless you need to. I want you to let me push your boundaries, just beyond what you think you can handle. Do you understand what I'm asking of you?"

He's checking with me. Walking me through an unfamiliar process.

"Yes." The word gets caught in my throat before it lands between us.

"I'm not going to stop because you beg, or scream, or even if you cry. You'll need to use the safeword. Otherwise, I'm not going to stop until I shatter you." He gently sweeps an errant hair off my face. "That's what you need, *Princesa*."

I shiver. Although I'm not afraid of him. And it's not because of some safeword. It's because I know he won't hurt me —not beyond what I can handle—not physically, anyway. I don't know how I'm so sure, but I am. Emotionally, though, I'm not sure of anything when it comes to him.

"What will you do after you shatter me? Sweep the pieces into a dust pan and dump them into the trash?"

He shakes his head. "I'll build back the walls, with grand doorways and floor-to-ceiling windows, where the light streams in."

"I never imagined you as someone who believes in fairy tales."

"I don't, *Princesa*. But I know how to get things done. And I believe in you. In your strength. In your goodness. In your resiliency."

He pauses for a beat, and for a moment I'm sure his mouth is going to crash into mine. But it doesn't. *Maybe I'm the one who believes in fairy tales.*

"How will you stop me if it gets to be too much? Say the word."

"Red."

"Say it again."

I lift my chin and meet his eyes. "Red." It emerges clear as day. A fiery splash of color, with magical powers. I see it, but I don't feel it.

He nods, gazing at me. "Don't be afraid to use it."

16

DANIELA

With deft fingers, Antonio untethers a few buttons of my tunic. But he's in no hurry. *Even a hungry cat plays with his food.*

The leisurely exploration continues, until the snow-white lace winks at him from under my shirt. His breath hitches as he skates a thumb across the intricate fabric. I feel it between my legs—small pulses of anticipation and need.

"You're mine," he says, without apology. "Your pain, your sorrow, your tears—I want it. And you're going to give it all to me. *Everything.* If you struggle to hold any of it back, to keep any part of it to yourself, I'll punish you until you're sobbing for mercy. I'll be ruthless."

His mouth brushes mine. The tender kiss is a startling contrast to the menace of the threat.

"Do you understand?"

My lips part, and my head bobs once or twice. His words are perilous, but his voice is seductive. He's reeling me in. I sense it. But I don't resist—not until my conscience pricks, and I remember Valentina. *And Isabel. Was she afraid when she died?*

Was it a painful end? I know so few details of her death. As the realization floods me, every muscle in my body tightens.

He feels it too.

"Already? It's going to be a long day if I start punishing you now. But maybe that's what you want."

I do. I deserve to be punished for seeking comfort in his body while Valentina is in danger. *What kind of mother behaves this way?*

"Stop overthinking," he demands. "Stop thinking at all." It's the last thing he says before tearing my shirt from my body. The tiny buttons sail through the air and bounce off the floor, scattering in every direction. Apart from the rumble in his chest, the patter of the buttons is the only sound in the room.

I invited the beast to play. Now he's here, and the energy throbbing around him is a tempest. I doubt there's a word, in any language, powerful enough to stop him. *Red? What a joke.*

My bra is gone before I blink, and his large hands are on my breasts, palming the taut flesh, his thumbs coaxing the nipples into tight peaks. He lowers his mouth, sweeping it over my throat. I surrender to the delicious sensations, letting him distract me with his skill.

I'm adrift in pleasure when he sinks his teeth into my neck, right into *that* cord. I shudder and try to pull away at the heightened sensation. But he cages my legs with his, holding me firmly in place while he laves the tendon with soothing kisses that ease the bruised skin.

I let down my guard, again, and follow him to a place where there is only dreamy bliss. And want. *So much want.*

I long for the cock that's thickening between us. *I need it.* It's all I can think about. That and his clean, masculine scent that permeates every breath I take. My head whirls as he leads me astray, until there is only him. His touch. His heartbeat. His need. *My need.*

The evil pinch comes right then. When I least expect it.

"Ahhh!" A tortured cry escapes into the room. But he doesn't stop. My nipples scream between his callused fingers, as his mouth works magic on my throat. Gentle and rough. Tender and coarse. My nerve endings are swaying in every direction—all at once. If he wasn't holding me steady, I would be a puddle on the bare floor.

"You're beautiful, *Princesa*. Too beautiful for words."

We're nose to nose. The intimacy curls around us, like a dense fog addling my brain.

"Your whimpers and cries make my dick hard. I want to fuck you until it hurts."

His cock twitches between us. I imagine it pushing against the zipper to free itself. I imagine it weeping as he buries it in my pussy.

"Would you like that?" he asks. "Would you like me to fuck you until you scream?"

A small moan twists its way out of my throat.

"Take off the leggings. And shoes. Leave your panties for me."

They're not suggestions. They're commands. This isn't a democracy. He's the king. *My king. God help me.*

While Antonio watches, I undress as he asks, a flush creeping over my skin. My inhibitions take over, drowning out the occasional twinge of conscience.

He admires me, quietly, while I stand before him in a scant piece of lace. My cheeks are warm, and despite my efforts to remain calm, I fidget.

"Are you embarrassed by your nakedness?" he goads, his mouth curling at the edges. Not a smile, but not a sneer, either.

I lower my eyes.

"You'll get comfortable with it." He steps closer, so close I feel the heat off his body. "I like you stripped bare. Body and soul," he murmurs, running a finger from the hollow of my throat down to the white lace panties.

I'm teetering. A gust of wind could send me to the floor. I draw a breath to steady myself.

Antonio cups my ass in one hand, while the other disappears between my legs. "Are you wet?" he asks, sliding his fingertips over my pussy and rubbing the sensitive folds through the gusset. "You are," he whispers above my ear. "I hope you brought a change of clothes."

It's hot in here. *So hot.* I arch into his fingers, and he rewards me by focusing his attention on my clit.

He smirks when I gasp for air.

"I spend too much time thinking about defiling your gorgeous body, but when you're a greedy little whore, like this, you're irresistible."

I bristle at the word whore and turn my head away.

"Look at me," he demands.

And I do. There's no guile in his expression.

"Does it make you uncomfortable when I call you a whore?"

I nod. Although it's not that it doesn't arouse me. It does. What makes me uncomfortable is that I don't want to be aroused by it. *I shouldn't be aroused by it.*

"What about slut? Do you like that word better, *Princesa*?"

I shake my head. "No."

"It won't be long before you're comfortable with all of it. Every *dirty* word. Every *dirty* deed."

He's right. And that's what I'm most afraid of.

He loosens my braid, shaking the waves free, until it falls over my shoulders. When he's through, he fists the hair at the nape, tugging my head back until we're eye to eye.

"You're my wife, my *Princesa*, and the strongest person I've ever met. But you're also my whore. You'll spread your legs for me, give me your ass, and choke on my cock. And you'll tremble while you submit, because it'll feel so good." His eyes flare, and the devil appears in the flames.

This isn't a game he's playing, or if it is, he's playing to eviscerate the opponent. *Is that what I am?* Is this what he meant by pushing my boundaries, or has he simply lost control?

As his eyes flicker with what feels like madness, I'm not certain he'll stop if I ask. I need to know. I can't afford to be broken—*more broken*. Not now.

I swallow hard. "Red." The word emerges loud and unequivocal, and I wait on tenterhooks, to see what he does.

He unfurls his hand in slow motion, releasing the grip on my hair, and steps back. His brow is furrowed. "Talk to me," he whispers.

I stagger back and blow out a breath caught in my chest, blinking away a tear or two. *He stopped.* "I know I'm not supposed to—that I agreed not to use the word unless my mind started to go somewhere that was too scary."

"Did it?" he asks, studying me carefully.

"No. But you seemed—possessed." I press my lips together. "I don't know a better way to describe it. I wasn't sure if you were in control of what was happening. Or if you'd stop."

"Were you afraid, or were you testing me?" His expression is neutral, as though it doesn't matter what I say, as long as it's honest.

I wasn't actually afraid—not at that moment. "I was testing you."

He nods. "It's fair," he says, cradling my jaw. "You're inexperienced. And I'm a ruthless bastard who wants to ruin you with every fiber of my being. I am possessed. You do that to me," he adds, in a whisper.

The world stops as Antonio peers into my eyes, rifling through the private layers of turmoil and grief, mourning my lost innocence. I don't cower or lower my gaze as he rummages. I peer right back, straight into his soul, searching for the light I know is there. *I've seen it.* A protective beacon, an unmovable force.

The man is danger personified. There's no denying it. Yet, when I'm with him, I feel safe. Maybe safer than I've ever felt. He won't destroy me. *Not intentionally.* He's already proved that.

"But you need to know," he continues, as though the world is still turning, "the power of the safeword is diminished when you abuse it. Don't throw it around carelessly."

"I—"

He holds a finger to my lips to shush me. "You didn't abuse it. But I want you to understand how it works. I trust you to use the safeword before you're traumatized, and you trust me to stop when you use the safeword. It's a trust that goes both ways. It has to. Otherwise, it doesn't work."

Trust. Is that what we're building? Something that firmly roots, and is unshakeable even during a virulent storm? Like my parents had. Or is it the kind of trust reserved only for playtime? The kind that evaporates as soon as the orgasmic glow fades?

"Do you always use safewords?" I ask, looking for answers to satisfy my heart—or maybe to strengthen the fortress that protects it. *Am I the only one?* That's the question I really want to ask, but I'm not sure I'm prepared for his answer. So I dance around it, probing at the edges, where I can back off at the first sign of heartache.

"Always?" He shakes his head. "No. But I have. Although not normally outside of a club."

"A club?"

"That's a discussion for another time, *Princesa*. Right now, I want you on that bed, on your back. Legs spread nice and wide for me, so I can see your pretty little cunt."

His eyes are flaring, daring me to defy him. And I don't. But first, I cross the room and lock the door.

17

DANIELA

"Close your eyes," he instructs in that buttery voice that's deceptively calming. "Raise your arms above your head. Just like that, *Princesa*," he murmurs. "Keep them right there, or I'll bind you to the bed."

The thought of being bound to the bed is at once frightening and exhilarating, making my pussy clench in response to the warning.

I don't hear him leave, but I hear sounds coming from the bathroom. The creak of a cabinet door, and some rustling. I don't hear him return, either, and I flinch when I feel his warm breath on my belly. Then his lips.

His tongue traces the waistband of my panties, before moving to the lace that encircles my legs. With the utmost patience, he pulls aside the gusset, and licks the exposed flesh. I ball my hands into tight fists, above my head, and gasp, fighting to keep my legs open. Struggling not to wriggle as every slash of his tongue sends a new zing of pleasure.

It's becoming more difficult by the second to keep my legs spread as he enjoys me. They begin inching together, trembling in a slow slide.

Antonio doesn't issue a single warning, and he doesn't say a word before his hand comes down on my inner thigh. I hear the *slap*, even before I feel the sting that makes my back arch off the mattress.

"Keep still," he growls.

I'm trying, but you're making it so hard.

His mouth is savage, now. His teeth. His tongue. His lips. It's all a blur.

I'm at the edge, and I clasp my hands above my head, twisting my fingers to stop thrashing.

"Let go," he demands. "Now, Daniela." He catches my clit on his tongue and sucks the swollen nub, cloaking it between his lips, yanking the orgasm from me while I writhe.

"Such a good *Princesa*," he coos, praising me as his tongue lavishes languid strokes over my pulsing flesh.

I'm panting. I feel nothing and everything all at once. For a long moment, my mind is an empty vessel, without a worry except for catching my breath.

He presses a kiss to my pussy before moving back. "Bring your arms down and open your eyes."

My eyelashes flutter as my vision adjusts. Antonio hovers over me, easing my panties over my hips and down my legs. He tosses them aside, and slides onto the bed near me. "You're delicious," he murmurs, "and I already need to taste you again. But first, I want something else."

He rolls me onto my side, tracing the contours of my hip, before he sits up, his shoulders resting against the headboard. "Get on your knees and straddle my thighs."

I'm still breathing hard. The pulses between my legs have slowed, but they haven't stopped. My brain is muddled in pleasure. I can't move.

"On your knees, straddling my thighs," he repeats, with more verve this time. It's enough to jolt me.

My mind begins to churn. I'm naked and a mess. He's fully dressed. In clean jeans. If I straddle him—

"I didn't tell you to think. I told you to move." He reaches for me, and I don't struggle. I go willingly, placing a knee on either side of his. "Come closer," he instructs. "I want to be able to reach you easily." His fingertips graze my thighs, as I creep forward. "What were you thinking a moment ago, when you hesitated?"

I swallow hard and pretend it was a rhetorical question, asked to embarrass me, not for a response.

"I won't ask again."

He's not going to let it go. *Oh God.*

"I—I was worried that I might . . . might make your pants wet." It's so embarrassing, I can't bear to look him in the face.

"Like this?" he asks, fingers digging into my hips as he grinds my pussy against his leg until the fabric is soaked.

I look away as shame floods me. Nothing about sex embarrasses him, and he won't be satisfied until I'm the same.

I nod and sputter. "Yes."

"Before we're done, you're going to come all over me. And by the third or fourth time, you're not going to give a damn what gets wet. Now touch yourself. Rub that sweet little cunt for me."

Unsure, I freeze. I don't think I can do this for him. I gaze into his face, pleading silently for reprieve, but Antonio's not having any of it.

He takes my hand and moves it between my thighs, pressing it there. "Do you grind your palm into that greedy pussy, or do you use your fingers to make yourself come?"

I'm a ball of energy, with misfiring synapses. The connections are haywire, and I don't know what to do.

"Show me," he urges, gently, when I don't respond.

There's something about his tone that calms me.

I draw a breath, and slowly, let my fingers circle my clit,

concentrating on how easily they swirl over the slick flesh. *And how good it feels.* My eyelids flutter, until they close. It's easier not to look at him while I stroke my pussy. Easier to not let him see my conflicted thoughts.

"Open your eyes."

No!

"Look at me," he demands. "I want to see you as the need mounts."

I force my eyes open.

"That's it," he purrs. His gaze has no judgment as it heats. *None.*

Now that I'm not hiding from him, I stroke tentatively. But not for long. My pussy is impatient, and as my arousal climbs, my fingers dance, teasing and kneading as I fly.

His eyes are dark pools of lust. The closer I get to the edge, the shallower *his* breathing becomes. *Antonio Huntsman affected by a dirty little show.*

My fingers quicken as I revel in the newfound power.

But Antonio is not without his own sway. He drags two fingers over the slippery flesh, before sliding them inside me. I gasp, and my head falls back when he joins the party. "Ride my fingers," he encourages, curling them toward my inner walls.

My hips rock, timidly at the start. But even the small movements send waves of pleasure through me, and I pull him deeper, until I'm seated on his hand.

"What do you think about when you're all alone, rubbing that beautiful pussy?"

I don't speak. Instead, I trace his jaw with my tongue.

He grunts and scissors his fingers, opening me wider.

The unrelenting pressure makes my thighs quiver.

"Answer me. What do you think about?"

"You. You," I repeat, as his fingers slow, easing their way back to the rough spot on my walls. The spot that makes me gasp for breath as he caresses it.

"I think of you too," he admits, his voice like crushed stone. "Every damn time."

My walls clamp down on his fingers, and I buck, and buck, as the orgasm washes over me like a giant wave. This one stronger than before.

Antonio pulls me toward him, holding my trembling body against his. I close my eyes and listen to his pounding heart.

"Never be embarrassed to show yourself to me. Or to come apart while I watch. Never be embarrassed about what makes you feel good. Your pleasure brings me pleasure, *Princesa*."

His tenderness is unexpected. I tighten my arms around his shoulders and melt into him.

"Don't get too comfortable. We're not done. On your hands and knees. Ass in the air. I want easy access."

Every muscle in my body stiffens. "No. No," I repeat. There's no way in hell I'm letting him do that.

He pulls my hair, angling my face toward his. "Pleading isn't going to get you anywhere. I already told you that."

He pauses, but his eyes don't leave my face as they watch and wait. "Say it, or get on your hands and knees," he says after a long moment passes. "We don't have all day."

The word is on the tip of my tongue as I stare into his eyes. The darkness eclipses the light—but it's there. It will return. I'm not worried.

And I'm not ready to stop him—not yet. "You can't expect me to move while you're holding my hair."

He nods. It's such a small movement, as though it's meant not for me but for himself. Without a word, he releases his hold on me, and I roll onto my stomach.

While I get on my knees, Antonio loses his shirt, but not his pants. Watching him undress feels like a small victory—like I've bought myself some time, or maybe he's changed his mind. My muscles unspool one at a time, as the cool sheet soothes my heated skin.

Nestled behind me, he wraps his arms around my body, cupping my breasts while his flat tongue forges a path along my spine, caressing each vertebra on his way up. "You're so sweet," he purrs, dipping two fingers into my sensitive pussy. After he draws them out, he holds them to my lips. "Suck, like a good girl. Clean your juices, just like you would off my cock."

I don't hesitate. I don't think. I just draw his fingers into my greedy mouth, feeling the rough denim against my back while I suck, like it's his cock. I'm aroused again. His voice. His touch. His filthy talk. Everything crashes over me, as he pushes his fingers deeper into my mouth. So deep, I gag.

"Such a good *Princesa*," he says, pulling his hand away.

I hear rustling behind me, but when I turn my head to look, his hand falls hard on my ass.

"I didn't say you could move."

The cheek where the blow landed is on fire, when the icy liquid drips into the hollow of my back. *"Ahhhh!"* I lunge forward, because I can't keep still. No one could.

He folds an arm around my waist, dragging me back toward him. "Until you use the safeword, you'll take everything I give you. All of it."

18

ANTONIO

I pull off my belt, and let it shimmy across her ass and the back of her thighs. But I don't strike her. And I don't threaten or warn. I'm patient, affording her ample opportunity to remember the bite of the strap when it strikes her flesh. I let her brain dwell on the possibilities as the leather caresses her smooth skin.

When she's perfectly still, I squeeze the lube into the dip of her lower back. This time, she doesn't crawl away. She barely flinches. Experience is an exceptional teacher.

Her skin glistens as I dip my fingers into the thick lube and drag it down her crack, circling the little bud that's going to bloom for me. I press my thumb over the tight hole, applying constant pressure. Her body stiffens, and my cock leaks.

"Only my fingers, *Princesa*. I'm not going to take your ass. Not today." *But I will.*

Not going to lie—I'd love nothing more than to sink balls-deep into that tight little hole. Even though the pleasure will ultimately dull the initial pain, I don't have the stomach to hurt her—even for a few minutes. Not after what she's been through.

"We're going to explore slowly. And you're going to use the plug I gave you when we get back to Porto."

I glide a soothing hand over her back, keeping my voice low. But I don't stop the dirty talk. She likes it as much as I do. "It'll train you to take my cock without pain. Soon you'll love having all your holes filled. You'll crave it, even when you're still too shy to ask for it." The image of her craving my debauchery sends a telltale tingle to the base of my spine, and my dick is still in my pants. *Jesus Christ.*

She whimpers as my thumb breaches the bud. *Fuck. It's tight.* "Breathe. That's it. Now relax and let me in," I murmur, reaching around to stroke her pussy with my free hand. After a few minutes of teasing her cunt, she's more pliable.

I slide my thumb out of her ass and replace it with a well-lubed finger, twisting it carefully while I lavish more attention on her clit. The little mewls and gasps are making my balls ache. I need her around my cock.

I can't hold out much longer, but I want to shatter her. I want her to come so hard, to be so wasted, she forgets about everything and falls into a peaceful sleep.

I stroke harder, sliding my finger in and out of her back passage, until she's whimpering and wriggling into my hand. When I add another finger, she groans. Long and low. The sound goes straight to my dick. "You're a dirty *Princesa*, and I'm going to make you come so hard."

"Yes," she whimpers. "Yes. Please."

I pull back, taking my fingers with me. She protests, but I ditch my pants and I'm behind her, before she can beg again. My balls are tight, and I'm long past needing to empty myself inside her. *Long past.* I can barely think straight. And I don't trust myself to be careful. I don't trust myself at all. "Say it. The safeword. Say it."

She doesn't respond. She just pushes her ass against my aching cock. *That's a mistake, Princesa.* "Say it," I growl.

She shakes her head. "No. I don't want you to stop."

A rumble escapes from my chest. *I'm not fucking stopping.* Nothing could get me to stop. "I'm not stopping. I just need to know you remember the word."

"Don't stop," she pouts, indignantly, before spitting out the word, "*Red.*"

That's all I need. I dig my fingertips into her hips and bury myself deep inside her cunt.

Her scream echoes in my veins. But I don't still. I reach around and rub her sensitive little nub, while I drive two thick fingers into her ass.

My mind is blank.

Every thought is the heat squeezing my dick. My fingers. My spine is tingling like a motherfucker. *Can't hold back. Can't.* Black dots cloud my vision. I pinch her clit, driving deeper and harder, until all I know is her smell and the ferocious heat of her body.

I shudder as her tight pussy holds me inside, while she comes hard around me, squeezing my heavy shaft until I empty myself with a roar that leaves her trembling under me.

By the time I'm spent, my limbs are so heavy, I can barely move. *Christ.*

She winces as I ease my fingers out of her, then my cock. I press a small kiss to her crown, and get up to wash my hands and find a warm cloth for her. My legs are jelly. I nearly lost control a half dozen times, and almost came in my pants like a damn teenager.

She does things to me—makes me feel things that are dangerous. She distracts me, beckoning me closer and closer to a place I can't afford to go. If I had half a brain, I would put her on Gray's plane and ask him to drop Daniela and Valentina on an obscure island, where they could have everything they wanted and needed, but where no one could ever find them. Not even me.

But I won't do it—not for her, not for the good of the valley, not even to save myself.

Daniela's curled up on her side when I get back. Her pussy is flaming red, like it's been well-used. I slide the washcloth between her legs gingerly. I know she's sore.

She grimaces and moans at invasion.

And my dick twitches, thinking about another round. "I'm just going to clean you up a little."

"Shower," she mutters, eyes closed.

"Not now. It'll leave you wide awake, and you need sleep. We have a long day ahead of us." A long fucking road ahead, one that might lead nowhere but to heartache. Not just for her, but for me too. I'm not ready to admit that—to anyone—including her. But I rarely lie to myself. It's too damn dangerous.

Daniela starts to sit up. "Valentina."

"Is fine." I guide her shoulders back to the mattress. "I'll wake you with enough time to freshen up before we land. Until then, sleep, my sweet *Princesa*."

I tuck the quilt around her and brush the matted hair off her face, while wishing I could make it all disappear. Every rotten thing that's made her soul weep. But even I don't have that kind of power.

My phone vibrates with a message. I pull it out, and stare at the screen.

Cristiano: **Tomas missed two meetings today. Hasn't left the house since the wedding.**

Antonio: **That sonofabitch better still be breathing.**

Cristiano: **He is. Just running scared from what we can tell.**

Antonio: **Good. I want to look in his eyes when I steal his last painful breath. Activate our man on the ground.**

19

ANTONIO

Daniela's out of her seat before the wheels touch down.
"Sit until we stop taxiing."

She glares at me, then sits her fine little ass in the seat. It's the first time our eyes have met since the bedroom.

She slept for most of what was left of the flight, while I worked. I checked on her a couple of times, and she was out cold. I only hope it was a peaceful sleep. I drained every ounce of energy from her, and every reserve I could find, but still, even exhausted, sleep isn't always restful. Sometimes it's filled with the worst of our demons.

When the plane stops on the private landing strip, the door doesn't open fast enough for Daniela. Her lips are pursed, and her well-fucked body is tight as a drum again. I can see it from here.

"If you don't make a conscious effort to relax, I'm going to drag you back into the bedroom and I won't let you out until you're blabbering again. I don't give a damn who's waiting on us."

She scowls at me, lifting her cute little chin. But she doesn't engage.

"You don't get to act like a haughty *Princesa* after you came hard around my cock with my fingers in your ass. You were begging for release."

"You really are an asshole."

"I really am. Now breathe. Deep breaths. You're not getting off this plane until you take a few."

She draws a breath, and then another, and another. It lowers her anxiety, but not anywhere near as much as I'd like to see.

I put a hand on her back as the airstairs are being secured. Orange blossom floats from her freshly shampooed hair every time she moves her head. "I'm here if you need me. Just throw me a sign."

She gazes up at me with those whiskey-colored eyes. "Thank you," she says, earnestly.

"For what?"

"For bringing Valentina back to me."

"We're a team, *Princesa*. We haven't quite found our way. We still work together like rabid dogs. But we'll figure it out."

She nods, but I'm not sure she believes it. I said it, but I don't really believe it either. It would take a goddamn miracle for us to make it work. And I've never been a big believer in miracles. "Have you decided what you're going to tell Valentina about us?"

Her body is rigid. "The truth. We're more than friends. We're married. But it might need to wait until tomorrow. I'm going to play it by ear and see how she's holding up after I tell her about Isabel."

"When will you tell her the truth about her mother? The mother who carried her in her womb and gave up the coveted title so the little girl could be happy and safe? When are you going to tell her about the mother who risked life and limb, and everything in between, for her daughter?"

All the color has drained from her cheeks. "I'm not telling her any of that. Ever. And don't you dare tell her, either."

"It's not my story to tell." I'm not sure it registers, or if Daniela even believes I'll keep her secret. Getting to Valentina seems to be her focus.

She takes a step toward the door, and I grab her arm. "I realize you want to get to Valentina, but you need to think of your own safety too. That's non-negotiable."

Daniela doesn't say a word, but when the all clear signal comes from below, she barrels down the stairs, toward Gray, who's on the tarmac.

I let her go. The advance team is on the ground, and they sent word that it was safe to land. Besides, Gray wouldn't be standing in a danger zone. He doesn't have that kind of death wish.

My stride is twice hers, and I'm just a few feet behind her when she reaches Gray.

"Where's Valentina?" she asks, panic in her voice.

"You must be Daniela. I'm Gray Wilder."

"I'm sorry." She's breathless. "I didn't mean to be rude."

"Valentina's just fine. She's asleep. Delilah stayed on the plane with her."

At the top of the airstairs, an attractive blonde, who doesn't look like she does difficult extractions for the government, is propped against the door. When Daniela looks up at the Wilder plane, the blonde waves.

"And no apology necessary. You have plenty on your mind."

Daniela squeezes Gray's arm. "Thank you. I don't know how I can ever repay you."

"Don't worry about it. This guy," he says, jerking his chin toward me, "is getting the bill."

Today has already cost me plenty, not in cash, but in emotion—a resource much more scarce.

"Thank you, Gray," she calls over her shoulder, as she takes the airstairs, two at a time.

I put out my hand, but Gray shoves it away and embraces me.

"I owe you."

"Big time," he quips, but he doesn't mean a word of it. "Send me a case of your best Port and we're even. Preferably the one my brother, JD, called you about."

"You're going to share?"

"Not a fucking chance. I'm going to rub his damn nose in it."

I snicker.

"I read about your wedding. The big bang is supposed to come after the ceremony. What the hell happened?"

20

ANTONIO

"We don't know." I spew the bitter words, my hands fisted at my side and the tension rising.

Knowledge is power. Anything you don't know makes you weak. Vulnerable to the enemy. It's that simple. "Someone either wanted to kill Daniela, or they were willing to risk her death to stop the wedding. Despite what the news is reporting, there were five deaths at the church." Not counting the bastard from the florist, who I killed myself.

"Isabel's murder?"

There's going to be no end to the probing. I can feel it already.

"Not a coincidence."

"And you know this how?"

I scowl at him. "I'm not an idiot."

"You are if you jump to conclusions and tie things together that shouldn't be connected. It could be a red herring."

Not a fucking chance. "It could be, but it's not."

"Valentina is twelve," Gray says, gauging my reaction through a pointed squint, "and Daniela looks like a coed. Tell me I'm wrong. Tell me she's older than she looks."

"She's twenty-four," I mutter through gritted teeth, venom running through my veins.

"Why is your cousin still breathing?" he asks through clenched teeth. Gray's a middle child, born after a hothead, and he doesn't rattle easily.

"I only learned about it this morning. He's going to have an unpleasant end. Trust me." I suck in a long breath, but it doesn't cleanse the Huntsman stench. Nothing can eradicate that. "My father was involved up to his eyeballs."

I'm not exactly sure why I share this with Gray. Maybe it's because he, of all people, understands what it's like to have a father who's more devil than man. Maybe I need empathy from someone who understands what it's like to be tainted by the worst kind of evil. Or maybe I'm just a pussy, and I need a little stroking.

"In what way?" he asks, with a deceptive calm.

Where do I begin? He was the fucking leader. I'm sure he created the plan. Reveled in destroying the enemy. After they took my mother in, protected her from his wrath, that's how he saw the D'Sousas. *The enemy.* "He raped and killed Daniela's mother. He would have raped her, too, but the sonofabitch couldn't get it up." The mere thought of it makes me want to puke all over my shoes.

"That's why we're friends," he replies coolly. "We have our Norman Rockwell upbringing in common."

I glance up at the Wilder plane. The women are just inside the door, heads together.

"Who else knows about the rape—and the kid?"

"From what we know, a handful of people knew about the rape. Even fewer know about the child. Most of them aren't suspects." *Most of them aren't even alive.*

"How's Daniela doing?"

"She's tough, Gray. Much tougher than most women who grow up in the lap of luxury with doting parents. Although after her mother was killed, the life she's had would toughen anyone who was able to survive it." *And I haven't done anything to help the situation. I've just been another bastard, heaping on more shit.*

"It's the tough ones you need to worry about. They function by burying their pain. Not a good coping mechanism for the long-term."

Tell me about it. I don't respond because complex emotions that aren't hatred and rage are beyond my bandwidth.

"You love her. This has got to be tough on you too."

Love? Another emotion outside my range. "Don't read too much into our relationship. I've already told you my world isn't like yours."

"Save the bullshit for someone else. I've known you a long time. If you didn't care about her, you wouldn't be here. And you sure as hell wouldn't have called me. You'd have sent Cristiano or someone else to get the girl, and hoped for the best. By now, you'd be somewhere with a whiskey in one hand and your dick in a pretty mouth, licking your wounds because your father fucked up your life again."

He's insufferable. *Especially when he's right.* "She's my wife. That's why I'm here."

Gray scoffs. "Tell yourself whatever you want, but I'm going to give you a piece of advice and you're going to listen to what I have to say because you called me in the middle of the night and I came through—just like you would have done for me."

I kick a pebble across the pavement like a churlish teenager who's about to get a lecture. But he delivered, as promised, so I keep my mouth shut. At least for the moment.

"This is hard shit," Gray says emphatically. "It's not for pussies. Sometimes our better angels dress up like demons. And our demons disguise themselves as angels. It's how they keep men like us on our toes."

"English isn't my native language, although I'm quite fluent.

Even the nuances rarely escape me. But I have no fucking clue what you're saying."

"What I'm saying, asshole, is it's your job to figure out what she needs, and it's probably not going to be under the first box you lift up. And even when you find it, it might not seem right to you. It might prick your conscience and test your humanity. She might need something from you that's hard to give in the moment. Something that makes you believe you are the monster that you worry you are. She might need something that actually shames you. Imagine that. The all-powerful Antonio Huntsman ashamed."

I know exactly the kind of monster I am. And so does she. "Not everyone sees the world through your lens. I'm not a Dominant, and Daniela's not a submissive."

"I haven't spent enough time around her to know what she is, and I certainly wouldn't trust your judgment in that area," he snarls. "But you're not a Dom. I'll give you that. You're an asshole like my brother. Why agree on rules upfront when you can make them up as you go along?" Gray shakes his head. "But you could stand to play by at least one of my rules. The hierarchy of needs. The golden rule." He pauses his little lesson to take a breath.

"You've played in my club, so I know you've had training. But let me remind you. Her needs come first. *Always.* Before anything else. Before you go on some half-cocked scheme to help her, you check your gut and make sure you're not just doing what's easy—for you. You make sure those aren't your own needs you're satisfying."

His words, with all their weight, fall squarely on my shoulders. I don't buckle, only because I'm used to carrying heavy burdens. But it takes everything I have to stand straight and keep my head up like a man.

Gut check. Make sure those aren't your own needs you're satisfying.

"It's easy to talk about but hard to do, and I don't know if you're up to it. But if you're not, and you keep a woman to play with, who's been through what she's been through, you're nothing more than an asshole who swings a limp dick around like it's a slice of sweet potato pie."

Satisfy my own needs. Is that what I did today when I tore through her boundaries? It's not what I intended. Not really. But how the fuck can a man like me ever expect to put her back together again? Erase the damage and make her whole? What do I know about that kind of thing? I'm so goddamn selfish that I have no fucking clue where to begin to assess another human being's emotional needs. Certainly not those of a woman who's been dragged through hell—by my family. She'd be better off if I stayed away from her, and the kid, too.

That's what she really needs. And I don't have to do a gut check to know it.

21

DANIELA

After we say hello, Delilah leads me to the middle cabin, where Valentina is sound asleep. She looks like an angel. A sense of euphoria floods me, as I watch her chest rise and fall. *She's safe.* My knees wobble, and I grasp the wall for support.

She's safe.

I press my lips together and hold my fingers to my mouth. But I can't stop the gush of tears as the sense of relief washes over me. I know it's not over, but for now, my baby is here and she's safe. I'll do whatever it takes to keep it that way. *Whatever it takes.*

Delilah rests her hand on my arm. "I know you want to hold her in your arms, but we need to talk first. Once she's awake, it'll be impossible for us to grab a minute alone."

After watching her sleep for a bit longer, I reluctantly follow Delilah into the forward cabin.

"Valentina's tired, but otherwise in good spirits," she says, keeping her voice low. "We distracted her as best as we could. She asked a lot of questions, and at first, she was apprehensive. The code word helped. Good thinking."

The code word. The one we had for the kind of emergency that I hoped would never come to be. "What does she know?"

"We told her that Isabel couldn't make the trip, and that you would give her all the details when we arrived. We didn't breathe a single word about anything else."

No, breaking her heart is my job. I wish there was a way to shield her from the pain, but I can't think of a single one.

"Thank you." I squeeze Delilah's slender fingers. "I don't know how I can ever thank you for bringing her to me. For keeping her safe."

"She's a great kid."

I beam, like a proud mama, because despite what we told the world, inside me, where it counts, she's always been mine.

"That guy out there." Delilah jerks her head toward the door. "The one with the chiseled jaw and the blue jeans wrapped around his fine ass. *Antonio*." Her brow crinkles above her clear blue eyes. "You sure you want to go back with him?"

Do I want to go back with him? Do I have a choice?

I peer out the door, at the man standing on the tarmac with the blue jeans wrapped around what is indeed a fine ass. The one who's often misguided and ruthless, with the kind of power and determination that can keep Valentina safe. *That makes me feel safe, too, even if it's an illusion.* He's our best chance for survival. I'm sure of it.

"Yes." I nod. "We're safe with him." *Mostly.*

"Are you sure? 'Cuz even from here, that man smells like trouble. I know, because I've got one of my very own. Men who look like that are always trouble," she adds, under her breath. "If you're not absolutely certain, you could come back to Charleston with us, where you can take some time to make the best decision for yourself," she tips her head toward the inner cabin, "and for her. I have friends there. Good people. We'll help you get settled."

There's so much I love about the US. But being back in

Porto—even against my wishes—it's home. And Antonio—he's definitely trouble. Our path has been treacherous as we've traversed storm after storm. The wind is still howling, the sun isn't shining, and the road is filled with snakes. But the pull I feel to him is like no other. In my heart, I know my destiny is with him.

I smile at Delilah, who is a better ally than I could have ever imagined. "You're very kind, and I have no doubt your friends are very nice, but Porto is our home. Valentina will be happy there. Please don't worry about us."

Her lips are pursed, and I'm not sure I've allayed any concerns, so I try again. "Antonio is a complicated man, and even though I've known him my whole life, I'm still unwrapping the package. But what I do know is that he's more than he shows the world." *God, I hope I'm right.*

"If you change your mind, or need anything, whatever it might be—you call me." She hands me a business card, and I clutch it in my hand. "I gave Valentina a card too, and I made her memorize my number in case she's ever in trouble and can't reach you."

"Thank you." *I pray she never needs to call Delilah, because if she does, something will have gone terribly wrong.* "I don't know how I'll ever repay your kindness."

"Take good care of Valentina." Her expression softens. "Help her grow up to be a woman who knows her own mind and has the courage to follow her dreams, wherever they take her. That'll be thanks enough."

"I want those things for her too." *And so much more.*

She's quiet for a moment, and the air around us grows mournful. I can almost hear the angels weep. "I was going to tell you that twelve-year-old girls can be resilient. I know from experience," she adds, her voice hoarse. "Even when bad shit happens, they can rise above the ashes, and go on to live a good life. But I don't need to tell you. I think you already know that the events of childhood, awful as they might be, don't have to define the women we become."

I nod, wrestling with emotion. Sometimes it takes a stranger to drill down into the darkness and sum up our worst fears, bathing them in light, where everything seems possible. Although I suspect Delilah is more of a kindred spirit than a stranger.

It remains to be seen how the next chapters of my life will turn out. Or if the events of my childhood will define me as a woman. But Valentina? She will rise like a phoenix, even if I have to drag her from the ashes until she takes her first breath. Her life will be amazing. *I'll make sure of it.*

Delilah takes my hands and squeezes. "I'm going to the tarmac to say hello to Antonio and save him from Gray, who I'm sure is giving him an earful. There's a flight attendant on board if you need anything. She won't bother you unless you call for her. Take as long as you need with Valentina. We have time."

She turns and walks off the plane, cloaked in the kind of confidence that money can't buy. I watch for a moment while Delilah descends the stairs. I don't pretend to know what they are, but I have no doubt that her scars run deep too.

Something stirs in the middle cabin, and I gather my courage and follow the sound.

Valentina's still fast asleep. The fleece blanket that was tucked around her is on the floor. I pick it up and take a seat next to her. She doesn't stir.

I would like to freeze this moment in time. Where she's a carefree child who hasn't been exposed to the burdens of life. *The evils.* When Jorge left, she fretted for a while, and she was angry at him for walking out without a single goodbye. But he'd become so volatile that I think part of her was as relieved as the rest of us that he left. This won't be like that. Isabel's death is going to cut deep.

I sweep my hand over her cheek, pushing some stray strands of hair off her face. "Hey, sleepyhead."

Her eyes pop open and she bolts upright, lunging into my arms. "Lala!"

My heart squeezes at the name she's called me since she began to talk. Now she uses it only when her friends aren't around. As a teenager, I played a game with myself, pretending Lala was her way of saying Mama. *L* is so close to *M*, I'd often tell myself. For a long time, I actually believed it.

"Where's *Mamai*? Is she coming with us?"

I wrap my arms tighter, rubbing her back, inhaling the sweet scent of the fruity shampoo she loves.

I'm going to break her heart. There's no choice.

"*Mamai* died a few hours ago. She's with God, and with my mother who loved her so much."

Valentina pulls back, cocking her head, while she searches my face. I'm not sure anything I said registered. "Died?" she asks, as if trying out the word, like a newborn colt tries its legs.

I nod.

The rush of emotion engulfs her, before the wail comes. It's painful to watch. She latches onto me, sobbing and shaking. I murmur softly into her hair and rub circles on her back, like Isabel did for me when my *mamai* died. But it's not enough, because the hole in her heart can't be filled from the outside.

When a young girl loses her mother, she loses a part of herself. Not a part that exists right then, but a piece of her future self. In its place, there's a grief so pervasive even her fingernails hurt. There's also the daunting fear of the unknown that takes on a life of its own, growing even more formidable when you're alone in your bed at night.

But the worst part of losing your *mamai* is that awful black hole, bleak and empty, with tentacles that burrow into every corner of your being, feasting on your soul.

I would do anything to ward off the demons. To spare her

the pain. But even if I could, some of it's necessary. She won't heal properly without the journey. All I can do is lift the torch so that it's not so dark, and walk with her.

"She can't be dead, Lala," Valentina sobs. "She wasn't even sick. Are you sure? Did you see her?"

"I'm sure," I answer quietly, wishing I could say differently. "I love her, too, *querida*. Cry all you need. I'm right here. I love you, Valentina, and I'm going to take good care of you. Be sad she's gone, but don't worry. We'll get through this together. I promise."

I'm not sure how long we cling to each other. Or how many questions she asks. *How? When? Who? Why? Where?* I answer every question as best I can without frightening her, but in truth I have so few answers. *Perhaps it's for the best.*

The time bleeds away as we try to come to terms with our fresh grief, mired by the sorrow.

22

ANTONIO

Delilah's a ball-buster, although she has the kind of face that allows her to squeeze hard before most men realize their balls are no longer intact. But I'm not most men, and she's not my type. I've about run out of patience waiting for Daniela to appear, and Delilah's frosty attitude isn't helping.

"I'm going up to see what's taking so long," I tell Gray, as I turn toward the Wilder plane. The words aren't out of my mouth before a small hand tightens around my forearm. I don't shrug her off—it would be easy enough to do, but she brought us the girl safely. Plus, Gray has been looking at her like she shits ice cream, so instead, I scowl at the place where her hand rests, and then at her face.

"I told Daniela she could take as long as they need. Unless you know something different, this is a secure location."

"We need to get back. There are things that require my attention. Important things. They can catch up on the way back."

She glares at me before removing her hand. "They're not catching up," she chides, with some disdain. "But before they come out, there's something I want to make clear. *Crystal clear.*"

Her lazy drawl is seductive, and I'm sure it's cost more than one man his dignity. "If you harm a hair on either of their heads, if you cause them *any* grief, you'll answer to me. I don't care how much money you have, or what kind of power you wield, I'll come for you."

I chuckle. Mostly out of surprise, but also because it's exactly the gauntlet I would lay down.

Gray's smirking like the smug bastard he is. "I'd take that threat to heart if I were you. Doesn't seem like she's playin'."

I ignore the sarcasm. He might not realize it yet, but he has his hands full. I make a note to ask his brother about her the next time he calls begging for Port, then I turn my full attention to the mouthy blonde. "You don't need to worry about either of them."

"That best be the case."

"Here they come," Gray mutters.

I glance over my shoulder. Daniela and a young girl are holding hands as they descend the stairs. From afar, they could pass for sisters, with their long, dark hair and slight builds. Daniela's taller, but not by much.

I take several steps toward the airstairs, remembering Daniela at that age. Mostly I recall her eyes. The way they twinkled with mischief and confidence. *I wonder if Valentina has that same sparkle.*

I've seen pictures of the girl—or rather, pictures of Daniela with the girl somewhere in the background. Because we never realized who she was, no one ever bothered to capture her on film—to really capture her. *We didn't bother with her at all.* In truth, I didn't care if she lived or died. My only concerns revolved around Daniela.

As the space between us disappears, I finally get a good look at the girl's face.

Jesus Christ.

She looks a lot like Daniela. The shape of her face, her

nose, and mouth are her mother's. But her eyes are not the color of an aged Tawny, like Daniela's. They're a brilliant violet-blue, framed by thick black lashes. It's an unusual color, outside of fiction. I've only ever known one other person with that eye color. *Vera Huntsman.* My mother's sister. Tomas's mother. Although as an adult, Vera's eyes weren't as vibrant as Valentina's. They were more of a muddy blue, almost washed out. *Probably from all the tears she shed at the hand of my bastard uncle.* But in some of the photos taken of her as a child—the similarity is startling.

"Valentina, this is Antonio Huntsman. I've been staying at *Senhor* Huntsman's house in Porto."

She didn't tell Valentina we're married. I'm not surprised. But from the girl's tear-stained face, she told her about Isabel.

"It's nice to meet you, Valentina. I'm so sorry to hear about Isabel's passing." I don't refer to Isabel as *your mother*, because while I'll keep Daniela's secret, I won't perpetuate the lie. It serves no one now—especially not Daniela. "I met her several years ago in Porto. She loved Daniela, and I'm sure she loved you too."

Daniela visibly relaxes when I behave like a decent human being. *Noted.*

"It's nice to meet you, *Senhor* Huntsman," Valentina says shyly, in perfect Portuguese.

Those eyes. There's no way we're going to be able to keep her parentage from anyone who knew Vera as a child. Fortunately, at this point in time, those people are few and far between. I'm not concerned about Tomas, because that sonofabitch's days are numbered. He won't see the harvest. With any luck, he'll be in hell before the first grape turns purple. *But what about Rafael? And my mother?* The very second my mother lays eyes on the child, there's no going back.

Gray and Delilah slowly make their way to where we're huddled. "We need to get back to Charleston."

"Thank you for bringing me here," Valentina says, with all the politeness and poise I would expect from Daniela's daughter. "And for teaching me about the South."

"You'll come to Charleston in December for our wedding, right?" Delilah asks the girl.

She gazes at her mother, who gazes back, the connection between them rock-steady and pure.

Despite how hard you tried to tear them apart—to sever that connection between mother and child. My chest tightens at the lengths I went to make that happen.

"I've never been to Charleston," Daniela says, with more cheer than she must be feeling. "It sounds like fun."

I expect it will be fun. *What I didn't expect is that I'd have two dates for the wedding.*

"I think that's a yes." Valentina smiles at Delilah. "Will you make shrimp and grits?"

"*Noooo*," Gray says, elongating the word. "You're our friend, darlin'. We won't let her make you anything to eat. But we know someone who makes them real good. Remember what I told you—" He jerks his head toward me, while winking at her.

Hopefully he kept out the part about me being an asshole.

Once Gray and Delilah walk away, we're on our own to muddle through the quiet sorrow and the awkwardness. Two adults and a child who can no longer distract themselves with the talk of weddings and Southern cuisine. Isabel's still dead—along with several others. *And I don't know who's next. I hate living with the unknown—especially when the stakes are so goddamn high.* Well, there are certainly no answers on an island in the middle of nowhere.

"We should go home, too." I gesture toward the plane.

Valentina freezes, before trembling.

Daniela wraps an arm around her. "It's going to be okay," she murmurs, pulling her close. "I'm right here."

"I don't want to go to Fall River," the girl cries. "I'm afraid. What if they kill you, too? Or maybe they'll kill me."

My chest rumbles. Little girls shouldn't have to worry about being murdered. Not even in my world.

"We're not going to Fall River. We're going to Porto," I explain, before Daniela can reassure her. "You'll be safe there. I won't let anyone hurt you, or Daniela. You have my promise."

She peers into my eyes in much the same way her mother does. Assessing me. Rifling through the bullshit in search of clues. *Can my word be trusted? Can I be trusted at all?* That's what she's wondering. *Smart kid.*

After several seconds, she appears to relax a bit and gives me a small nod. I either passed muster, or she decided that I was her best option for remaining alive.

"Let's go, ladies."

While they board, I scan the tarmac and surrounding area. The Wilder plane is taxiing onto the runway. Nothing seems amiss. But danger awaits us. Every cell in my body knows it.

The promise I made Valentina was from the heart. But it's been on shaky ground from the moment the words tumbled out of my mouth. Until we identify the enemy, they're both vulnerable. There's no getting around it.

23

DANIELA

When the car pulls up to Antonio's house in the valley, Valentina's asleep.

"Don't wake her," Cristiano whispers to me. "I'll carry her inside."

"I'll do it," Antonio mutters, with a pointed look at his friend. The one that screams *Back the fuck off. I'm in charge here.* "Go ensure that the activation we discussed earlier is on track."

Activation?

Cristiano doesn't respond—not with words. But the knob in his throat bobs up and down.

I don't waste my breath asking about the *activation*. There will be no forthcoming explanation.

"I'll take her up," Antonio says quietly, "and you can get her settled. She needs sleep, and so do you." He gets out of the car, and then reaches in and lifts Valentina off the seat like she weighs nothing. She mumbles something incoherent but doesn't open her eyes.

While I'm trying to make sense of Antonio with Valentina in his arms, a muscular arm reaches for my overnight bag.

"I'll take care of the luggage," Thiago, our driver, says

kindly. He glances at Antonio, who is almost at the entrance of the house. "Will you get the door for him?"

"Of course. Thank you." I flash him a small smile and hurry to open the door.

"Where are you taking her?" I whisper, when we get inside. I hadn't given the sleeping arrangements much consideration. When Valentina asked me about it on the plane, I told her that the house had lots of bedrooms and that we'd find her a nice one. I never gave it another thought. I vacillated between being grateful she was safe, to the road ahead of us, unpaved, with divots and potholes that, even if they don't swallow us, will leave us stumbling.

Antonio's response is to beckon me to follow.

"Don't drop her," I whisper, when we're at the bottom of the staircase. "Maybe it'll be safer if she walks."

He glares at me over his shoulder and starts upstairs.

I follow closely behind. *To catch her if she falls.* It's a fanciful thought, because she's not a toddler I can snatch from midair. *Not anymore.* Besides, despite my concerns, Antonio won't drop her. I'd stake my life on it.

When we reach the upper landing, he goes directly to my suite, stepping aside so I can open the door.

The light in the sitting area has been dimmed, and someone left a tray with water, a tea kettle, and an array of food. Without stopping, I stride past it and into the bedroom with Antonio on my heels.

The bed has already been turned down, and I pull back the covers completely. When I glance up to tell Antonio to put her down, my heart stops.

He's not paying attention to me. He's looking at her. It's not a leer that would make me rip her out of his arms—it's nothing like that. His expression is serious as he studies her face, but his features are soft. My heart melts.

One of the many things I hadn't considered today was how

Antonio's life would change—again.

He's taking in another child. Valentina is older than Rafael was when he came to live with him, and I'll be the one taking care of her and making decisions. But the household will change. He recognizes it, like I do. I'd give anything to know what he's thinking.

He meets my eyes and holds my gaze for a moment. The responsibility of having a child in the house is not lost on the man who already has too much responsibility.

After he lays her on the bed carefully, I slip off her shoes and socks, and cover her with the luxurious sheet and comforter. She's safe. In my bed. There were moments—hours—when I wasn't sure we'd pull it off. I say a small prayer of thanks before tearing myself away from her.

Antonio waits for me by the sitting room door, his shoulders braced against the plaster, his eyes glued to his phone. He's lost the soft look he had a few minutes ago. In its place is a deadly serious expression. I don't ask what's on his phone that has him worried. He won't tell me, and I'll feel shut out, spoiling the warm feelings I have for him right now.

"Thank you," I murmur, placing my hand on his arm. "There are no words to describe how grateful I am to you for getting her back safe. She's my life."

He nods and runs his fingers through my hair, gently pulling it back. "Victor prepared a light meal. You should eat something before you go to sleep."

"I'm not hungry. But maybe I'll have a little something with a cup of tea," I add quickly. I have no desire for a little something or for tea, but Antonio has a lot on his mind, and he doesn't need to worry that I haven't eaten.

"Your things are in my—our room," he informs me. "I'll stay here, while you get what you need for the night."

I'm exhausted—more mentally than physically—and he must sense my confusion.

"We're married, remember? It's customary for married couples to share a room—at least in the beginning."

How could I forget? I nod.

"This will be Valentina's suite. She can decorate it however she wants. Victor will coordinate the project. These are no longer your rooms."

He's decided, and it's final. That's the way it is with him. My heart clenches. "I can't leave her. She'll be terrified if she wakes up in an unfamiliar place."

"That's why I told you to go and get what you need for tonight."

Just tonight? Nothing will be different tomorrow. "It's going to take her awhile to adjust."

"It's going to take us all awhile to adjust."

There's a weariness in his eyes, and a couple days' worth of scruff on his face that only makes him seem more dangerous. *More attractive.* I itch to run my fingertips over his stubbled jaw, but I don't want to give him the wrong impression. Not that Antonio is the kind of man who waits to be seduced. *He takes what he wants.*

But he's patient right now, more patient than I would expect from an exhausted Antonio, with Santa Ana's in ashes and several dead bodies on his hands. But for some godforsaken reason, I need to make him understand that Valentina needs me, and that she'll continue to need me, and that she's my first priority.

"She's a child, and we're adults."

His expression is unreadable. "I've never been a twelve-year-old girl, but I assume they require the same kind of privacy that twelve-year-old boys require. After tonight, I expect you in our bed every night I'm here. She'll be happy to have some space."

I'm tired, and I should just go get my things and go to sleep. But I'm worried if I don't set a tone with him tonight, while he seems more amenable, I'll lose my chance. *She's my child, not his, but he has to be the boss of everyone.* "You don't know her. You have no idea what makes her happy."

His eyes flare, and I feel his composure slipping. *That didn't take long.*

"Maybe not. But I do know this: You need to tell her we're married. She's been told enough lies. It's time for a little truth."

Something takes hold of me—terror, rage, I'm not sure—but it has me reeling. *He's going to make me tell Valentina that I'm her mother—and Tomas is her father. Or he's going to tell her himself.* That's next. I can feel it.

I pound my fists on his chest like a crazed woman. He lets me release my anxiety, without a single word. When he's had enough—or maybe when I've had enough—he grabs my wrists and holds them still against his chest.

"Don't you dare say a word to her—about anything," I hiss. "Don't you dare."

He reaches over me and shuts the bedroom door. The click is barely audible. At least one of us has the presence of mind not to be overheard.

"I don't take orders from you, *Princesa*. This is still my house."

"Antonio, for the love of God. It'll crush her."

"Stop. Just stop." There's a flicker of light in his eyes. "I have no interest in hurting that little girl, nor do I have any interest in usurping your newly acquired parental status, unless you force my hand. I won't say a word—for now. But sooner, rather than later, you're going to tell her everything. Until you do, a black cloud will hang over your head. You'll always be waiting for the other shoe to drop."

"The other shoe isn't going to drop. She'll never be the wiser as long as you and your friends keep your mouths shut." The words come out far surlier than I mean to be, and even as I say them, I know they're not true. I'm taking a chance keeping the truth from her. I've known it for years, but in the US, it didn't seem as risky. "She doesn't need to know everything." I mimic the tone of finality that he's so fond of using.

Without warning, Antonio drags me through the outer door of the suite.

At first, I think he's taking me to *our* room to punish me. Separating me from Valentina would be the worst kind of punishment, especially tonight. But he's shown me before that he'll stop at nothing to teach me a lesson.

But he leads me in a different direction, to a different wing of the house.

"What are you doing?"

"Giving you a little dose of reality."

24

DANIELA

When we arrive at Rafael's suite, Antonio gropes atop the doorframe, until he finds a key.

"I guess Rafael isn't entitled to the privacy of a twelve-year-old girl," I observe aloud, while he unlocks the door.

"He gets plenty of privacy. But what you don't seem to understand is that this is my house and nothing here is off-limits to me."

Once we're inside, he hauls me into the bedroom, to a tall chest of drawers, where he hands me a framed photograph.

"What—" The question lodges itself in my throat, nearly obstructing my airway. It's a photo of Valentina. *Isn't it? Has someone been following her? Have they known she was Tomas's child all along? No. That doesn't make any sense. I saw how Antonio reacted when he learned about her.* "Where did you get this?"

"It belongs to Rafael."

Why does Rafael have her photo? Does he know she's his niece?

When the initial shock wears off, I notice the details. The young girl in the photo looks like Valentina. *A lot like Valentina.* But it's not her. Those aren't her clothes, and the last formal portrait we have of her was taken when she was five. This girl looks to be about nine or ten, and the photograph has a vintage feel to it.

"Who is this?" I demand, my eyes never leaving the girl's face.

"Vera Huntsman."

Of course.

I ease myself to the floor because my legs can no longer hold me up. Squeezing my eyes shut, I try to remember her. But I can't—not in any great detail. I was young when she disappeared, and before that, she rarely came to our house. I never knew her as well as I knew Antonio's mother.

"The resemblance is striking. Someone's going to make the connection. You need to tell Valentina before that happens."

He's right. Eyes are a defining characteristic.

"With Isabel's death," he continues, "now is a good time to talk to her. The longer you wait, the harder it will be for her to hear the truth. Eventually, so much time will pass that it will become almost impossible for her to forgive the lies." He lowers himself to his haunches, beside me. "I don't want that for you," he murmurs so softly, I can barely hear him.

Anger rips through me, chased by sorrow and frustration. I don't want that for me, either. But I can't bear to tell her. "What am I supposed to say? *You're the parting gift of a monster. A bonus baby from a rape.* There are no words to make it okay. I can't tell her."

"You can. And you will."

The end. He's going to force my hand. Maybe not today, or tomorrow, but he will. I hear the determination in his voice.

"I'm her mother. You're not entitled to make this decision—or *any* decision with regard to her."

"I'm through discussing this—for tonight." He cups my face. While his hold is gentle, I can't wrest myself away. "But know this. I intend on keeping you both safe. At any cost. We're not always going to agree on the methods, but you need to trust me.

Otherwise, your life is going to be more difficult than it needs to be. The last word when it comes to safety—yours and hers—is mine. Always."

I'm tempted to tell him he can go straight to hell. But I bite my tongue.

Without another word, he stalks out of the room, leaving me with something new to keep me awake at night. Not exactly a new concern, but it's more pressing now.

I stare at the little girl for a while longer, before I set the frame on the dresser and go back to my room. *Valentina's room.*

After I brush my teeth, I crawl into bed beside *my* daughter.

Before he marched out of Rafael's room, I wanted to tell him that the last word, when it comes to Valentina, is mine. *I'm not giving her up again.* But I didn't argue, because a part of me is terrified he'll send her away if I make his life too difficult.

I rest my hand on her warm arm. *I won't let that happen.*

25

ANTONIO

"Have you found an assistant for Daniela?"

Cristiano nods. "I think so. Jacinto recommended Lara Ramos."

Lara Ramos. She wouldn't have been the first person I thought of. "That's it? One name? He didn't have anyone else?"

"He said she fit the bill: smart, personable, and loyal. Good family. She's Gloria and Lorenzo Ramos's daughter."

"I know who she is." I've known Lara all my life. Her family has worked for mine for generations, and now she works for me. She's a couple of years younger, but we essentially grew up together.

"Never liked her," Lucas pipes up.

Cristiano scowls at him. "Did she leave you with a bad case of blue balls or something?"

"*Pfft*. Fuck you."

"I trust Jacinto's word on this," Cristiano assures me. "He understands the stakes."

He recommended Paula too, but Victor thinks she's not up to the job. Cristiano might be willing to trust him on this, but

I'm not. We're talking about someone who's going to be inside *my* house with unrestricted access to *my* wife and all our personal business. I want to know everything there is to know about her.

"Why don't you like her?" I ask gruffly with my palms flat on Lucas's desk.

He shrugs. "No reason in particular. Something about her always seemed off."

"Off? What the fuck does that mean?"

"She was an ass-kisser. Always trying to improve her social position. More than most. It always rubbed me the wrong way."

Everybody kisses my ass. If that's the hiring criteria we're using, the whole damn place will have to be shuttered. She was an ass-kisser, I'll give him that. And once or twice I got the impression she was offering to kiss more than my ass, but I never took her up on it, and she backed off. I never gave it another thought—until now.

I glance at Cristiano. "Have you done an independent check? Because there's no way in hell I'm taking Jacinto's word as gospel."

He nods. "I trust him on this, but I'm a big believer in 'trust, but verify.' I dug into her pretty deep. The only thing I found that gave me heartburn is that her neighbor is your Uncle Abel's therapist."

Abel. It makes me sick just to hear his name. But I take solace that the bastard is immersed in his own hell. "Therapist?"

"Occupational and physical therapy."

The stroke left the right side of Abel's body paralyzed, and he has only partial use of his left arm and leg. He doesn't speak, and from what we know, he only understands bits and pieces of what goes on around him. "Why the fuck does he need an occupational therapist? Is he planning on staging a coup from his hospital bed?"

"Palliative therapy. It's not unusual, certainly not for someone like your uncle, who has a lot of resources at his disposal. We'll know more about what goes on in that house soon."

Not soon enough. "What's happening with that?"

"We've made contact," Lucas replies in a clipped tone. He wanted us to sit tight awhile longer, and he's not happy we activated our guy inside. *Too bad.* I want someone we trust with eyes on Tomas. And since he's not leaving the house, we don't have any other choice.

I turn to Cristiano. "Lara and this therapist, just neighbors?"

He rubs a hand over his chest. "Looks that way. Friendly neighbors—but there's no indication there's anything more."

"Is there anything in his background that should concern us? Because it looks like you still have heartburn."

He shakes his head. "No surprises. He runs a small business doing private in-home therapy for several well-to-do clients. Married, no kids, no evidence that he steps out on his wife—she's clean too. He drives a refurbished van, rents his place, no boats or expensive vacations outside the perks of his wife's job. She's a flight attendant with TAP. He's never been in any trouble."

"What about the wife?"

"Clean, as far as I can tell. She's gone a lot because of her job. Not a single red flag with either of them. Lara moved there after her husband and son died. It's another reason I thought Jacinto might be right about her being a good match for Daniela. She understands grief better than most."

I'd forgotten about the car accident that killed her family. It happened around the same time of my *accident*—the one that plunged my car into the raging river and almost killed me.

"Do you want me to interview her, or should we keep looking?"

She has a lot of upside. *A lot*. But given her proximity to Abel's therapist, it's not as clean as I'd like.

"I'll do it. She's going to have access to my life. I want to talk to her myself. Set it up for this afternoon. But keep looking in case it doesn't pan out. If I have a single reservation, she's not the one." *I don't give a shit what Jacinto thinks.*

26

ANTONIO

"*Bom dia,*" Victor says brightly, through the phone. I'm sure having another person in the house to fuss over, a child no less, has energized him.

"Good morning. How are things there?"

"Daniela isn't quite herself, but it's to be expected after what she's been through in the last couple of days. She's putting on a good show in front of Valentina, who, by the way, is a charming little thing. I've been making a list of things for her to do so she's not always thinking about her mother. It's a tragedy to lose one's mother at such a tender age."

I'm sure it's horrible. It certainly was for Rafa. I'm also sure Victor's noticed how much the girl looks like Vera, but he'd never ask me, and he certainly would never breathe a word about it to anyone else. While I don't have the same relationship with Victor that I do with Cristiano and Lucas, he's no less loyal and discreet.

"How long will Valentina be staying?"

No, he wouldn't dream of asking directly, but he'll probe until he strikes gold.

"She'll be with us for a while." I'm not showing all my cards, yet. Not even to Victor. "I'll let you know if anything changes. In the meantime, she should have free rein to decorate her suite—within reason," I add, remembering the regulation-sized basketball hoop Rafa begged to have installed in his suite, complete with painted lines on the wood floor. That did not happen. Not inside the house, anyway. "Anything over-the-top, run by me first."

"Decorating the room might make a nice distraction for her."

"What do you know about Lara Ramos?"

"Gloria and Lorenzo's daughter?"

"Yes."

"Haven't seen her in years. As a child, she was always very polite, maybe a little spoiled, but well-behaved. Her parents doted on her endlessly. Her husband and son died some years ago. I run into Lorenzo from time to time, but the last time I saw Lara or Gloria was at the funeral."

It's difficult to ignore her experience with grief. It could be a double-edged sword, though. She might be an emotional wreck, who would make the situation worse. I'll ask her about it during the interview.

"I'm considering bringing her into the house as an assistant for Daniela."

"Hmmm." He pauses for a few seconds, as though considering it. "Not a bad idea. With Valentina here, she'll need some help juggling her social commitments as your wife and taking care of a child. She'll get the hang of it quickly, I have no doubt, but it's all new to her. Besides, she could use a woman to confide in. The more I think about it, the more I'm convinced Lara's a good choice. In addition to her regular education, she had tutors and the like. Her mother had big hopes that she'd marry above her station." He sighs. "When will she start?"

"I haven't made up my mind. I'm interviewing her in a few minutes."

"Will Daniela have a chance to meet her before she's hired?"

Fucking Victor. "Do not mention a word of this to Daniela until I've sorted it out," I growl. But he has a point. Daniela should have an opportunity to meet with anyone I'm considering for the position. It doesn't cost me a thing, because she won't interview anyone who hasn't already been vetted by me, and it might buy me some goodwill I can cash in later. *No doubt I'll need it at some point.*

"Should I prepare dinner for eight o'clock?" Victor asks, changing the subject.

"Check with Daniela. I won't be there this evening."

———

NOT FIVE MINUTES after I hang up with Victor, my secretary buzzes to let me know that Lara has arrived.

"Send her in."

A slender woman with mousy-brown hair coiled into a bun enters the office. She looks harmless enough, but looks can be deceiving. It might be cliché, but that doesn't make it any less true. In my briefcase, I carry a small jackknife that usually passes through security without issue. That knife can do a lot of damage—and it has.

Because she's a woman, I stand to greet her. "It's nice to see you, Lara. Have a seat, please."

"It's so nice to see you again too." She lowers herself to the chair, crossing her ankles demurely, like someone who's been to finishing school. "Congratulations on your marriage," she gushes, before catching herself. "I'm so sorry about what happened. Thank God no one was hurt."

If you only knew.

"Do you have any idea why I asked you here?"

She lowers her eyes. "Not the details. But when I heard you

wanted to see me, I got so nervous that I—well—let's just say Jacinto told me not to worry, that you weren't angry with me, but that you wanted to discuss changing my position. He didn't give me the specifics."

I size her up while she talks, looking for anything that seems off, like Lucas described.

She's still a bit of an ass-kisser, but mostly I see an articulate and polished woman who's dressed professionally. I can see why Jacinto recommended her, and why Cristiano thought it made sense.

"That's correct," I reply. "I *might* have a position for you—no promises."

"Of course," she says, sitting taller.

"My wife needs a personal assistant. We have a twelve-year-old staying with us for the time being, who recently lost her mother. She was a friend of my wife's. They're both grieving, and I expect the next few months to be challenging. After what you've been through with your own family, do you feel as though you're ready to deal with this kind of situation, day-to-day?"

"Certainly. But I'm not a counselor," she adds, backpedaling a bit.

"I'm not looking for a counselor. What I'm asking is, will it be too much, too soon?"

She pauses, contemplating for a moment, which I appreciate. "To tell you the truth, you never get over losing a child, or a spouse. But it's easier now than last year, and that was easier than the year before. Although during the holidays, it's still quite painful. But sometimes focusing on someone else's pain can ease your own. To answer your question, *no*, it's not too soon."

I have no reason to disbelieve her—not yet, anyway. "Tell me about your relationship with your neighbor, Elliot."

She tips her head to the side. "I'm sorry. I don't understand what you mean."

"What type of relationship do you have with Elliot?" Her reaction to the question will tell me more than her answer.

Lara's jaw falls open, and she looks aghast. "He's married, *Senhor* Antonio. I have no relationship with him. We're neighbors."

"There are plenty of neighbors who enjoy all kinds of relationships."

She sticks her chin out, ever-so-slightly. "I'm sure that's true, but our relationship begins and ends as neighbors."

Lara's uncomfortable having her morality questioned, but there's no outward sign she's lying—she maintains eye contact, no tics, and her hands remain in her lap.

"While I'm doing the preliminary vetting for the position, my wife will make the final decision. I'm going to pass along your name to her, and someone will be in touch, if she'd like to meet you."

"Thank you," she says, standing.

"There's one thing you should know before accepting a position in my household, should it come to that." She peers at me with great intensity. I have her complete attention. "Any breach of loyalty, however inconsequential, will be punished. The consequences will be severe. And I'll be the one to mete them out, not my wife. There are no second chances for traitorous infractions."

She pales at my candor. Or maybe it's my icy tone. I couldn't care less. Everyone knows I don't tolerate disloyalty from any Huntsman employee. But the closer you get to my inner sanctum, to my family, the higher the bar. I don't care how long I've known her. If she betrays my trust, her blood will be washed into the storm drains of Porto like any other criminal.

She holds her head high. "My family has always been

discreet and loyal to yours. And I have continued in their proud tradition."

Then we'll have no problems. "Good day, Lara. Send my regards to your parents."

"Thank you for the opportunity. If I'm fortunate enough to get the position, you won't be disappointed," she says, before leaving.

I'm not entirely sold on her, but I wouldn't be entirely sold on anyone who hadn't already proved themselves. The true test of loyalty isn't a few words spoken in a comfortable office. The true test, even for a person of good character, happens when money is short or when they feel they've been wronged, and someone comes along and waves a wad of cash at them or offers an opportunity for revenge with anonymity. That's when the loyalists separate themselves from the traitors.

Lara didn't give me any reason to withhold her name from Daniela, and she has a lot to offer. If it doesn't work out, I'll lower the boom.

27

DANIELA

The phone rings, and I know right away it's Antonio. Other than Cristiano, he's the only one who calls this number. I really don't want to continue our discussion from last night, but I answer anyway.

"Good morning."

"Good morning. How are you?"

"I'm well, thank you. And you?"

"You really are charming when you're not beating on my chest."

A warm flush creeps into my cheeks. I was exhausted last night—and I didn't handle him very well. "Valentina and I were just going for a walk. Is there something you need?"

"Is she there with you now?"

I almost answer *yes*, just to save myself from whatever it is he's going to say, but I don't. I've lied to protect Valentina—and myself, at times—but I'm not a liar. "No. She went to get her sneakers."

He pauses for a few seconds. "Isabel's body arrived overnight. We'll arrange a private funeral and burial. It'll be a few days."

Isabel's body arrived overnight. I close my eyes while a fresh wave of sorrow engulfs me.

"Daniela?" he says gently, after some time passes.

"I'm here." I take a breath and compose myself. "She didn't have any family, but there are a few people from my father's household who I would like to include."

"Give Cristiano their names by the end of today. Everyone who gets within a block of Santa Maria's will need to be fully vetted."

Santa Maria's? "Not Santa Maria's," I say, without thinking through the safety ramifications. "I want the funeral held at Santa Ana's. The sanctuary wasn't damaged. It was Isabel's church when we were in Porto." She loved Santa Ana's. I want to do this for her.

"You don't need to put yourself through a service at Santa Ana's. A church is a church," he says matter-of-factly. "God doesn't discriminate between ornate churches and humble chapels."

"I didn't realize you were such an expert on God's proclivities. But if you don't have the resources to secure Santa Ana's, I understand."

It's somewhat of a low blow, and more than a little manipulative. For a man like Antonio, it's like hearing, *If your dick isn't big enough, I understand.* But I'm not the least bit sorry for the manipulation. Isabel deserves to have her life honored in a place that she held dear.

"I have another piece of news," he says, choosing to ignore my request, like I might forget about it if he moves on.

Not happening.

"We might have found an assistant for you. After the funeral, you can interview her, and if you like her, she can begin immediately."

An assistant? It catches me off guard. Of course, I expected that eventually I would have someone, but it's been the last thing on my mind. *You can interview her, and if you like her, she can begin immediately.* He's allowing me to choose my own assistant? *How magnanimous.* But completely out of character for him.

"I have Paula," I tell him, dismissing the idea of more change.

"You'll need some help, especially with Valentina living with us. It's a large household to run, and we'll have lots of social obligations to coordinate, especially as it gets closer to the harvest. Paula's a maid. Nothing more."

She's been loyal to me, and I really like her, and I hate the way he dismisses her so easily. "I have a relationship with Paula. She isn't *just a maid*. The people who work for us aren't *just* anything. They're human beings with full lives beyond your castle."

"Are you through?"

"For now."

"What I meant is that Paula has had no experience with the sorts of things that you'll require. If I'm wrong, let's hear it."

The smug bastard knows he's not wrong.

"Who do you have in mind?"

"Lara Ramos. Do you know her?"

I sort of remember her, but she's several years older than me. I don't think we ever exchanged a word. "Not really."

"Her family has worked for mine for generations. She's been working in one of the Huntsman offices since she graduated. But I don't have a horse in this race. The final decision is yours. If you don't like her, we'll find someone else."

He knows her and has decided that she'll do. Maybe she'll spy for him—contact him every time I hiccup. "Assistants aren't like dogs. When one dies, you don't run out and get another to make you feel better. I'll speak to Lara, but I don't want anyone here who I can't trust." *A part of me already doesn't trust her.*

"Agreed. But I live there too, and I need to be able to trust whoever you choose."

I live there too. He just handed me an opening. "What time will you be home?"

"I'm staying in the city tonight."

Really? Why? I feel the jealousy in the pit of my stomach. I could pretend it's something else, but I don't. I certainly would never admit it to him, but I won't lie to myself. "I told Valentina that we're married, like you wanted. So now you need to behave like a husband."

"Oh *Princesa*, is that what you really want?"

I can almost see the smirk and the twinkle in his dark eyes, and my body responds in ways that are impossible to ignore.

"In exchange, will you do your wifely duties? Will you get on your knees and swallow my cock into your pretty little mouth?"

It's not what I meant. But, yes, I would. There's no sense in pretending otherwise.

I want him home at night. The house feels safer when he's home. *I feel safer* when he's home. That's the truth. Now that he knows about Valentina, about Tomas, his father, *the rape*, I worry he won't find his way to our bed as often. Let's face it, none of it's a turn-on. *What about what happened on the plane?* It was an anomaly. He was taking care of me, in the way I took care of him the night before. *Paying a debt. That's all.*

He'll get his needs met elsewhere. *In a different pretty mouth.* I essentially gave him permission. *Why did I do that? How will we ever make a marriage?*

If you want a marriage, a family, you'll have to fight for it.

"Families have dinner together in the evening," I say with all the allure of a schoolmarm. "They share news of the day. Husbands and wives don't live separate lives, in separate homes. Those are values I want to instill in Valentina. It's my responsibility as her mother."

"Your responsibility? And here I thought you wanted my cock," he tsks, taunting me. "But don't worry, I won't have any trouble finding someone who does."

This is vintage Antonio. Every time he gets too close, every time we cross a bridge, he pushes me away in the most vile manner. At some point he'll go too far, and the damage will be irreparable.

Will it? Because up to now, you've forgiven everything.

After we hang up, I swallow the hurt, the anger, and even the jealousy. In this world, the one I was born into, men make their choices, and women live by them without making too much fuss. They choose their battles carefully, and fidelity isn't something that can be demanded. It's something a man has to give freely, because there's no way to police it. My father was faithful to my mother, but their marriage was more than a sham. He loved her.

Ours is a marriage of convenience. His convenience—and now, mine. There's safety for Valentina here, and for me, too.

Love isn't part of this equation—it's nowhere to be found. Not that I give a damn. I have more important things to worry about, like helping Valentina acclimate to a new life without the woman she believes was her mother, and keeping her out of harm's way. Antonio is nothing more than a distraction. For all I care, he can sleep in a new city every night.

I repeat this to myself each night before I fall asleep alone, and again in the morning when I open my eyes to the undisturbed covers on his side of the bed. But it doesn't matter how many times I say it, or how adamantly. My heart can't be fooled.

I won't live like this. I can't.

28

DANIELA

Five long days later, Antonio meets us at Santa Maria's church, sliding into the pew beside me right before the casket is wheeled up the center aisle.

After our phone call, I never raised the issue of holding Isabel's funeral at Santa Ana's again. Once I had a few minutes to think carefully about it, I decided that bringing Valentina there wasn't smart. As much as Isabel loved the old church, she would never want our safety compromised.

There were few funeral arrangements for me to make, as much of the planning was on a need-to-know basis to ensure our safety. But Antonio went to great lengths so I could honor my friend.

Despite the elevated security concerns and ongoing investigations, Cristiano accompanied me to the funeral home to choose the casket. I picked a polished cherry, lined in plush white velvet, with a luxurious nap. Isabel loved velvet. When I got home, Valentina and I spent hours choosing just the right flowers and music for the service. It was cathartic, but even more, it gave us both an opportunity to care for Isabel—to love her—in death.

While Antonio skillfully pulled the strings behind the curtain, he all but disappeared. Despite his assurances, I wasn't entirely certain he'd show up for the funeral. *Such is our marriage.* But he's here, and during the Mass, he does all the right things: lowering the kneeler for us, handing me the hymnal before I reach for it, and wrapping his large hand around mine while the priest eulogizes Isabel.

Somehow, I keep it together for the precious girl at my side. I've been putting on a good face for days and days, trying to be the rock Valentina needs. But inside I'm raw and trembling and as much as I hate to admit it, Antonio's presence steadies me.

During the final blessing, the frankincense overwhelms the tiny chapel, taking me back to Santa Ana's, to my mother's funeral, and then to my father's. Isabel was at my side for both. Her loyalty never wavered. The angel who comforted me after my mother was murdered, who held my twelve-year-old hand while I labored, offering ice chips, cool compresses, and unconditional love. The woman who didn't bat an eyelash when my father asked her to raise my child as her own. Some people are blessed with one mother. In many ways, I was blessed with two.

The processional begins, and Valentina sobs as the casket is rolled out of the church. I rifle through my purse to find her a tissue, but she's exhausted both her supply and mine. When I come up empty, Antonio leans over me and presses a monogrammed handkerchief into her hands. It's a simple gesture, but I'm bursting with emotion that has no place to go, and his kindness is almost enough to open the dam.

"Thank you," I murmur, gazing into his beautiful face.

He uses his thumb to dry a tear from my cheek. "Handkerchiefs are for emergencies."

Indeed. Such a complicated man. He knows what proper etiquette requires. He also knows what being a good person requires. But chances are far greater that he'll use the correct fork during dinner than show mercy to someone who has wronged him.

Will I ever understand him? Truly understand him in the way a wife understands her husband, or will he forever remain an enigma?

———

THE BRIEF SERVICE at the cemetery is a lot like my wedding, where the priest administers the sacrament while we're ringed by armed guards who wouldn't hesitate to kill anyone who appears suspicious.

Antonio scans the perimeter the entire time the priest prays, then shuttles us quickly toward the car when it's over. But not before I stop at my parents' grave.

I haven't been here since my father's funeral. So much has happened since they died that some days it seems like they've been gone a hundred years. Other days, the grief is fresh.

As we approach the burial site, Valentina slips her hand into mine. I feel her warmth in my soul, as we stand at the grave in a heavy silence.

The area around the headstone is immaculate, with the shrubs recently pruned. Someone left an urn with fresh garden roses. It's oddly comforting.

"We can't linger long, Daniela," Antonio says softly, from beside me. "You can come back when things settle down."

After a quick prayer, I let go of Valentina's hand, and crouch down to see if there's a card with the roses. But there's nothing. *Maybe Antonio sent them.*

He touches my shoulder. "Let's go."

"Did you send the roses?" I ask on the way to the car.

He shakes his head. "It was probably something your father arranged with the cemetery as part of the ongoing maintenance."

I made the final arrangements for my father, although he'd

taken care of much of it when he learned he was dying. I wasn't in a great frame of mind at the time, but the funeral director went through every detail with me. Antonio's right. There was a contract for perpetual care of the graves. It was quite detailed, although I don't remember anything about flowers.

Antonio has a private word with Thiago as Valentina gets into the back of the car. I turn to the caretaker of the cemetery, who has been accompanying us since we arrived. "Do you provide flowers for my parents' graves?"

His brow furrows. "The roses?"

"Yes."

"No. I assumed the family arranged the weekly delivery."

Weekly delivery? "Someone brings flowers every week?"

He nods. "Roses. Always in the evening. If you're uncomfortable about it, we can put them in the trash when we arrive in the morning."

I shake my head. Garden roses were my mother's favorite flower. My father must have arranged something, not with the cemetery, but directly with a florist. "They're beautiful. Please leave them."

"Get in, Daniela," Antonio chides, as he comes around the vehicle. He takes my elbow, and guides me into the car, but not before scowling at the caretaker, who stumbles back.

I slide over to make room, but Antonio only sticks his head inside.

"She loved you," he tells Valentina and me, with the utmost sincerity. "She loved you both." He squeezes my hand. "What she would want is for you to go on living. To live long and happy lives. You can honor her best by doing just that."

It's true. That's exactly what Isabel would want.

Antonio reaches into his pocket and hands Valentina a cell phone. "You'll have your own security, like the rest of us, but you're old enough to have a cell phone too. Daniela's number, mine, and a few others are programmed in the phone."

There's no sense in telling him that he should have checked with me before giving her a cell phone. This is a safety issue, and he's already made it clear that he's the last word on our safety. In some ways, I don't even mind—especially when it comes to Valentina. He knows more about security than I ever will. I do want to ask him about her security detail, but now's not the time.

"If you need anything," he continues, "you call one of us. Understand?"

She nods. "Yes. Thank you, *senhor*."

"We're family. My family calls me Antonio, and you should too."

Her eyes are washed out, but I see a ghost of a smile, and maybe a small sense of relief at his kindness. Antonio has a big presence, and he's intimidating. Valentina hasn't had a chance to see the other side of him.

"We're working on a way for you to be able to talk to your friends. But for now," he adds, "those are the only numbers you can call."

Antonio presses a kiss to my hairline. "Thiago will take you back to the house."

"You're not coming?"

He gazes at me. "I have business in the city. There's a lot going on at this time of year."

I'm disappointed—crushed, really—but I don't reply. I won't have the discussion in front of the child. But I will have it —as often as necessary, because I'm determined to make this family work.

29

DANIELA

We text here and there, but the last time I saw Antonio was a week ago at the cemetery. Even my decision to hire Lara as an assistant was relayed by text.

Great, he replied. ***Cristiano will handle the details.***

"Daniela," Lara calls from the doorway, "if you don't need me right now, I'm going to help Valentina choose a paint color for her room."

I sigh quietly. Lara would take over every tedious detail of my life if I let her. That's what a competent assistant does, after all. But picking out paint colors for Valentina's room isn't mundane—not to me. I'm not giving up anything, not one thing, regardless of how inconsequential, when it involves her. "I'd like to help, too."

"You must have more important things on your plate. We'll be sure to consult you for final approval on the color."

"There's nothing I have to do that's more important than helping Valentina." It comes out sterner than I intend, and I feel bad for a moment. But she's very assertive for someone who has just taken the position, and perhaps it's better to reach an understanding early in the relationship. Although I could be less bitchy.

"Valentina is my priority." My tone is softer, but my intentions are clear.

Lara nods, a bit chagrinned. It seems she got the message. "Of course. We'll wait for you," she assures me before leaving the suite.

"Give me five minutes," I tell her on my way to the walk-in closet to get a sweater. When I pass Antonio's section of the closet, I stop to run my fingertips over the smooth leather jacket he wore on the plane. I lift the hanger off the rod and bring the jacket to my nose, inhaling the scent of leather, cedar, and that boozy cologne he wears. *It smells just like him.* I close my eyes and remember how he took care of me on the plane. How he roused every nerve, played each one expertly, until they danced for him. Until I surrendered—*everything.*

Now's not the time.

I return the hanger to its place and grab a fleece sweater, hurrying out of the closet before I sniff anymore of his clothing. *I miss him.* We had turned a corner in our relationship—until the ugly past unearthed itself. *Hadn't we?*

I'm not sure. I'm not sure of anything, including what the future holds for us. For now, I take him at his word, that he's working and trying to gather information that will keep us safe.

On my way out of the suite, I glance at the weekly magazine from the newspaper, sitting on the console. My childhood friend, Susana, is on the glossy cover, wearing a navy gown and silver shoes that sparkle almost as much as she does. I smile, picking up the magazine. The photograph is from a benefit gala held a few days ago. I thumb through the pages to see who else I might know.

That's when I see it.

Antonio and *Sonia.*

The woman who confronted me in the bathroom at the

Camelia Ball. The gorgeous woman in the stunning blue dress who only gave me her first name. Her dress is crimson in the photo. But it's still stunning, as is she.

Antonio's in a tux—handsome as the devil, and just as shameless. He's chatting with an elderly woman on his right, but his arm is draped casually over the back of the chair to his left. *Sonia's chair.*

A wave of nausea hits, and I press my lips together firmly.

It certainly didn't take him long to find someone who wants his cock.

"Lala," a sweet voice calls from the hall. "We're waiting for you."

I turn over the magazine so Valentina doesn't see it. I'm not protecting *the cheater*. I'm protecting her—and my dignity.

Unlike what I expected, Valentina didn't blink when I told her about my marriage. I think she's relieved we have some place safe to be, with someone who seems capable of keeping us safe. I did tell her that I had loved Antonio all my life. It was only a childhood crush, but it felt like love to me at the time. *It was just a small fib. Unlike the whoppers Antonio has been telling me.* "I'll be right there. I just need to use the bathroom first."

Avoiding the mirror, I splash cold water on my face until the urge to vomit goes away.

It's bad enough to have a private affair, but there's no damn way he's going to embarrass me publicly.

30

ANTONIO

"Anything on Tomas?"

"He's still holed up," Lucas replies. "Not only is he guilty as fuck, but he's also a coward. Although that's not a surprise."

It's been almost a week since I've seen Daniela. I've kept the correspondence to texts, mostly, because her voice makes my dick hard and my resolve weak. *I want to see her.* But I also want to give her some time to help Valentina adjust.

I laid down the gauntlet when I told her she'd be in our bed any night I was home. I can't go back on that. Daniela will smell the weakness and wield it at every turn. I'm not worried she'll use it to ruin me. I'm concerned she'll use it to buy herself some control, which I'm not prepared to give her—right now.

Although the real reason I'm staying away is that Tomas is still breathing. Until that sonofabitch is in hell, I won't touch her. I made that vow to myself on the plane returning to Porto. I will avenge her mother's death and her innocence. *Until then, I don't deserve her.*

But just because I don't deserve her doesn't mean I don't think about her. Her sassy mouth, her soft heart, her beautiful face, her sweet pussy—it's tattooed on my brain, all of it. Every smile, every whimper, every tear. *She's mine. Or at least she will be, after I gut that fucking pig.*

I glance at the phone ringing on my desk. *Daniela*. It's like she knew I was thinking about her. I start to reach for the damn thing but let it go to voicemail instead.

Not a minute later, Cristiano answers his phone. "I'm not sure he's available. Is there something I can help you with? Okay," he replies after a pause. "I'll ask him to call you. I understand," he mutters, seconds later. "Hold on."

Cristiano mutes the call and turns to me. "Daniela wants to speak with you. She claims it can't wait."

If it were a true emergency, she would have told Cristiano. "Did she give you any clue as to what's so damn important?"

He shakes his head. "No, but she sounds upset."

I hold out my hand for the phone, and put the call on speaker, cursing myself for being soft. "I'm a busy man. I hope this is important."

She doesn't say anything for a moment.

My shoulders tighten at the prospect of something, or someone, upsetting her. *I'm getting too emotionally involved with her—I can't let her weaken me.*

"Do you need something, or did you interrupt my day to listen to me breathe?"

"You haven't been home in a week."

What the hell?

"Let me stop you right there. I've been home every night. I keep two homes, and several apartments around the world. I've been working until all hours, and it's more convenient to stay in the city."

"But you found time to attend a benefit gala with Sonia." She spits out the words, with a tenuous grasp on her composure.

How does she know about the gala?

"I don't need to justify anything I do, but I didn't go to a benefit or anywhere else with Sonia."

Lucas shoves a laptop under my nose, with an image of me seated beside Sonia. *Fuck.* Now my neck has joined my tight shoulders.

The paper knows better than to print photos of me that haven't been preapproved, but this was a fundraiser. Normally we give them carte blanche to print those types of images because they're good for business. *Not anymore.* They messed up, but I'm not entertaining Daniela's tantrum. I take the phone off speaker.

"Should I send you an emerald trinket to go with the lovely shade of green you're sporting?"

"Listen carefully, Antonio," she says after a moment. "I don't pretend to be able to control anything you do, and that includes Sonia, but you will not rub my nose in it, and you will not humiliate me publicly. But more important than any of that, you will *not* send a message to Valentina that this is acceptable behavior."

"Get out," I growl at Cristiano and Lucas, who waste no time leaving the villa.

I won't chastise her for taking this stand, because she's my wife, and she's entitled to demand fidelity—in private, anyway. I would be disappointed if she didn't. But she needs to save her wrath for when we're alone.

"So you don't care who I fuck as long as it's done with discretion?"

"That's right," she says so unconvincingly I almost laugh.

"I wasn't with Sonia."

"I know what I saw. Photos don't lie."

"But they can be manipulated, *Princesa.*"

"That one wasn't."

"No. It wasn't." For a moment, I contemplate what to tell

her. If I justify my behavior every time she raises an eyebrow, I might as well just hand over my balls now. But the photo is misleading, and if the shoe was on the other foot, I'd have already murdered the guy sitting near my wife.

"The seat near me was unoccupied—it had been reserved for you, but I didn't want to drag you away from Valentina for an entire evening. The gala wasn't important. Before dessert was served, Sonia came by the table and joined us."

"And?"

"And that's it. I've already explained myself more than I would normally. Don't expect it to happen again."

I'm not sure she's convinced, but hopefully we'll finish this call before she demands I come home this evening. Hate sex with a jealous Daniela is something that I would have trouble turning down.

"How do you know Sonia?"

"We run a small business together."

"What kind of business?"

We are not going there, and you don't get answers from me by making demands. "The kind that doesn't concern you. If you're done throwing around baseless accusations, I need to get back to work."

"Before you go—"

"More pictures?"

She ignores the sarcasm. "You said that Cristiano would take me to my parents' house. Valentina and I would like to go."

I did say it. But it's not a good time. "You can't go right now. Quinta Rosa do Vale is not as heavily fortified as our house in the valley. Until we have more information about the explosion at Santa Ana's, and Isabel's murder, I can't allow it."

I hate to deny her something that would be so easy to make happen—especially this—but there's no choice. "As soon as we know more, you and Valentina can spend as much time as you like there. You have my word." The promise seems to placate her, at least for the time being.

While I can't let her go to the house, I do have something that will take the edge off the disappointment. I don't know why I've been saving it—*maybe for this moment.*

31

ANTONIO

After we hang up, I text Lucas and Cristiano to come back to the villa.

"Everything okay?" Cristiano asks when they walk in, his eyes twinkling.

I'm sure these two assholes had a good laugh at my expense. I scowl and toss him his phone.

"Call that fucking reporter and tell him if he ever takes another picture of me without my express permission, it'll be the last thing he does."

"Should I contact the publisher?" Cristiano knows I'm not fucking around, and there's less levity in his voice now.

"I'll deal with that stupid bastard myself," I mutter. "After you talk to the photographer, go to the house and take Daniela and Valentina to the stables."

Cristiano side-eyes me like I'm batshit crazy, sending him on that errand when we have so many pressing matters.

He's right. I am. "Take Thiago so you can work on the way there and back. Daniela hasn't been to the stables, and I want to be sure that everything's safe before they go on their own."

He cocks his head. "Happy to do it. But don't you want to be there?"

"If I wanted to be there, I wouldn't have asked you to go." *This is a lie.* There's a surprise waiting for them—for Daniela—and I'd do anything to see her face. But if I go, it'll be too much like an apology, and I don't apologize, especially when I haven't done anything to warrant it.

"Take Santi, Mia, and Alvarez to the stables with you so that they can get the lay of the land too."

We put Mia in charge of Valentina's security team because she's that good, and I knew Daniela would prefer a woman so close to her daughter. Alvarez is Daniela's guard when I'm not around. Next to Cristiano and Lucas, he's my most trusted soldier by far.

"I'll call on my way back," Cristiano says, stuffing some equipment into a backpack.

"A black Mercedes sedan with tinted windows just entered your uncle's property," Lucas mutters, after a few minutes. His eyes are glued to one of the monitors hanging along the wall. "I'm tracing the plates, but it looks like it's tied to the Italians."

Bullshit. "That's too damn obvious. Someone wants us to believe that. Just like they wanted us to believe that the Georgians were responsible for the threat to my car at the Camelia race."

"Agreed. I'm all over it."

"What about our guy inside?"

"Radio silence." He's distracted, tracing the plate, but there's a tightness in his voice that I don't like.

"When did you last have contact with him?"

"Two days ago."

Two days isn't that long to be out of touch with an operative, but Lucas was never on board with the plan to activate him. "Any specific concerns?"

Lucas shrugs. "Nothing specific. But my gut's telling me there's trouble."

A human plant is a risky proposition. Although our man inside knew it when he accepted the assignment.

We worked for nearly two years to get someone into that house. Then, after Abel's stroke, the routine of the place changed to protect his privacy. There are entire sections where only the most trusted staff are allowed to enter. But even with those restrictions, our guy can provide invaluable intel that will help us determine what kind of game Tomas is playing, and more importantly, who's backing him. I still don't believe he has the brains or the balls to come after me himself.

"It's unlikely he would have been outed so quickly after being activated."

"If he was, we have a problem."

I know what kind of problem—the worst kind—but I ask anyway, hoping like hell he's talking about something else. "Exactly what kind of problem would that be?"

Lucas turns his head and glares at me. "If he's been outed, we're leaking internally."

Not just internally, but from somewhere near the top.

One fucking day of peace. That's all I ask.

32

DANIELA

"Valentina, please put those shoes in the closet and your pajamas in the laundry. Paula shouldn't have to pick up after us. But hurry. Cristiano is waiting downstairs."

"I don't mind," Paula says quietly, smiling at Valentina.

Maybe not, but I don't want Valentina to grow up to be the kind of woman who depends on others for everything, especially for cleaning up her messes.

"The household is so well-staffed," Lara chimes in, "that Paula is probably looking for things to do."

I gaze at her with a brittle smile. "That might be so, but she'll have to look elsewhere, because Valentina knows exactly where the laundry hamper is located." Fortunately, no one challenges me on this.

Lara is lovely and very knowledgeable, but we have different styles, and clearly different ideas about how to raise children. I'm hoping to avoid a discussion with her about it, or worse, to have to send her back to the Huntsman offices. Valentina adores her, and I like her too, but I won't be undermined at every turn.

Maybe I'm being too sensitive.

"Where are we going?" Valentina asks for the fifth time, as we leave the suite. "Are you sure you don't know?"

"I don't know. I couldn't get anything out of Cristiano, except that it's a surprise." It's not exactly true. I made him look me in the eye and promise that there would be nothing that would upset Valentina.

"Cristiano is good-natured," Lara explains, "and he always responds to a question, but he never actually answers it."

I chuckle. "Isn't that the truth."

"Cristiano's so nice. And he's hot too." Valentina waggles her eyebrows at us.

Oh God. That's all I need. "He's much too old for you to be crushing on. Stick to boys your own age, please." I try to sound matter-of-fact, but the prospect terrifies me. Not Cristiano per se. Valentina's safe around him, but this place is teeming with men—guards, the household staff, the vineyard workers. It's like a frat house.

Antonio has assured me that only the most trusted men are allowed anywhere near us. While I have no doubt that's what he believes, I still worry about Valentina with her budding breasts and easy smile.

When we get to the bottom of the stairs, Cristiano is waiting, with a hand buried in his pants pocket. Valentina's right. He is hot. Not scorching hot, take your breath away, like Antonio, but I'm sure women throw themselves at him too.

"Ladies," he says with a wide grin. "Are you ready?"

Valentina nods, flashing him a grin of her own. She hasn't once complained, but I'm sure she misses her friends and the freedom she had in Fall River. A surprise will be good for her.

"We're ready," Lara replies. She sounds like a teenager who needs a little excitement in her life, too.

Cristiano stops and turns to her. "We won't need you for this."

Whoa. Where did that come from?

Lara seems less taken aback by his attitude than I am. "Valentina invited me. I like surprises too." She smiles at him, but the smile doesn't reach her eyes.

"Not this time." His tone has the ring of finality.

Even Lara, who is a bit pushy, doesn't challenge him, and I don't intervene on her behalf. She needs a better sense of boundaries. Valentina might have asked her to come, but she's my assistant and should have checked with me.

The interaction between Cristiano and Lara is interesting. Both their parents worked for the Huntsmans, and they're around the same age. They should know each other well enough to speak their minds, but the air is thick with unspoken words.

"Valentina will fill you in on every detail when we get back," I promise Lara, hoping to diffuse the awkwardness. She means well, and I do feel a bit bad for her. He slapped her pretty hard —for Cristiano, anyway.

"Have fun." She touches Valentina's shoulder as we leave. "I want to hear all about it when you get back."

"So where are we going?" I ask when we're outside, not really expecting a straightforward answer from Cristiano.

"Somewhere we can walk."

I roll my eyes and follow him.

"Is this a good surprise?" Valentina asks, beaming up at him.

"Of course. Do I look like the kind of guy who likes bad surprises?" He winks at her, and she giggles, batting her eyelashes, like the preadolescent she is.

I make a note to tell Antonio that she has a crush on Cristiano. I want him to give his friend a heads-up so he doesn't inadvertently encourage her behavior.

I've always been more relaxed about this sort of thing, to counterbalance Isabel's fears about the male species. But now that she's gone—or maybe it's being back in Porto—I'm on high alert when it comes to our girl.

Valentina chatters incessantly, playing twenty questions with Cristiano, who tells her only enough to whet her appetite. Lara was exactly right. Despite his easygoing manner, he's a pro at subterfuge.

As we approach what appears to be the barns, Alvarez, Mia, and Santi—who I'm not entirely sold on—are huddled near the fence.

"Does Antonio keep horses?" I ask Cristiano, excited about the possibility, but missing my horses too. I've thought about them a lot over the years. They helped keep me sane after my mother died.

"You'll have to see for yourself."

There's a familiar shadow in the doorway of the main building. The man resembles Silvio, who managed the stables at Quinta Rosa do Vale. He taught me to ride and care for the horses. I left my beloved animals in his care when we fled to the US. As much as I would miss them, I knew they'd be in good hands.

It can't be him. Why would he be here?

I hurry down the path, with Valentina and Cristiano lagging behind. My eyes never leave the barn door. *It's him.*

"Silvio!"

"Daniela, *querida*," he says, embracing me. For a moment, I feel like a young girl again. This man was such an important part of my life as a child, and even as a young woman.

"I've missed you," I murmur. "How's your wife?"

"She's a very contented avó. She babysits for our grandchildren while my daughter and son-in-law are at work. How are you, *senhora*?"

My heart clenches at the word *senhora*, a reminder that so many years have passed. "I'm happy too, especially now that I know you're here."

"Valentina," he gushes, gazing over my shoulder. "Look at you. All grown up."

She smiles shyly at him. "Do you work here?"

He nods, his eyes gleaming. "I believe I once made a promise to teach you to ride when you got to be six years old. Are you six, yet?"

She nods and laughs, her violet-blue eyes dancing a happy jig.

It hits me then. *If Silvio's not at Quinta Rosa do Vale, who's taking care of Atlas and Zeus? They trusted him as much as they trusted me.* Zeus isn't young. He needs a steady, familiar hand. Antonio assured me they were well cared for—I don't think it's something he would lie about. If he had sold them, he would have had no qualms about telling me.

"Come inside," Silvio murmurs softly to me, as if sensing my concern. "There's something I want to show you."

33

DANIELA

I follow him into the barn, with Valentina on my heels. When we reach the center stalls, I stop as the blood *whooshes* in my ears. *Zeus and Atlas.*

I rush over, first to one, then the other, being cautious not to spook them. Six years is a long time. But they recognize me right away. Zeus nuzzles me immediately, and Atlas, the proud stallion, takes only a few moments longer to forgive me for leaving him.

"Silvio, they look like they haven't aged a day. You've taken such good care of them. Thank you."

He nods. "They're fine animals. You trained them well."

Before I abandoned them. "Why are they here?"

"This is their home now. *Senhor* Antonio would come out to Quinta Rosa do Vale regularly to check on them, and to ride, but it was easier for him to have them stabled here."

I swallow the lump in my throat. *Antonio, you never cease to amaze me.* "He rode them?"

"They needed to be ridden, *senhora*."

Of course they did. But Silvio could have done it.

"*Senhor* Antonio has been generous with me, and he spares no expense when it comes to the horses."

I glance around the stable. Zeus and Atlas aren't the only horses here. When my gaze meets Cristiano's, he gifts me a tender smile. *Rascal.* He's enjoying this almost as much as I am.

"Silvio, will you really teach me to ride? Please?" Valentina gives him that angelic look she has whenever she begs.

"I would be honored, but Daniela might like to teach you herself. She's an accomplished rider, and I have no doubt she would be a marvelous instructor."

"Which horse would be better for me to ride, Zeus or Atlas?"

I don't respond to her question because I'm still trying to wrap my head around the idea that Antonio Huntsman would make sure my horses were well cared for—not assigning the chore to someone else, but overseeing it himself.

"Zeus is old and set in his ways, and Atlas is still feisty," Silvio explains to Valentina, "but I have a mare that's perfect for you. Come on, I'll introduce you."

Valentina takes my hand and pulls me along. It's a good thing, because my emotions are all over the place, and I'm a little lost.

"Ohhh!" Valentina cries. "She's beautiful. What's her name?"

"Demeter," he replies, "after the goddess of the harvest." Silvio glances at me. "*Senhor* Antonio thought you would approve of the name, but you can call her something else, if you'd like."

"I love it," Valentina squeals.

"Me too," I say, so softly I'm not sure anyone hears.

"Her sister is here," Silvio murmurs, looking at me. "She's less docile than Demeter. *Senhor* Antonio thought she could use your steady hand. Her name is Hera."

I smile. He named the horses after Greek goddesses, like I

named mine after the gods. Hera is the queen of the gods. The goddess of women, marriage, family, and childbirth. A few tears escape while I say hello to Hera. I brush them away before anyone notices.

I know in my heart, maybe I've always known, that Antonio has a good soul. It's hard not to see all of this as a gesture of love from a man who can't find the words. But I try not to read too much into it. If I get too far ahead of myself, I'll be hurt. He has the power to break my heart. *That's the honest truth.*

Valentina and I are in no hurry to leave, but Cristiano excuses himself almost immediately, although not before I steal a moment with him.

"He's a difficult man to get on the phone. Will you thank him for me?"

The edge of his mouth twitches. He's run interference for Antonio more than once when I've called. "I'm happy to, but I'll bet he'd love to hear it from you."

Cristiano knows his friend better than anyone. If there is a person alive who knows what makes Antonio tick, it's him. Whether he'll share it with me is something else entirely.

"Cristiano, who is he? Is he the man who dragged me off the ship without a kind word, or is he the man who bought my mother's jewelry after I sold it, and filled this barn for me? Who is he, really? Because those two men aren't reconcilable."

Cristiano blinks a few times and swallows hard. "He's complicated, Daniela. Proud. Infuriating. Loyal. A formidable soldier. A courageous leader."

"But not an easy man to love."

"I expect that's true. Although I'm not sure he's ever been open to the idea of a woman's love—or to loving a woman."

This is hardly a secret, but I'm looking for the motive behind it. "Why?"

"I suspect the reasons are as complex as the man. Love leaves powerful men vulnerable to their enemies. And he has plenty. But even someone like Antonio, with great discipline and a willingness to sacrifice, will eventually succumb when faced with the right woman. The heart wants what the heart wants." He pauses for a few beats. "Before long, everyone will know you're his Achilles' heel."

His Achilles' heel. Is that what I am?

I don't want to be his weakness. *Maybe I do.* But I certainly don't want his feelings for me to be weaponized and turned against him. *That's what happened to my parents.* "I won't be used by his enemies to destroy him."

"None of us wants that." Cristiano is wistful, as though it's been predetermined and out of our hands.

It's so unlike him.

I have news for anyone who plans to use me as a pawn to get to Antonio. I'm a fighter, especially when it comes to my family. I'll fight to the death, if necessary. And I sure as hell am not surrendering Antonio's destiny, or mine, to fate.

34

DANIELA

My mouth is bone-dry as we wait for Antonio to call. I texted with him after we returned from the barn, and explained how excited Valentina is about Demeter, and how she wants to thank him for making her dream of riding come true. It took some prodding, but he eventually agreed to video chat with us this evening.

Now I'm so nervous, I can't sit still. What if instead of the three of us bonding over his gift and our love of horses, it makes things more awkward?

My stomach turns somersaults when Valentina cries, "It's him," and engages the chat.

"I love Demeter," she gushes before we even say hello. "I've always wanted to learn to ride. Thank you so much."

He grins. *Grins.* First his features softened, and his eyes glittered, and then came the curl of his full lips.

I grin back at him, like a fool.

"She's a beauty. I'm happy you like her."

"I love her. It's the best present I've ever gotten. I won't even miss my friends now. Well, not too much."

My heart clenches when she mentions missing her friends.

"I want to bake you a cake. When will you be coming home?"

Oh my God. He's going to think I put her up to this.

If Antonio's caught off guard, he recovers without a hiccup. "A cake? What kind of cake?"

"What's your favorite kind?"

"Chocolate."

"I can make a chocolate cake," she replies, excitement bursting from her, like fireworks in the night sky.

I hold my breath, pleading with my eyes, for him not to crush her.

"Will this cake have frosting?"

She nods. "Yes. And decorations."

"Excellent," he replies. "Are you a good baker, or are you going to feed me cake that's so dry I'll choke?"

Valentina erupts into a fit of giggles, which makes Antonio smile, again.

If I wasn't sitting here, I'd never believe it.

"I can't get to the valley until Thursday because I have a lot of work here, but maybe by then you'll have had a chance to ride a little, and you can tell me all about it. Is that a deal?"

Her head bobs up and down. "Yes."

I can feel the excitement vibrating off her. *If you renege on this deal, Antonio, I'll strangle you.*

"If you could give Daniela and me a moment to talk, I would appreciate it."

"A private moment," I explain with a wink that seems more lighthearted than I feel. As much as I want some time alone with him, I'm nervous.

"Oh," she chirps, jumping up. "Good night, Antonio." She blows him a kiss through the screen, and I twist my fingers in my lap.

I'm not sure how much he's willing to give, and I don't want her to be disappointed.

"Sleep well, *menina*. No dry cake," he calls after her.

At first, we say nothing. We just gaze at each other, while days' worth of pent-up emotion gathers in my chest.

"Did she shut the door behind her?"

I nod, and the words tumble out, each one brimming with heartfelt emotion. "Thank you for everything. For taking care of Zeus and Atlas. For being good to Silvio. For the way you just were with Valentina—and for Demeter. And Hera. I'm sure I'm forgetting at least a dozen things." I swipe the back of my hand across my wet cheek.

"I want you to be happy," he murmurs, humbly. "I want Valentina to be happy. It's that simple."

If only it were true.

"You made her so happy—and me too," I add softly. "How did you know she's always wanted to ride?"

He shakes his head. "I didn't. Kids who have lost a parent, or who have experienced trauma, benefit from having a pet to care for and love. Unconditional love is a powerful healer. That was the advice I was given when Rafael came to live with me. I figured, having your genes, a horse would be a natural for Valentina."

Kids who have lost a parent, or who have experienced trauma, benefit from having a pet to care for and love. Unconditional love is a powerful healer. It's true. After my mother died, before I knew I was pregnant, I spent hours and hours with Zeus. When I was with him, my grief and sorrow bled away.

"Aside from missing her friends, how's she coping?"

"That's the first I heard about her friends. She hasn't really mentioned Isabel since the funeral. When I bring her up, she changes the subject. I'm a little worried about it."

"We can arrange to have someone available for her to talk with, or you can talk to someone who can give you some guidance about how to help her cope. It can be the same person. Let me know when you're ready, but don't wait too long."

Unlike my father, I don't care what secrets she spills. I want her to have all the help she needs.

"I think it's a good idea, not just for Valentina, but for me too. I don't want her to bury her grief, but I don't know how hard to push."

"Rafa and I worked with a child psychologist, Dr. Lima. She doesn't pull any punches. You'll like her."

"You worked with a psychologist?"

"Don't sound so surprised." He smirks—his trademark panty-melting one. "Rafael had been through a lot. Even I'm not arrogant enough to believe I can fix childhood trauma without a little guidance."

Antonio Huntsman, you never cease to amaze me. You have one foot in an old world with misogynist customs, and the other in the modern world where therapy is an acceptable practice and little boys are allowed to have feelings.

As I gaze at him through the screen, my heart is filled with hope for him—for us. *We can work on the misogyny.*

"A cake? That's very sweet," he says, gauging me carefully.

"I didn't put her up to it. When we were in Fall River, we always baked cakes for special occasions—and for special people," I add in a whisper.

"You'd never use Valentina to manipulate me. That's not who you are."

Sometimes I'm surprised by how well he knows me, how he can see into my heart. It's what makes him so dangerous.

"She'll be disappointed if you don't show up on Thursday." I feel as though I need to say it, even if it breaks the mood. She's a child, and she's been through a lot.

"I'll be there. For cake," he clarifies quickly.

For cake. Not for you. He doesn't have to say it. I hear the message loud and clear, and despite my quivering stomach, I won't ignore it.

"You'll fill a barn, a whole life with things you know I love, but sharing my bed repulses you."

He blinks a few times. "Nothing about you repulses me. *Nothing.* Put that idea right out of your head, *Princesa.*"

Cristiano's words come careening back. *I'm not sure he's ever been open to the idea of a woman's love—or to loving a woman.*

Perhaps it's that simple—not simple, exactly, and it certainly won't be easy to sway a man like Antonio.

If you want a marriage, you'll need to fight for it. Don't let pride get in the way.

"If you want me to beg, I will. I want this marriage to be more than a sham—for all of our sakes. And I believe it can be. Spend the night on Thursday."

As he gazes at me, I see the turmoil eating at him. "I can't."

Not letting this go, Antonio. "Can't, or won't?"

"I'll be there for cake. Then Thiago will take me back to the city."

Not if I have anything to say about it.

35

ANTONIO

It's been the better part of a week, and we still haven't heard a word from our guy inside my uncle's house. It could be nothing more than he has no news and doesn't want to risk making contact. But too many days have passed and we can't sit on our hands for much longer.

We swept every inch of Huntsman real estate thoroughly, for recording devices. It's something we do regularly, especially my offices, the villa, and any car where we discuss business, but we spared no quarter this time.

There was nothing. That leaves us searching for a leak. *A traitor.*

As far as I'm concerned, only Cristiano and Lucas are beyond reproach—and maybe Thiago, my driver. Alvarez and Santi have proven themselves, but to a lesser degree. Everyone else is suspect, although the culprit is unlikely to be a low-level guard who has no actionable information.

Despite the prospect of a traitor in our midst, I show up Thursday night. Not just for Valentina, but for Daniela, who would feel the child's hurt feelings acutely, like a heart attack, or a bludgeoning.

There will be times when I'll cause her pain. I am who I am, and I do what I do. Many things can't be avoided, but showing up for cake is a small thing. *Staying the night, however, is another matter.*

Why? Because *staying the night* is just a euphemism for sex.

That won't happen, again, until Tomas has paid for what he did. He's *my* family, *my* blood, and along with *my* father, he made Daniela's life a living hell. I don't deserve her goodness until I've made that pig bleed. *After that, she's mine. Every day and every night.*

"You rode Demeter around the enclosure, groomed her when you were done, and she loves you as much as you love her." I repeat the highlights of Valentina's last few days, between bites of cake, which is delicious. I don't even need to pretend.

"How do you know?" she asks, her wide eyes a shimmery violet under the light.

It reminds me that I need to talk to Rafa, and my mother, and I need to rip out Tomas's bowels. The first two are going to be unpleasant, but I'm going to enjoy the hell out of the last one.

"I know everything," I tell her as though it's fact—and to some extent it is.

"Did you tell him?" she asks, scrunching her nose at Daniela, who has been quieter than normal during dinner, but fidgety.

And beautiful—I've had to force myself not to stare, but more than once she caught me red-handed.

Daniela shakes her head. "Not me. I didn't blab."

"I spoke with Silvio to make sure you didn't need anything for Demeter."

Valentina nods. "I don't need anything. Demeter has everything. And even the riding boots fit me perfectly. They're real leather. So beautiful." She beams. "Thank you."

Daniela smiles softly at the girl, her entire face radiating love. There have been moments when she looked at me with something that resembled *love*. But they're few and far between, and honestly, it's better that way. *Better for whom?* I shove aside the nagging voice and focus on Valentina's gratitude. It's safer, and less likely to lead me to trouble.

They're real leather. Something I take for granted, and I'm sure for most of her life Daniela took it for granted too. But Valentina left Porto and the riches of Quinta Rosa do Vale at a very young age. I'm sure she doesn't remember many details from that time in her life. And those years they spent in Fall River—leather was a luxury that they couldn't afford. *I made sure of it.* It's not something that makes me proud. It never did, but now, sitting here with them, I feel nothing but remorse.

"Do you want more cake?" Valentina asks.

I shake my head. "I've had two pieces. It's delicious, but I'm stuffed. Would you mind if I take some back with me?"

Valentina nods. "Do you think Cristiano would like a piece, too?"

Daniela side-eyes me. She texted me that Valentina has a thing for Cristiano. It's harmless, and perfectly normal, but Daniela doesn't like it. Given her own experiences, I get it, and I gave Cristiano a heads-up, but that's it. I refuse to make a big deal out of a schoolgirl crush. That serves no purpose. "I'm sure he would enjoy some cake. But I better take a piece for Lucas too, or he's liable to eat mine."

She smiles, broadly. "We have a lot left. You can take half, if you want. But do you need to go, already?"

"I'm afraid I do."

Daniela stiffens, her lips pursing.

It's been a relaxing evening. As it turns out, I needed it. *I needed her.* But if I stay any longer, I'm going to tear off her clothes and lick that sweet pussy before I bury my cock inside it. I won't be able to stop myself.

"I think you've had enough cake too, *menina* Valentina," Daniela says kindly, but firmly. "It's time to go upstairs and do some reading before bed. Between cake baking and horse riding, you haven't done any today."

"Can I stay a little while longer? Antonio is never here."

"You need to listen to your"—*Mother* almost slips out, but I catch myself. Although not before Daniela pales—"friend. Until you have a tutor, we need to make sure you stay caught up on your schoolwork."

"When will I be able to go to school?"

"Valentina," Daniela chides, "we've been over this. You'll have a tutor for the rest of the year, which is over in a few days. We'll talk about school over the summer."

Valentina's never going to school. Not in Porto. Her association with me makes it too risky. Eventually my enemies will all know she's an important part of our lives—a way to get to me. It's too dangerous. Despite kicking the issue down the road, her mother knows it, too.

"Good night, *meu amor*," Daniela coos.

"Good night. I love you, Lala." Valentina kisses Daniela on both cheeks, without a thought. It's customary in our culture for children to say hello and goodbye to relatives and close adult friends with a kiss on each cheek. But Valentina's not quite sure what to do about me. She doesn't utter a word, but her shuffling speaks volumes.

"We could shake hands," I offer, "but if your lips are warm, you can kiss me so I don't feel left out. But if they're freezing from all that ice water you were sipping, forget it. Ice water—such an American thing. Victor must have heart failure every time he sees you drink it."

Custom or no custom, I don't want her to do anything she's not comfortable with, and I want to give her an easy way out.

"Just a little cold." She giggles, before pressing a small kiss to each of my cheeks and then practically skipping out of the room.

"Thank you for making her feel comfortable—like part of the family. I'm impressed by how easy it is for you to be around her."

She doesn't say, *So much easier than it is for you to be around me,* but I'm sure it's what she's thinking.

It's only hard to be around Daniela because of the promise I made to myself. If I could touch her, it would be easy. But I don't trust myself to stop at a simple touch. I don't share any of this with her. There's no point.

"She's part of the family. She's a good kid, and she's been through a lot. I am a human being—although I've given you plenty of reason to doubt it." I pause for a beat, thinking back to when my cousin moved in. It was quite an education, and it's not over yet.

"Rafa was even younger than Valentina when he came to live with me. He had friends, boys and girls, constantly in and out of the place. Plus, my stepsister Samantha has a daughter Valentina's age. I'm comfortable with most kids."

Daniela gazes at me for a moment, before getting up and locking the door.

My pulse kicks up a notch, and my dick jumps, pressing against the zipper.

On her way back, she untethers the small pearl buttons of her sweater and shrugs it off. The silk camisole she's wearing highlights her beaded nipples.

"What are you doing, Daniela?" My voice is rough, and I am seconds from helping her remove the rest of her clothing, but I won't do it. She can flash those gorgeous tits at me all night. I'm not going back on my promise.

36

ANTONIO

"I thought we'd have some Port."
Sure you did.
"Don't you need to check on Valentina?"

"Paula is going to look in on her. I'll stop by her room later to say good night. Valentina knows not to expect me right away. Victor promised he'd keep an eye out too. He helped me set up the tasting room earlier."

"Did he?" So this is a conspiracy. I'm going to ream Victor a new asshole before I leave.

She nods.

"You didn't wear a bra because it enhances the taste of Port?"

She smiles coyly.

"Did you leave your panties upstairs too?" I know I shouldn't engage. I know I should leave *now*. But she's breathtaking in the firelight, and her eyes are sparkling with mischief—and lust. *A beautiful seductress.*

I'm enjoying this too much to leave. But I'm on borrowed time, and if I let this go on much longer, I'll never leave.

"Panties? You'll have to check for yourself."

She's a brazen little vixen tonight, and sex with her, like this, would be mind-blowing. It's always mind-blowing with her—but this—*I'm so fucked.*

"Don't worry, Antonio, I don't have a magic pussy. You're not going to fall in love from fucking me."

Too late for that, I'm afraid.

"I thought we were having Port?"

"A tasting," she murmurs, licking her full lips. "I've always wondered if the vessel it's served in changes the character of the wine. What do you think?"

If you're ever leaving, now's the time.

Daniela tugs on my hand, and I let her lead, until we get to the bookcase that opens to the tasting room. This is the moment of truth. I can keep my promise, or I can indulge my darkest desires. I feel the beads forming on the back of my neck.

With one hand on my chest, she brushes the other over my cock. There's not a single fucking decision to be made at that point.

I pin her against the shelves and ravage her mouth until her back arches and needy gasps escape from her throat.

"There's something you should know, *Princesa*. You can seduce me, bare your tits, and leave your panties in the drawer, but I'm in charge of everything that comes after that. Tonight, I'll be the one who chooses the vintage and the vessel." I brush my mouth along the shell of her ear. "I hope you're prepared to finish what you started."

She lifts her chin, until her eyes meet mine. "I hope you're prepared to taste—*everything*." Her voice is husky, and my dick is begging for a small taste of whatever she's offering.

I crossed the line and there's no turning back. Not for me. I'm not going anywhere tonight—not without her.

I flip the door latch and drag her into my private tasting room, where the light is scant and the walls are soundproof.

37

DANIELA

I blink several times as my eyes adjust to the dim light. Victor and I were here this afternoon, choosing Port, and setting out glasses and snacks for the tasting. But the space is different now that Antonio is here. It's sultry, reeking of sin and the promise of pleasure that only he gives me.

The contours of the room are fuzzy. There's only him—his searing gaze, and the stark masculinity that fills every crevice, every turn of the room.

My body burns for him. He knows it too.

With two graceful strides, he reaches the long wooden table and lowers himself to the beveled edge.

Time stills as his shimmering eyes rake over my body, admiring me like a prized possession. I don't shy away tonight. I let him look to his heart's content, while I soak in the admiration in his dark gaze. The unfettered passion.

He's all I see. All I taste. All I smell. And I want to touch him. I *need* to touch him. Just the thought of his warm skin under my fingertips makes my pussy flutter.

"Take off your clothes," he commands from his perch. "Let's

see if you were really brazen enough to leave your panties upstairs."

I smile softly. I'm wearing panties. Not because I wasn't feeling brazen, but because I was anxious about losing the jeweled plug I inserted before coming downstairs for dessert. He'll be disappointed when he sees the red lace, but my jeweled ass should more than make up for it.

I slide the camisole off, shaking out my hair. His eyes are pitch black when I hold out my hand and offer him the flimsy lingerie.

Antonio takes it from me, rubbing the silk between his fingers before dropping it on the table beside him.

"I want your skirt," he demands in a voice like coarse stone that makes my skin tingle.

Slowly, I pull down the zipper and shimmy the gauzy fabric over my hips until it pools at my feet.

"You're a tease," he murmurs, getting to his feet. I forget to breathe as he steps closer, his eyes glued to mine. "There's a special punishment for teases."

My ass clenches at his seductive tone, and I can barely contain the triumph when I feel the plug. *He's going to be surprised.* There's nothing headier than surprising Antonio. *Nothing.*

"The punishment—will I like it?"

He throws his head back and laughs.

It's such a wonderful sound and it fills my heart with joy.

"That's a loaded question, *Princesa.*" He glides a thick finger between my breasts. "The journey might be rocky, but the destination will be everything you could ever want. We'll leave it at that," he murmurs.

I'm trying to remain composed, but I'm seconds away from launching myself at him and begging him to take me on the trip—wherever it leads us. But he steps back before I can act, his heated gaze roaming over my flesh. It's vulgar and lewd, and I revel in the warmth that drenches my skin.

"Would you like my panties?"

Antonio doesn't respond. Not right away. It doesn't matter that I'd like nothing more than to hand over my underwear—a flush still creeps over me.

"Are you embarrassed, *Princesa*? Are you ashamed to be standing practically naked in front of me while I fantasize about defiling your gorgeous body?"

I shake my head. "You're my husband."

"And what else, *Princesa*?"

I don't know. I shrug.

"Your body belongs to me."

I nod, once.

"Say it."

"My body belongs to you." I don't hesitate or equivocate. I repeat it like a familiar prayer. I shouldn't like this so much. *But I do.*

"I'll take those pretty red panties from you in good time, but not yet."

I nod, only slightly disappointed.

"I didn't come prepared for a *tasting*. I'll need to improvise," he adds, reaching for my camisole. "I'm going to use this sexy little thing to blindfold you," he murmurs.

"Blindfold?"

He nods. "What kind of tasting would it be if you could see the color of the Port? That's a game for amateurs. You're much too clever for that."

"Are we playing a game?" I ask while he secures the lingerie over my eyes. A blindfold hadn't been part of my plan, but even as I plunge into the darkness, I have no intention of stopping him.

"I rarely play games, *Princesa*. You should know that by now. But when I do play, it's deadly serious, and I always win." He slides his mouth over my jaw. "When we play together—we should both win."

My heart is hammering. *Hammering,* like it's going to jump out of my chest. *It must be the blindfold.* There's something thrilling about it.

Antonio slides his hand between my legs, over the gusset. I hear him sniff, long and exaggerated, before placing his fingers at my nose. "It's the scent of arousal. Uniquely yours. More alluring than the call of the Siren. I'd follow it to hell."

I can barely breathe.

"I need you to stand here, quietly, *Princesa,* while I prepare the tasting. Can you do that?"

I don't respond at first because I'm feeling a little woozy. Standing while blindfolded is more difficult than it seems.

"Daniela?"

"I'm not sure. I'm a little light-headed."

"It's much too soon for that. Let me help you to your knees. You'll be safer closer to the floor."

"I could sit in a chair."

"Too comfortable. You don't want that," he whispers above my ear. "You didn't bring me here to be comfortable."

38

DANIELA

He's right. *Sex with him is never comfortable—it's a spine-tingling roller coaster ride, and highly addictive, like a potent drug, but it's never comfortable.*

He places both hands on my waist. "Hold onto my arms, and I'll help you to the floor so you don't hurt yourself."

Without my vision, it takes a good dose of trust to let him guide me. But I do, because if I know anything, it's that he won't let me fall. Sometimes the safety net is so far out of reach I can't see it, like on the ship, but with him, it's always there. No detail is too small when it comes to my safety.

When my knees hit the cold tile, he eases me back until I'm sitting on my heels.

"Distribute your weight evenly. Place your hands on your thighs for leverage, so you don't list and topple over. That's it."

His lips graze over mine, slow and sublime. I feel the kiss *everywhere*.

"It'll take just a few minutes to get things ready," he says, after pulling back.

When he steps away, I experience his absence acutely. He

hasn't left the room, but blindfolded, with him out of arm's reach, I'm alone and vulnerable.

I take several deep breaths to settle my nerves, and it's enough to ground me so I'm fully present.

Although I can't see what he's doing, I hear everything. Bottles uncorked, Port decanting, the clink of glasses, and the rustle of his trousers as he moves. Each sound paints a vivid picture against the dark canvas.

After a few minutes of just listening, I sense him approaching. His spicy cologne woos me before he says a single word.

"Do you need anything before we start, *Princesa*? Maybe some water?"

I shake my head.

"You're breathtaking on your knees. I almost hate to have you move, but we have a *tasting* to conduct." He cradles my cheek in a warm hand. "I'll help you up. Follow my lead," he instructs, before lifting me to my feet and scooping my body into his arms.

I cling to him because I'm high off the floor and I can't see a thing. We move for mere seconds—although it seems infinitely longer—before he sets me down, on the table—I think.

As I root around to get my bearings, he stands between my legs. I'm suddenly acutely aware of the plug. *Maybe it's been in for too long.*

"You're on the table. At the edge," he explains, "so don't wiggle around too much. You're safe, *Princesa*. Even when it feels like you're not, you are. I won't let anything happen to you."

It's the reassurance I need, and the pent-up anxiety that masquerades as energy begins to unspool. Not because he won't let anything bad happen, but because he's watching me closely enough to know I'm off-kilter without my vision.

Before I have a chance to get fully comfortable in this position, his hands are on me, gliding over my sensitive skin. He sucks a nipple into his mouth, and I reach for him as my body sways forward. "Is this the tasting?" I gasp.

I feel the curl of his mouth on my breast before he pulls it away.

"So much going on inside that pretty little head. Too many questions."

I shiver at his warm breath on my shoulder.

"You'll wait for what I give you. And you'll drink greedily, sucking every drop into that sassy mouth, like a grateful *Princesa*." Without another word, he sinks his teeth into the base of my neck, marking the soft flesh at the top of my spine. It rouses every nerve, and a whimper tumbles from my lips in response.

He brings a glass to my lips, and I take a generous sip, and then another. It's luscious. *A vintage Port from a vintage year.* I'm sure of it.

"It's a vintage Port," I announce confidently.

"Very nice, but anyone with a moderate amount of knowledge would know that. I want to know the year."

"The year?" That's almost impossible. I'm not that good. "I have no idea."

"Take a guess."

"What happens if I guess wrong?" I ask, buying myself some time to narrow down the possibilities.

He laughs. "You'll be punished, of course."

"What kind of punishment?" I sound entirely too eager —*and I am.*

"Oh, no, *Princesa*. You don't get that information up front. The anticipation is all part of the fun."

"Your fun or mine?"

"Stop talking and open your mouth," he urges gently.

When I let my jaw go slack, he pushes two fingers into my mouth. They taste of Port. *This one is vastly different than the last.* As I suck on his fingers, I know it right away.

"It's a thirty-year Tawny."

"Good girl."

I hear the pride in his voice.

"Now let's go back to the vintage. In a different vessel this time. Maybe it'll help you identify the year."

He places a hand on the back of my neck and presses my head down. "You'll need to lap it up like a pampered pet who eats from her master's hand."

A myriad of emotions swirl inside, engulfed by heat and laced with a tad of shame, just enough to heighten the seduction.

Slowly, I stick out my tongue until it reaches the fortified wine in his cupped palm.

"Drink, my pretty," he purrs.

And I do. I drink until the vessel is empty, and then lick the sticky residue from his skin while my arousal leaks onto my panties.

"1960." It's a guess, but that was a great year—and the Port I lapped from his hand is a special vintage.

"Good guess. Impressive. But you're wrong."

You're wrong. The words shimmy through me in a seductive dance, dragging thin silk scarves behind them as they await the delicious punishment. "What happens now?"

"My turn to taste. But it was such a good guess, I think you should be rewarded."

He hooks his fingers in my panties, and I lift my hips off the table to help. I want them off as much as he does. *Maybe more.*

When his breath hitches, I know he sees the jewel.

"Are you wearing this for me, *Princesa*?" he asks, tapping the red stone in a way that makes my pussy quiver. His voice is raspy and his breathing is heavy and shallow.

The pressure from the plug is no longer uncomfortable. I smile.

"Yes," I reply. "I'm wearing it for you."

I'm certain I feel his hand tremble before it tightens on my hip.

"*Mmmm*," he murmurs, his nose grazing my ear. "Have you ever used the plug while you stroked your pussy? Have you come with it in?"

"No," I squeak. It's the truth. I've been experimenting with having it inside me, but I've never come—although my fingers might have wandered between my legs, but not for long enough to orgasm. With a preteen in the house, I don't have quite as much time in the morning to linger in bed and play.

"Lie down," he says, nudging me until my back is flat on the tasting table.

I feel his hands on me, then his tongue. I'm not accustomed to the new position, and when I squirm, he slaps my thigh.

"*Ah!*" I gasp at the unexpected sting.

"Stay still."

While he licks me, I press my fingertips into the tabletop, and let the pleasure wash over me. My soft mewls turn into gasps and whimpers when he slides two fingers into my pussy.

"Oh, *Princesa*," he practically groans. "You're so tight plugged. I'm going to fuck you while it's in."

He wiggles the plug, and my back arches off the table. It's a snug fit with his fingers and the plug inside me. *So snug.*

As his wicked tongue paints circles on my wet flesh, my walls clench. I feel my belly contracting into a tight ball. The orgasm he's demanding from me will be long and brutal, and I hold back for as long as I can. But it's futile. I'm powerless to stop the avalanche, and as I surrender to the giant swell, every muscle in my body screams before it submits.

"*Princesa*, you are *so* beautiful when you come for me. *So* tortured as you surrender to the bliss. I feel your tremors in my balls—the anguish in my soul. It makes my cock weep every time."

I'm trembling on the table when I hear Antonio's zipper. *I can't take any more—not yet.* But I don't object beyond a whimper. I don't have the strength to utter a single word, let alone wage a protest.

He flips me onto my stomach and drags me to the edge of the table. It's quick and rough, and when he takes his pleasure, he'll be rough too. My muscles tighten, almost painfully, around the plug that's still wedged inside me, and despite the twinge of soreness, my body begins to hum in anticipation.

He's settled between my legs. His bare skin caresses mine, nudging the pleasure sensors open.

"Enjoy one last taste before I enjoy you."

When he reaches over to bring the glass to my lips, his thick cock lies in the small of my back. Hot and hard. I'm certain I feel the throb.

I take a small sip of the fortified wine. Even in my hyper-aroused state, I recognize the young Port. The one he shared with me the first time we had dinner together.

"It's the special Port from the first night we had dinner," I pant. "The one that will be declared a vintage later this year." *The one that filled my heart with joy.*

His cock is at my entrance, now. It takes everything I have not to wiggle against it until it slips inside.

"My prized Port from the barrel inside the cave. The barrel you rubbed your pussy all over, squirming until your ripe juices seeped through the wood, making a succulent Port even sweeter. Do you remember that, *Princesa*?"

He doesn't wait for me to answer before he sinks his cock into me. The slide is heavy and merciless, especially with the plug. But I welcome every inch of him into my private heaven, basking in the carnality. Although it's not enough. *I want to see him.*

Without asking permission, I pull off the blindfold and rest on my forearms, so I can look over my shoulder. *I need to see him.*

He's beautiful in the low light. A handsome wolf with hooded eyes and a tight jaw bathed in scruff. It takes my breath away.

"You're a naughty *Princesa*," he growls, pounding harder.

"I had to see you. I couldn't wait any longer."

He twists the plug, pulling it out, and then pushing it back into my tight passage. *The beast inside him has taken over.* I feel the shift, as he manipulates the plug, again. And again. In and out. Rocking his hips, deeper and harder, and stealing my sanity as he drives me to the edge. It's wanton and reckless—and I want more and more—until I can't.

I lower my forehead to my clenched fists and scream as my body convulses. It's a hollow scream, muffled by my hands and the lack of air reaching my lungs. But it sends him to the edge too. And with a few savage thrusts, he empties himself inside me.

39

DANIELA

I don't know how much time passes before we move. I might have drifted off.

Antonio nudges my protesting muscles into a sitting position, as my eyes struggle to adjust to the light.

My camisole is a few feet away—it looks like it's been sitting in the bottom of a clothes hamper for months. *That's because it was used as a blindfold. Oh God.*

Sometimes even a brilliant idea concocted in the light of day loses its luster when set into motion. Especially ideas that involve butt plugs. *What was I thinking?*

"Small sips," he murmurs, bringing a water goblet to my lips. Although my mouth is dry, I only manage a couple of sips while he pulls on his pants.

I hand him the glass, and he guzzles what's left of the water, the muscles in his throat rippling gently. I inch myself off the table until my feet are on the floor, but I keep one hand on the wooden lip. I'm disoriented and it offers security.

Antonio grabs my skirt and panties from the floor. I reach to take them from him, but he shakes his head, and begins to dress me, with the utmost care. I've been undressed before, but no man, or woman, has ever dressed me—at least not as an adult. Not until today—when Antonio Huntsman with his strong hands and nimble fingers decided that it was his pleasure.

He deems the panties expendable and wads them into a ball before shoving them into his pocket. After my skirt and top are on, Antonio steps out of the room and returns with my sweater. His fingers seem much too large for the dainty pearl buttons, but he doesn't stop until the last one is tethered. Having him fuss over me makes me feel like a little girl. *Like a cherished little girl.* And helpless—I don't like that feeling, and I manage to push it away by distracting myself with the mess around me.

"We need to clean up," I whisper, surveying the room. It's not a total disaster, but it reeks of sex and booze and too much fun.

"Not tonight. I'll cap the bottles. The rest can wait until tomorrow."

He picks the plug up off the table and wraps it in a cloth napkin before sliding it into his pocket. I don't mention how disgusting it is to have that thing in a pocket, because God knows I don't know how else we'd get it out of here. *I'll sanitize the table in the morning before Victor has a chance to get in here.*

"Come here," he says, placing a tender kiss on my head before scooping me into his arms.

The sense of helplessness is back, and it makes me feel too vulnerable. "I can walk."

"You need to drink some water. You carry these." He hands me three small bottles of water. "I'll carry you."

"This is silly," I whine.

"I'll decide what's silly. You're still not that steady on your feet. I promised you earlier that nothing would happen to you tonight. And I'm sure as hell not breaking that promise now."

The house is quiet as he carries me up the stairs. Neither of us says a word until he sets me on my feet outside Valentina's suite. "Go in and check on her. I'll wait here."

I gaze up at him—*he remembered*. I'd forgotten. It would have occurred to me at some point, and I would have berated myself as I climbed out of bed and trekked down the hall to check on her. *But he remembered.*

This is what it's like to raise a child with a partner. One person picks up the slack when the other's mind is somewhere else. It's how Isabel and I operated too.

I touch his cheek. "I'll only be a minute."

"I'm not going anywhere."

All bravado and lying to myself aside, those are the words I've been hoping to hear since I was a young girl. But I don't let myself get swept away by vowels and consonants strung together that aren't backed up by actions. Even though my true heart wants him to stay for a lifetime, my brain knows he's talking about the moment.

———

IT TAKES me just a few seconds to pull up the covers Valentina kicked off, and I use the rest of the time to admire her. *My brave, strong girl.* My miracle sleeping so peacefully.

She deserves to live every day in peace. *I can't tell her about the rape. I have to find another way.*

I take one last peek before I turn off the overhead light in the sitting room and shut the door behind me.

"She asleep?" Antonio asks, putting away his phone.

I smile. "She didn't bat an eyelash, even when I covered her."

He wraps his arm around my shoulder and pulls me into his side. "Before you sleep, you need a shower, *Princesa*."

"Are you suggesting I stink?"

"Of me. I'd like nothing more than to keep you dirty like

this all the time, my scent all over your gorgeous body like cheap perfume, but I suspect you'll sleep better if you've showered."

I'm bone-tired, but I do need a shower. "Just a quick one."

He leads me directly to our bathroom and turns on the water while we undress. I can barely keep my eyes open.

After checking the water temperature, Antonio pulls me into the shower.

"Sit." He motions to the marble bench that spans the width of the space, before unhooking the handheld shower head from the wall.

"Tip your head back," he instructs, spraying warm water over my hair. After he works the lather into my scalp, he rinses the suds and reaches for conditioner. It feels heavenly to have Antonio massaging my scalp, but there's also something about it that feels too indulgent, as though I'm helpless. *It's too much.*

It doesn't evoke a specific memory, but a feeling. The feeling I had in the meadow when I couldn't save my mother or myself, the feeling of looking over my shoulder for years, waiting for Tomas to rip Valentina away from me.

For years, I've combated the feeling by controlling everything I can. Sure, it's maladaptive, but it worked—until I met the man who craves control even more than I do.

"I'm not an invalid. You don't need to bathe me." I grab the bottle of conditioner, but he doesn't let go.

"I'm not easy, Daniela. I'll never be easy, and we will never have the kind of marriage little girls dream about. But I can take care of you the way you deserve. If you let me."

The steam has taken over every corner of the shower, but through the fog, I see the emotion in his face. *I feel how much it costs him to open his heart to me.* It's staggering.

I stand and drag my hand over two days' worth of stubble, enjoying the rough prickle on my fingertips.

"Little girls don't all have the same dreams. Some of us

dream about dark princes, on dark horses, who defy danger, bravely slaying dragons and monsters. I'll take the extravagant library and the glass slippers, and even the little mice who chatter endlessly, but in my heart, I'm a dirty *Princesa*, and I want the dark fairy tale. The one with the dangerous, broody prince who has a good soul that he never allows anyone to see." I stroke his jaw. "I can take care of you, too, if you let me."

He takes my hand and brings it to his mouth. His eyes never leave mine. "You deserve more than me. So much more."

I shake my head. "What I deserve is what every girl and every woman deserves: to choose my own fairy tale, and my own prince. Tradition and outdated customs be damned."

"You make it sound so simple."

"It is, Antonio. You're too close to see it, but it's not a novel idea. That kind of freedom will strengthen our world rather than weaken it."

A muscle in his jaw twitches. "You would have never chosen me after your father died, or if I'd gone to Fall River and asked you to come home." Anguish is woven around each word.

"I don't know. Maybe not." It pains me to tell him, but it's the truth. "There have been so many seasons of my life when I would have chosen you over anyone. But I don't know. What I do know is that I choose you now."

He holds me against his beating heart, my head tucked under his chin as the water cascades over us. Long minutes pass while we cling to each other.

"You're my greatest temptation, *Princesa*. My weakness. The woman I spend every day and every night lusting over. It wasn't supposed to be like this," he whispers into my wet hair. "If I had a shred of decency, I would send you away, far away from me, where my life can't dim your light and stain your soul, where you'd be safe from my enemies. But I'm a selfish man, and I need you."

It's a humble prayer from a man who doesn't know humility

or prayer. My heart clenches for him as he traverses the unfamiliar soil, and I wrap my arms around him tighter. "I'm right here, Antonio. I'm right here."

I once read that there's a turning point in every relationship that binds two souls, and no matter what happens after that, there's no going back. *Ever.* Not even if you end up hating each other. Not even when one of you dies. Once you reach that mystical point, once you take the turn, your souls are inextricably tied to one another, never to be fully free again.

This is our turning point.

40

ANTONIO

I fucked up. Not just a small mistake, but I dug a hole so big you can drive a tank through it. *Or Daniela can, anyway.*

Last night should have never happened. I wasn't going to stay over at the house. I wasn't going to fuck her until Tomas is in hell. And I certainly had no plans to bare my damn soul like I'm a teenage girl prone to drama.

But the second she sashayed across the room and locked the door, I was screwed. By the time she had her sweater off, and those dusky nipples were taunting me through the fabric, it was a foregone conclusion. No damn way was I leaving without tasting her.

I'm tired of denying myself, of denying her. It needed to end. That's what I told myself over and over, last night, and again this morning. It's true.

But the world is full of truths we shouldn't act on. In the end, it was a bullshit excuse for being a weak bastard without an ounce of self-control. And I'm going to pay for it—dearly, because now, Daniela's going to expect things from me that I can't give her.

The worst part of the entire mess is that, given the opportunity for a do-over, I'd dig the damn hole again. Maybe leave out some of the soul baring. But the rest? I wouldn't change a goddamn thing.

I pass Lucas on my way to the villa. He's moving at a good clip. "Where are you going in such a hurry?"

"There's a delivery for me upstairs. I need to sign for it."

"A delivery?"

"Fuck if I know."

"Cristiano inside?"

"Nah," he calls over his shoulder. "He had an errand to run."

"What are we, suburban housewives?" I grumble under my breath. "Deliveries and errands? The next thing, someone's going need time off to get their pussy waxed." No one responds to the sarcasm because Lucas is long gone.

The silence in the villa is eerie. Screens flicker high on the walls, like a row of soldiers, monitoring the comings and goings of select places all over the region. But the sound is off, and it feels too quiet.

I pour a coffee and sit at my desk, reviewing the agenda for a meeting this afternoon.

Either the proposed agenda is a big snooze, or my concentration is shot.

I glance at the time on the screen. *Is Daniela awake, or is she still curled up under the covers, her dark hair fanned over the white pillowcase, like it was when I left this morning?*

By the time we got to bed, it was well after one, and after a short nap, we were at it again. *Sleepy sex.* The kind where you're both on your side and you slip effortlessly into her warm body. The kind I've never had with anyone but her, because I never stick around for a midnight snack—or at least I haven't since I was a college kid.

I stole away under the cover of darkness, long before anyone in the house was up. I didn't wake her to say goodbye, because it was early. *There really is no shortage of bullshit that I'm willing to swallow when it comes to her.*

She's a chink in my armor. No one knows the extent of the vulnerability but me—and now her, because I couldn't keep my damn mouth shut. I can't afford that kind of vulnerability. Especially now.

Once we know more, I might be able to afford more risks, but until then I need to assume danger is everywhere.

The Italians and the Russians are the most formidable opponents. But the Italians won't touch her. It's not their style, and we have an understanding. But if the Russians get their hands on her, they'll take photographs and video while she's tortured, and send them to me so that her screams are forever imprinted on my consciousness—haunting me until I take my last breath. Maybe beyond. Maybe that's destined to be my eternal hell.

I glance up when the door slides open. "Someone sent you flowers?" I scoff, as Lucas enters carrying a vase of colorful blooms.

"I love these flowers," he quips. "The card with them has news we've been waiting for."

He opens the small enclosure card, and his face drops. "It's a mixed bag," he grumbles, handing it to me.

You're leaking at the neck. Coordinates unknown. I'm out.

"Our guy?"

Lucas nods. "The florist delivers fresh flowers to your uncle's place a few times a week. Our guy got friendly with her. She told me he asked her to deliver us a message last week, but she was too nervous to follow through. She hasn't seen him since."

A cold chill runs up my spine. "Is this the same florist who prepared Daniela's wedding bouquet?" *The one that concealed a plastic detonating device.*

"No. It's the first thing I thought of too."

Still, I don't like it. What kind of idiot delivers a message through a florist he recently met? *The kind who doesn't have any other choice.* "Do we need to be worried about her talking?"

He shakes his head. "I don't think so."

"Why did she feel the need to deliver the message today?"

"She claims to have run into him every time she's there, until last Friday. Apparently, his disappearance has been eating at her, and she didn't know what else to do."

"You believe her?"

He nods. "But I'm going to do a background check to see if there's any reason I shouldn't."

I glance at the card. Discretion is one thing, but could he have been any more cryptic? "This doesn't tell us much."

"It confirms we have a problem. And it's not a foot soldier. It also tells us he's off the grid."

"Or dead," I mutter.

"You're right. It doesn't tell us much. We still don't know if someone turned, or if they've been inadvertently compromised, or if it's a device we haven't been able to pick up. The Russians are masters at that sort of thing. It goes back to the KGB. It's got Dimitri Fedorov's name all over it."

Fedorov is the *Pakhan* of the Elite group of the European Bratva. He's made Porto his home. The lore surrounding him is legendary—and chilling—although, like all legends, I expect some of it is exaggerated. Still, he's not a man to be underestimated.

"Like I said, it doesn't tell us much." I toss the card on the desk. "Get those flowers out of here. They stink."

"I'll bring them up to Cecelia. I'm always doing something to piss off your assistant. Maybe this will curry me a little favor."

"No," I bark. "Get them out of the building."

He glances at me but doesn't say a word before he takes the vase and leaves.

This has gone on too damn long. Something feels off. Not just the flowers—it's everything. I can't put my finger on it, but my gut has been uneasy since the wedding.

I'm done waiting. We can get what we need out of Tomas once we have him.

I give myself a few minutes to change my mind before I place a call from the secure line to another line that I'm also confident is secure.

41

ANTONIO

"Antonio. How's married life treating you?" My brother-in-law Will snickers. His wife Samantha is technically my stepsister. But it's semantics. In my culture, we don't think about relationships that way. Family is family.

"Does Daniela have your balls yet?"

Pretty much. "Last time I looked, they were still attached to my dick, but the day is coming. I've got a job for you."

Will runs an operation that eclipses our scope, and in terms of pure real estate, he plays on a bigger playing field. The United Kingdom is larger than Portugal. Plain and simple. But our organizations have unique capabilities, and we help each other out from time to time.

"Do tell." It's only two words, but it's evident from his tone that he's cast aside all joking.

"I need a package delivered."

"Does this package piss itself? If so, it's going to cost you extra."

"My wallet's wide open."

"Does this have anything to do with the wedding?" he asks, after a brief pause.

"It does."

"You don't owe me a goddamn extra penny. Nobody blows up a church while my wife's inside. *Nobody*."

Despite his cool British reserve, Will is a mean sonofabitch when he's crossed, and nothing, *nothing*, rankles him more than someone taking aim at his wife or daughter. Even if they're not the intended targets. It's a trait I respect.

"How soon do you need it delivered?"

Yesterday. But it's going to take some time for it to happen seamlessly. "Sooner rather than later. But there are several factors to consider, including that it can't be traced back to either of us. I also need to clean up a few things before the delivery. I suspect it'll take at least ten days before you can pick up the package and I can take delivery. There can be no mistakes."

"Works for me. I'm in the middle of something myself, and it would be better if we could hold off a couple of weeks. But after that, I'm all in."

"I'm planning on visiting my mother next week. I don't have a firm date. But I'll get back to you. Let's hash out the details in person."

"In the meantime, I'll start pulling together assets. I'll tweak them after we chat."

"One more thing before you go. Tell me about St. Philomena's."

"The girls' school?"

"Yeah."

42

DANIELA

It's been a week since Antonio skulked away in the middle of the night without a word. I haven't seen him since.

We're back to texting. We also had a video chat that included Valentina so she could report the progress she's made with her riding. *But he didn't have time to talk to me alone after Valentina said goodbye.* While Antonio had the charm turned up high during the chat, he's mostly been his usual closed-off self.

He's put back up the wall and it's been more difficult to penetrate since the night of the *tasting*, but there are moments —small moments when he gives me something to hold on to.

"I'm not ready to spend my nights in the valley. I need you to be patient." That's what he said when I asked him when he'd be back. I'm not sure what to make of it, but it leaves me raw and angry every time I think about.

Part of me believes his ambivalence is because of the rape. Because his father got so close—and his cousin clinched the deal. But I don't probe. To begin with, he wouldn't tell me the truth—I'm not even sure he's honest with himself about it.

Antonio and I are magnets, drawn together by a pull neither of us can resist. At times, like in the tasting room, something primal claws its way to the surface and he doesn't think. He acts purely on instinct. But in the light of day, when the animal crawls back to its lair, he's left with the remnants of the past, something neither of us can change. He can say whatever he wants, but I don't believe it doesn't bother him.

But the main reason I don't bring it up with him is because it's how I've learned to cope. It's how I've gotten out of bed for the last twelve years with my head high. How I've moved forward with my life.

While others have been impacted by what happened that day, I don't owe anyone an apology and I won't engage in any discussion where my worth is called into question—or Valentina's—because I was assaulted. There are times, few and far between now, when I beat myself up about what happened, or when I'm disparaging to the little girl who lost her innocence or the woman she's become, but I'll be damned if I allow anyone else to disparage me.

Antonio's a big boy. If I learned to live with it, so can he. Or maybe he can't, and as heartbroken as I'll be if that's the case, it's not my problem. It's not my fight. I have my own.

Although maybe I'm wrong about all of it. Maybe Antonio's hot-and-cold behavior goes back to my discussion with Cristiano. I keep going back to it. I can't help myself.

"Love leaves powerful men vulnerable to their enemies. And he has plenty. But even someone like Antonio, with great discipline and a willingness to sacrifice, will eventually succumb when faced with the right woman. The heart wants what the heart wants."

More than anything, I want to believe I'm the right woman and he just needs to open himself up to the idea of love. But either way, after the last time we were together—maybe before—I'm willing to give him time. My days are full of distractions. It's the nights that are long and lonely.

"The mail has arrived," Lara announces from the doorway of my office.

The mail is an unpleasant chore. It's left at the front gate and the guards check it to be sure there isn't a bomb or poison or anything sinister before they drop it at the house. Some days I'd prefer if they dumped it in the trash instead.

"Should I go through it, or do you prefer to do it?" Lara asks, holding two packages and a sack of letters.

"Let's do it together."

"There's more downstairs. I'll be right back. Don't start without me," she teases.

We're still getting wedding presents from all over the world, and notes of congratulations, not to mention the never-ending invitations, and letters from charitable organizations requesting money. As much as Lara loves to be in my business, even she complains about the daily mail delivery.

When she gets back, I hand her a letter opener and we get to work. About forty minutes in, I get up to make myself some tea. "Do you want a cup of tea?"

Lara doesn't respond. She's gawking at something, with her lips puckered. She can be so judgmental about some of the invitations that come through. *Gaudy, classless, poor taste.* The list goes on and on.

"What is it?" I ask, pouring hot water over the tea leaves.

When she doesn't reply, I know this isn't about the wrong font or party venue.

"Lara," I say gently. "What do you have there?"

"I—I'm not sure," she mutters.

"Let me see it." I take a few steps toward her. *Photos.*

A shiver runs through me before I've seen a single one. "Can I have a look, please?"

She gazes up at me. "It must be a prank—I'm not sure—"

I take the photographs. There are several. *All of Antonio and Sonia at the Intercontinental Hotel downtown.*

I draw a large breath and sink into a chair. The world stops spinning as I study the photos. One of them huddled in the ornate lobby, another at a table in the swanky bar. There's a photo of Antonio with his arm slung around her shoulders as they leave the hotel. They're happy. Smiling. Sharing a private joke, maybe.

Is that what post-coital bliss looks like?

There's a photo of them saying goodbye. She presses a kiss to each of his cheeks before he helps her into the back of a car. There are eight photos in total. I've counted them twice. But each time nothing changes, not the number of images or the stark betrayal.

My stomach churns, driving bitter bile into my throat.

"I'm sure it's nothing," Lara assures me.

I hear the pity in her voice, and it makes me furious. Not at her, but at *them. At him.*

It's nothing? Really? Because it looks like something to me.

The events of a week ago come careening back. Sex in the tasting room. *The trust that allowed us to explore. His tenderness in the shower.* It doesn't matter how intimate we are or how good the sex is—it'll never be enough.

He wants what he wants—and Antonio wants everything. Men like him always do. Or maybe it's just his way of sabotaging our marriage. *Congratulations, Antonio. There's no better way to push me into the periphery of your life.*

"Daniela?"

I'm a heartbeat away from spewing everything I'm thinking and feeling all over this room and making a huge scene. But I'm not going to do that. I don't feel close enough to Lara to let her see my pain. My embarrassment. If a new bride can't keep her husband satisfied, what does that say about the future?

I set the photos aside with a shaky hand. "I'm sure you're right. You know how the media is always hounding Antonio, hoping for something juicy to print." I plaster on a smile, but my heart is weeping. "I'll speak with him about it later. Let's finish going through the mail. We're almost done."

Lara seems somewhat surprised, as she takes my measure carefully. "Are you sure?"

No, I'm not sure, but I want some time to think. "Absolutely."

We finish triaging the mail in silence. When we're done, Lara gathers the piles we created, and reaches for the damning photos.

"Leave those." I smile sweetly at her, because now I have a plan.

43

DANIELA

After she's gone, I call Victor. Valentina doesn't need a babysitter, but she's never been here without me. I'm sure Lara would keep an eye on her, or Paula, even. But there's no one I trust more than Victor.

"I have a small surprise for Antonio," I explain. "I'd like to deliver it myself. Valentina's with the horses, but I'll leave her a note. Would you mind keeping an eye out for her until I get back? She has reading to catch up on, so she shouldn't be a bother. I'll only be gone a couple of hours."

"I'd be delighted. Valentina's never a bother. I have some pastries to fill. Maybe she'd like to help."

My insides are quivering, but fortunately Victor's too caught up in entertaining Valentina to notice.

"I'm sure she'd love to help you in the kitchen."

After we hang up, I go to the closet and pull out a classy dress in a warm white shade—and add a piece of my mother's jewelry and a pair of leopard print heels. But first, I slip on a gorgeous red bra and panty set—for me—to remind myself I'm sexy and desirable.

When I'm satisfied with my appearance, I leave Valentina a

note, and call for a ride. This will be my first hurdle, but I'll be damned if Alvarez is going to stop me.

"I'm going to Huntsman Lodge. I have a surprise for Antonio."

"Is he expecting you?" He's polite, but his tone is tight. I like Alvarez, but he's a member of the old boys' club, and he prefers when women ask his permission to come and go.

"It wouldn't be much of a surprise if he was expecting me."

He might be my guard, but he's Antonio's man, and I've put him in an uncomfortable position. *You can't worry about it now.* If Antonio had kept his dick in his pants, no one would be uncomfortable.

"If you're too busy to take me, I'll call an Uber."

"That won't be necessary, *senhora*."

"Good. Will you keep my secret?"

"Of course."

Bullshit.

WHEN I GET inside the main building at Huntsman Lodge, I'm given immediate access to the elevator. Either the security personnel recognized my face, or they were expecting me. Even if Alvarez didn't tattle, Antonio certainly knows at this point.

Now that I'm here in a building with his name splashed all over it in big letters, I'm a little nervous. But I won't let a few jitters stop me. If I allow him free rein to cheat, he'll never stop.

His assistant, Cecelia, is waiting for me when the elevator doors open, and she escorts me to his office. "You can go right in. He's expecting you."

Of course he is.

I've never been inside his office. *Maybe that tells me everything I need to know.*

I take a deep breath before entering.

44

DANIELA

The fury, the disappointment, the embarrassment, and yes, the hurt that I've tried to control since I first saw those pictures several hours ago are a tempest now, with a flood threatening. But I will not give him my tears. *Not a single fucking one.*

Antonio's leaning back in his chair, with an elbow resting on the graceful arm. *He's beautiful. But only on the outside.*

The truth is, I'm almost angrier at myself than I am at him. How could I have been so foolish as to believe he'd be faithful? That I would ever be enough—*me*, enough for a man who believes that a marriage is nothing more than a business transaction. He said it himself. I just didn't want to believe it. *Stupid, stupid, stupid woman.*

Antonio's a cheater—that's on him. But my heartache is my own doing.

He appraises me from head to toe, with the gaze of a predator. "*Princesa*, to what do I owe the pleasure of your visit?"

I'm consumed with the urge to hurl everything within reach at his head, but I'm not playing that game. It's too easy to dismiss an out-of-control woman. He's going to have to deal with someone who's calm and composed—at least on the outside.

"I'd like a few minutes of your time."

"Then you'll need to make an appointment." His tone is dismissive, but I'm not going anywhere. "I make it a rule to keep my personal life separate from my business. It couldn't wait?"

"Perhaps. But I came because I have no idea when you'll be home again. It can't wait forever." I flash him a saccharine smile, and he glowers. He's not amused. That makes two of us.

"Say what you came to say."

I take the photos out of my tote bag and toss them on the desk in front of him, and then I sit in the chair across from him.

"They arrived with today's mail." It occurs to me that I should have made a copy, or at the very least taken a picture of the images.

He glances at the top photo and shoves the entire pile aside. "I've already told you that you don't need to worry about Sonia."

"And I've already told you that I won't be embarrassed publicly. There are few places in Porto that are as public as the Intercontinental." *And gorgeous. It's always been my favorite hotel. But I'll never set foot in it again.*

He doesn't say a word about the photos before he picks up the phone. "Do you have any information about the matter you brought to my attention this morning?"

Really, Antonio? You're going to do business while I'm sitting here waiting for an explanation? If he's thinking I'll storm off in a huff, he's mistaken. I lean back in the chair, cross my legs, and fold my arms across my chest.

"It's enough for me," he says to the person on the phone. "Send Thiago to pick up our friend. My office. Right now," he adds before hanging up.

He places another call, never taking his eyes off my face. There's no remorse. If anything, there are flashes of anger, but I don't know if they're meant for me or for the person he's talking to.

"I've sent a car for you. It should be there within ten minutes—perhaps less." Antonio pauses for a few seconds. "I don't care if you have the president of Portugal's dick in your mouth, I advise you to get your ass into the car the minute it arrives."

He's not playing. If it were me, I'd be waiting at the curb.

Is this how he's planning to get rid of me? *I'm sorry, dear, this will have to wait. My appointment is here.* "Who was that?"

"That was business."

"You don't seem to understand. I'm not going anywhere until we've had a discussion. It doesn't matter who shows up. I don't care if you summoned the president of Portugal himself, he'll have to wait his turn."

His mouth quirks at the corners. "We have a little time, and there are some pressing matters I need to discuss with you. As much as I hate people showing up in my office without an appointment, this might be a good opportunity to talk."

I sit up tall. "I'm not people. I'm your wife. First, we discuss my business."

He smiles, but it doesn't reach his eyes. "My office. My business. We'll get to yours in due time."

He's stalling. "I'm not leaving until I have answers. If you don't like it, you'll have to have security drag me out."

"If I don't like it, I'll drag you out myself."

He's such a smug bastard. "What do you want to talk about?"

"I want you to listen carefully to what I'm about to say," he cautions, like I'm a teenager who has broken curfew again. "Put aside your misplaced anger and use your common sense to think it through."

My common sense? Because I normally shoot from the hip, making all my decisions based on emotion? The man is insufferable.

He goes over to the bar and pours himself a drink. "Do you want something?"

"I'll have some water."

Antonio hands me a glass before sitting at the edge of his desk.

I consider dumping the water on his crotch, but that's foreplay for him.

His Adam's apple bobs, and a sense of unease settles over me. Antonio doesn't hedge—but that's exactly what he's doing. *This can't be good.*

"I want Valentina to spend a couple of weeks at summer camp."

The unease has become pure dread. Is he punishing me for interrupting his workday? *No.* "Camp? What are you talking about?"

"St. Philomena's School runs a camp outside of London. She'll have an opportunity to spend some time with girls her age. It'll be good for her."

What will be good for her is if I strangle you right now and shove your body out the floor-to-ceiling windows. I stand. "I'm not sending her away."

"I wasn't asking for your permission. She will be going to camp."

"Are you insane or just evil?"

"Perhaps both."

I turn to leave, because while he's in this kind of mood, I'm not going to get anywhere. Better not to have the discussion at all. The photos are nothing compared to this. He can fuck Sonia anywhere and everywhere he wants. But he's not taking my child from me.

"Sit down."

"I need to get back."

"You showed up here uninvited. Now we're going to see it through. But first, you're going to listen to everything I have to say."

As usual, he holds all the cards. I'm not sure what to do, but after some time passes, I lower myself into the chair because he could send her away, and I wouldn't be able to do a damn thing about it.

He takes the seat next to me, turning it so we're facing each other. "Things are about to get dangerous in Porto. We're close to learning more about the explosion at Santa Ana's and Isabel's murder. St. Philomena's is an exclusive private girls' school outside of London. The kind of exclusive where kings and presidents send their daughters and granddaughters. The security at the school is unparalleled. Samantha and Will send Alexis there. Valentina will be safe in London while the war is being fought here."

There's a sense of urgency about him. I don't think he's lying about the danger, but there has to be another way.

"She can stay in the valley with me. It's not like we go to the mall or the nail salon, or anywhere, really."

"No. We don't understand the risks well enough."

This is a difficult argument. Perhaps if I were in another frame of mind, I might see it differently. Of course I want her to be safe. But I also want her with me. I'm not convinced that I can't have both.

"You expect me to send her to another country, to a place I know nothing about?"

"You'll have an opportunity to visit before she's enrolled. It's required. And my mother and Samantha are close by."

"She's twelve. I can't send her away alone."

"She won't be anywhere near the youngest girl there. Besides, you'll be going too."

"To camp?"

He rolls his eyes. "No. To stay with Samantha and Will."

This is crazy. I'm not staying with people I don't know. "I've met them just once."

"My mother and Rafael will be there too."

I gauge him carefully. This isn't just any danger. He's talking serious danger. I can't afford to dismiss it—not that he'll let me anyway. Maybe if we're both in London, it won't be so bad. "Will I be able to visit with Valentina while she's at camp?"

He shakes his head. "No. St. Philomena's is safe because people aren't in and out. But she'll have Mia with her, and Santi nearby."

I glance at the photographs on the desk behind him. "Is this so that you can do whatever you want with whomever you want with me out of the way?" It's snarky. I know sending us away has nothing to do with his whoring, but he deserves a bit of snark.

"I don't need you out of the way to do whatever or whomever I want."

"You are a despicable excuse for a human being." I get up to leave. I need some time to think through the possibilities, and I can't do it here.

"I suggest you put your cute little ass back in that chair. I'm thin on patience today, and from the moment you walked through the door, I've wanted to tear that dress off your gorgeous body and fuck you against the windows overlooking the old city."

My eye catches the photos on his desk.

His expression is dark and salacious, and despite the growing anger, my lower belly tightens in response.

Fuck me against the windows? "It'll be a cold day in hell before that happens."

He throws his head back and laughs. It takes me by surprise, and if I wasn't so angry, I might laugh too.

Before either of us says anything more, the phone on his desk buzzes, and he answers. "Send her in."

"Our guest has arrived," he murmurs, a moment before Sonia traipses through the door.

45

ANTONIO

I'm not sure who's more surprised, Sonia or Daniela. Sometimes getting everyone in the room at the same time is the best way to air the dirty laundry.

I stand and lean against my desk, with my arms folded.

"What's she doing here?" Sonia asks, tentatively.

I'm sure Daniela is wondering the same thing.

Two sets of eyes are glued to me. Hopefully they're not holding their breaths waiting for me to explain. They both know better.

"Sit down," I tell Sonia. She peers at me, begging silently for a reprieve. But she's not getting a fucking thing from me. "Now."

She sits at the edge of her seat, and I hand her a stack of photos. Not the photos that Daniela brought, but the ones Lucas printed this morning from the internet.

"Let's cut right to the chase. You gave the photographer permission to run those photos. You vouched for their accuracy. And you led him to believe that there was something going on between us." I am no less livid now than I was when Lucas told me about it this morning. If anything, I'm more furious now that Daniela knows.

Sonia doesn't say anything in her defense. It's all true. What I haven't figured out is why she wants to cause trouble for me. She has a lot at risk—it doesn't make sense.

"Tell Daniela why we were at the Intercontinental."

Sonia gapes at me.

I'd like to hold her up by the hair and make her beg for my wife's forgiveness before I slit her throat.

"Are you crazy?" she mumbles.

"Apparently there's a growing list of people who think so. Tell her," I repeat firmly.

"We were meeting at the bar to discuss a diverted shipment."

I don't as much as glance at Daniela while I interrogate this bitch. I won't take a chance that Daniela pleads with those expressive eyes for me to go easy on Sonia. It would be just like her to ask for mercy on Sonia's behalf.

"Were we alone?"

"Only for a few minutes. No."

"Did we go up to one of the guest rooms either before or after the meeting?"

"No."

"Did I fuck you in the bathroom in the bar?"

"No."

"Have I ever fucked you?"

"No," she huffs.

I watch Daniela out of the corner of my eye while I fire that final question at Sonia. Her mouth is open, and her brow furrowed, trying to make sense of the little scene unfolding.

I'm done for the moment, and I turn to my wife. "Do you have any questions?"

"What shipment?" Daniela asks.

I should have known that she'd focus on the diverted shipment.

I turn back to Sonia, who stares at me like her world is about to come crumbling down. *Too fucking bad.*

"Tell her. You put this shitstorm in motion, and now you're going to deal with the fallout."

"Women," Sonia mutters, smoke coming out of her ears.

Daniela gasps. "Women? You're trafficking women?"

46

ANTONIO

Daniela glares at me with a disdain that I hoped to never see from her. It's worse than anything she's ever thrown my way, and it cuts me to the quick.

"Of course not," Sonia spits out.

But Daniela doesn't seem convinced, and the disgust and horror on her face hasn't faded anywhere near enough for me. It's in this weak moment that I decide she needs to know everything. It's a mistake to read her in. I'm sure of it, *but I don't care.* So when the voice inside my head shrieks, *What the fuck is wrong with you?,* I tell it to go to hell, and I jump headfirst into disaster.

"In a way, we are," I clarify. "Trafficking women from dangerous people and dangerous places to where they can be safe."

She chews on her bottom lip. "I don't understand."

I glance at Sonia. "Why don't you explain?"

"This is the end, isn't it?" she asks me, tears in her eyes.

"If it is, it's your doing." I have no real sympathy for her. If she were almost anyone else, I'd have hunted her down this morning and killed her with my bare hands.

She buries her face in her hands for a long moment before she speaks. "We run a small shipping business together. Through the business, we send women who are victims of domestic violence or other atrocities to safe harbors, away from their abusers, and provide them with resources to create a new life elsewhere."

Sonia has Daniela's rapt attention, but more importantly, the contempt is gone from her face.

"We occasionally intercept a boat where women are being trafficked through the city, but that's not our main focus."

Daniela turns to me. "How long have you been doing this?"

"More than a decade." My tone is matter-of-fact, but in truth, the work makes me proud. We've saved more lives than I've taken—many more.

"Eleven years," Sonia says under her breath.

"Tell her how we met."

"Antonio. Please."

"Tell. Her."

"My friend, Petra, disappeared while we were studying at the university. Just disappeared." The sorrow on Sonia's face is palpable, even after all these years.

But after what she put Daniela through today, she has it coming.

"She was my best friend. She'd been receiving hateful messages and threats from her family when they learned she was a lesbian. I went to Lydia, Antonio's mother, who had cobbled together an extensive network to help locate missing women. That's when I met Antonio."

"For the most part, my mother's activities were local," I add. "Until she met Sonia." Although, to be fair, my mother was on a hiatus, but before that, she had been involved in the underground network for years, and was jonesing to jump back in. "I got involved because I didn't want her involved with anything that had anything remotely to do with trafficking."

"Have you ever found Petra?" Daniela asks, softly.

"No."

I have never outed Sonia to anyone, including my mother, who was always playing matchmaker. But the idea of Sonia and I getting together ends today—at least for Daniela.

"Petra and Sonia were more than friends—they were lovers. We live in a shitty world filled with shitty people. Sonia works for the president, and it's easier for her if people believe she's straight."

It's quiet for a few moments while the two women digest it all. Daniela, who I essentially abducted after entering into a betrothal contract with her father, is wondering how I can be involved in helping women escape misery. And Sonia, I'm sure, is trying to come to terms with what she sees as my betrayal. She proved herself to be a huge liability today. It can't happen again. She needs to know that I'll do anything to protect Daniela.

"What I still don't understand," Daniela says, swiveling to face Sonia, "is why you sent me the photographs. What were you trying to accomplish?"

Sonia looks horrified. "I swore to their authenticity, and I gave the photographer permission to put them up on the site. I hoped you'd hear about them, but I never sent photographs to you or to anyone."

I'm not so sure about that.

"Why did you do it?" Daniela probes. "Why did you allow those pictures to be splashed all over the internet?"

It's a good question.

"Because. Because you have the power to shut down our business. The work is important. Vitally important. It seems childish in the light of day, but I thought if I drove a wedge between you—embarrassed you—maybe you'd go back to the United States. There were no good options. I was desperate."

Daniela doesn't blink, but I'm struggling not to wrap my

hands around Sonia's throat and squeeze until she's blue and limp.

"Why would I want to shut your business down?"

"You wouldn't shut it down—not directly—Antonio would. He doesn't like Lydia anywhere near the business, and he doesn't want you near it. He believes it's too dangerous. Since you arrived, it feels like it's only a matter of time before he abandons it completely."

She's not wrong. It's crossed my mind. The truth is, I should have shut it down years ago, but I didn't because my mother would just go behind my back. I'd find out eventually, but maybe not before something tragic occurred.

"I have a brain," Daniela says firmly. "And my own opinions. I'm not some puppet who dances when the master pulls the strings. You should have come to me."

Hell no. I glower at Sonia so she doesn't ever think that's an option.

"What you're doing—both of you," Daniela murmurs, "is of the utmost importance."

Not more important than you, Princesa.

"You have no idea," Sonia whispers.

"I think I do. And I want to help."

We're done here. "No fucking way will I allow you anywhere near that business."

"We'll discuss this privately," she replies, her eyes sending me a pointed dagger before turning their attention to Sonia.

You won't get a different response from a private conversation, Princesa.

"I fully support the endeavor, and I'll do whatever I can to assist you. But if you ever, *ever*, try to make trouble in my marriage, or hurt my family in any way, you'll have to contend with me. And trust me when I tell you it'll make dealing with Antonio feel like a spa day."

I bite back a smile, as I'm filled with pride. My little vixen has sharp claws, and she's willing to use them to protect our marriage. But there's no fucking way she's going near anything that smells of trafficking. There is nothing more dangerous than men with a stake in the flesh trade.

Sonia blinks her eyes several times, still gawking at Daniela.

I'm sure she never expected this. Daniela's a formidable adversary. Anyone who underestimates her does so at their own peril. I've learned that lesson firsthand.

This tête-à-tête was useful, but it also raised more questions.

"You're absolutely certain you didn't send the photos? Because now's your time to come clean." I peer at Sonia, gauging her reaction. I'm hoping she walks back her denial. It would be easier if there was only one culprit to track down. Ordinarily, I wouldn't be too concerned about photos like these, sent anonymously. This kind of thing is usually meant just to stir trouble. If the photos had been sent to me, it would have been about extortion. That's another matter entirely. But right now, I need to take all threats seriously.

"I did not send them to anyone. Electronically, or otherwise. I was emailed a link, but I never made a copy of the photos."

She's telling the truth.

I'm done. "Get out," I tell her gruffly.

"Are we done?" Sonia asks.

She's not wondering about the meeting, but about something bigger. I'm not in the mood to make her feel better. As far as I'm concerned, she hasn't suffered anywhere near enough. "For today."

"What about tomorrow?"

"If you were anyone else, you wouldn't even live to see tomorrow, let alone continue as my business partner. Don't push your luck."

47

DANIELA

They run a business that takes vulnerable women to safety and helps them create a new life. I did not see that coming. Am I surprised? *Yes.* Should I be? *Probably not.*

Antonio's a bundle of contradictions. He lives by his own rules, soulless as some of them might be, and he has his own brand of honor.

After Sonia leaves, Antonio and I spend a few moments eyeing one another—each waiting for the other to make a move.

I'll go first. I begin with a humble pawn. It's an undervalued piece, somewhat dispensable, but capable of striking gold at times. "Is she still searching for Petra?"

He nods. "She chases every lead into every dark corner and dead end."

I sigh deeply.

"But that's no excuse for what she did."

"Desperate people do desperate things. You might not appreciate it because you're always the one in control of every situation. You can't begin to understand the tortured feelings that come with that kind of desperation."

"That's not true," he says soberly, gazing at me, although he seems faraway. "I know that desperation. It ran wild through me when I learned you were headed for the docks to board a cargo ship, and we had to stay one step ahead of you, even though we had started from behind and were flying blind."

As he speaks, the raw emotion snakes and curls, making the wounds seem all too fresh. I lower my eyes because it's too difficult to look at him still wounded, by what he viewed as my betrayal.

"The world is a dangerous place, especially for women and children." His tenor has shifted to something more familiar. It's a tone that belongs to someone in control, to someone who isn't prone to displays of rank emotion—unless it's rage.

I glance up at him. "I'd like to help in some way. I can gather supplies or whatever needs to be done to get the women safe passage."

"I'd like some peace, but neither of us is getting what we want. It's too dangerous, Daniela, I won't discuss it."

Yes, you will.

"I need to do something besides go through mail and write thank-you notes."

"You have Valentina."

"She does need me, but she's not an infant. There's a lot she does for herself. Sometimes I think I need her more than she needs me." It's embarrassing to admit, but true.

He doesn't respond right away, but the wheels are turning, as though he's weighing options. I sit quietly, giving him the time it requires, hoping the scales will tip my way.

"My father and Abel were involved," he says softly, "—in the sex trade. At least peripherally. Mostly, they closed their eyes to the atrocities, while accepting kickbacks from the devils who moved women through Porto." He pauses for a quiet breath. "I believe my Aunt Vera stumbled onto something and that's why she disappeared. And I'm beginning to feel your mother was murdered because she got too close, too."

The air leaves my lungs in a long *whoosh*. "My mother? How was she involved?"

"For years, the three amigas—Vera, my mother, and yours—ran a small underground operation. They smuggled women out of the country who were abused by their husbands, helped others acquire birth control, which was illegal in the country at the time, and I suspect more than one bastard was poisoned with a recipe they concocted."

I feel as though a steel beam has been lowered onto my chest, and it's making it difficult to breathe, let alone think.

My mother always deferred to my father in public, but she had strong opinions about—everything. She was involved with various charities that benefited the poor and helped distribute food to impoverished pockets of the valley. But smuggling women and illegal activities? *I don't know.*

I have no reason to doubt Antonio, but this is all news to me. I try to think back, but it was a long time ago, and I was young when she died. I can't make a single connection. "My father never mentioned anything about it. Did he know?"

He nods. "I don't think your parents had many secrets between them. But I'm not surprised they shielded you. We had a dictator running the country, with neighbors ratting out neighbors. They would have been jailed just for distributing birth control, let alone the rest."

"Did my father help them?"

"At times. Begrudgingly. He wanted them out of the business, but he also wanted them safe. From what I know, it was mostly the three women, although they had friends in lots of places. You can ask my mother about it. I'm sure she'll share more with you than she's shared with me."

I sit with the revelation, trying to make sense of it. But I keep coming to the same thing. My mother and her friends risked their lives doing angels' work, while I'm cloistered away responding to party invitations and approving menus. While she would have wanted me out of harm's way, it's not the life my mother would have envisioned for me.

"Do you really believe that's why they murdered my mother?"

"I'm not sure. It's very possible my father killed her because your parents took in my mother."

I've often thought I was spared that day not to punish my father, but to bring sweet Valentina into the world. But maybe God spared me for something even bigger. All I do these days is sit at home, waiting for Valentina to finish riding or her schoolwork, so I can enjoy her company. It's not good for either of us. She could use some friends her own age, and most importantly, she needs to be somewhere safe. *It's two weeks.*

I sit up tall in the chair, and pull my shoulders back. "Valentina can go to camp. Maybe. I want to see it and meet the director. I also want to check with Dr. Lima. But I'm not going anywhere. I'm your wife, and until you begin treating me like a partner, no one will see me as one."

He tilts his head. "You need to go too, *Princesa*. I don't want you to become the spoils of war. It might get ugly here."

I stand and go to him, placing a hand on each of his thighs. "I guess I didn't make myself clear. I'm not going. I know all about the spoils of war, and I want to be here at the end of each battle, to remind you of your humanity. You owe me that. You owe yourself that. And you owe it to us—to our family."

"Daniela."

"No, Antonio. You signed an agreement to marry me, but I've read the betrothal contract. Nowhere did it specify the terms of the marriage. What's not expressly stated is up for negotiation."

A moment passes where his tight jaw tics, but now, his eyes glitter with mischief. "Is that so, *Princesa*?"

"It is."

"If you're planning on remaining in Porto, I want you to get comfortable with a gun."

I don't think he's trying to frighten me. I think we're headed into uncertain times. I want to know more, but I don't waste my breath asking. "I can do that." If he senses the hesitation, he doesn't mention it.

He nods. "You'll work with Santi every day until he leaves with Valentina and Mia."

Santi? It doesn't make sense. He's Valentina's guard. "Why not Alvarez?"

"Santi's more patient, and that makes him a better instructor. Plus, it will allow you to get to know him so that you're more comfortable with him around Valentina. But listen carefully."

Bossy Antonio is back.

"The first time you do something, *anything*, to put yourself or anyone else in danger, I'm putting your gorgeous ass on the plane and sending you to London."

He's not expecting anything unreasonable. "I can live with those terms."

Antonio picks up his phone. "I don't want to be disturbed," he growls, before tossing the phone aside.

He rests his hands on my hips. I feel the energy radiating from him. "Now, about that apology you owe me."

I lift my brow. "Apology?"

"The one that comes after marching into my office and tossing around baseless accusations."

His eyes are glittering again, but the mischief is dark now. The throb between my legs begins in anticipation for what's to come.

"Perhaps you're right. Maybe I do owe you an apology." I turn, and go to lock the door with an exaggerated sway of my hips.

"You can lock it, but there's no need. Cecelia wouldn't barge in if flames were engulfing the place."

I flash him a smile over my shoulder. "You never know. My apology might be noisy."

He stalks me to the center of the room, tangling his fingers in my hair, before crashing his lips into mine. By the time he pulls his mouth away, I'm gasping for air.

"The sincerest apologies happen from the knees, *Princesa*. Don't make me wait."

48

DANIELA

Today is my fourth day working with Santi, who has an infinite amount of patience. Guns are heavy, even the small ones, and there's more to handling and pulling the trigger than the movies let on.

My hand-to-eye coordination leaves something to be desired, and it's a miracle I haven't shot Santi yet, or myself.

"Is your gun clean?" he asks, the bronze highlights in his chestnut hair glistening in the sun.

Santi makes me clean the weapon every day, so that I get comfortable handling it. I've been using a small .22 that looks almost like a toy, but today, he's given me a larger pistol to contend with. "Squeaky."

"All right, let's try a little target practice."

Ugh. I'm determined to learn to do this, but each day I become more discouraged. "Will it be easier with the bigger gun?"

He shrugs. "You never know. But it's important to become accustomed to handling different weapons." Santi is tall, with lean muscle and an easy way about him. He looks to be in his early twenties, and when I first met him, I was taken aback by how young he was for a guard. *For Valentina's guard.* But after a few days with him, my initial reservations are gone.

"I thought that everyone had a favorite gun they carried."

He nods. "Most people who regularly carry a weapon have one they prefer. It often becomes their binky. But that's a mistake."

"Why?"

"Why? What happens when all hell breaks loose, and the only weapon you can get your hands on is someone else's binky?" He's animated, waving his hands around. "You can't just say, wait a minute. I need to go home and get my favorite gun. Ain't *nobody* letting you do that."

I chuckle. This is exactly why Valentina adores Santi.

"Enough fun and games." He hands me a pair of muffs to block out the worst of the noise. I hated them the first time I put them on, but now they don't bother me as much.

"See that target?" he asks, pointing to one of the straw men he's set up in the not-too-far distance. "I want you to aim and hit him. Remember everything we've worked on."

I eye the straw dummy, dressed in worn clothes with a bandanna covering his face. *Hit him, he says, like it's so easy.* "Where should I hit him?"

"Wherever you can, *senhora*. It's best to kill him, but even a flesh wound will slow him down momentarily."

I put on the muffs and practice for about twenty minutes, with Santi making small corrections. This gun has a heavier recoil, but the longer barrel helps with accuracy. Although, much to my annoyance, the target is still pristine.

"Do you think it might be better if I was aiming at a bull's-eye? Isn't that what some people use for target practice?"

"They can be useful, especially for more advanced training. But I've never seen an attacker wearing a bull's-eye you can aim at. You need to find your own bull's-eye. That's the way I was trained, and it's the way I teach. I think it's the best way to learn."

"I'm never going to be able to protect myself, or anyone, with a gun, am I?"

"Things will have to go very bad for you to need to draw a gun," he says casually. "It's merely a precaution. You'll get the hang of it. No one learns to shoot after a few lessons. It's not natural for most people. That's why I make you clean the gun every day and stock ammunition, so you get used to it."

I realize this is a new skill, but for some reason, I feel the urgency to be proficient.

"Let's take a break," he says, taking the pistol from me. "Sometimes it helps to step back and reset. A lot of it's up here," Santi explains, pointing an index finger to his head.

There's no question I've been psyching myself out. I know if I stick with it, I'll improve. The first time I got on a horse—that's a bad example. Riding has always come naturally to me.

"I'm going to have a coffee," he says, "but you're better off with water. Caffeine can make your hand shaky. You don't need that."

It's the last thing I need. Although I don't see how my aim could get any worse. I sit on the bench and take a long swig from my water bottle. I know what Antonio said, but I'm still surprised he's having me work with Santi rather than Alvarez. "How long have you worked for Antonio?"

"Almost thirteen years."

Thirteen years? "How old are you?"

"Twenty-three, next month."

"You started working for him when you were ten?"

He laughs. "You sound like you're going to have him arrested for violating child labor laws."

"I'm thinking about it."

He sits and puts his foot up on the large slab of stone we use as a bench, and takes a drink of coffee. "He caught me stealing food out of the trash one day, after the vineyard workers had lunch. Pulled me aside, and while he was interrogating me, he noticed a bruise on my arm. He didn't believe the story I peddled, and he told me to take off my shirt. I thought he was going to beat me, so I ran."

Please don't say he did. I take a breath and hold it while I wait for Santi to continue.

"He chased me and held me by the scruff of the neck until I showed him my scarred back."

"Someone beat you." It's not a question, but he responds anyway.

He nods. "After my parents died, my brother Nino and I went to live with my mother's sister. They lived up north. All the way up, right behind the Huntsmans' *Quinta do Minho*. Her husband arranged the sale of our house and took control of the proceeds. Nino was four. Most days we weren't given much to eat, and he would cry himself to sleep because he was hungry. I'd steal scraps of food for him when I could, but my uncle was a miserable man, and after he caught me the first time, he kept a tight rein on the food. Anytime he even suspected something was missing, I'd get a beating."

"Oh, Santi. I'm so sorry."

He slides a boot over the dirt. "It was a long time ago, and it ended better for us than it does for most boys in that situation. After Antonio saw what was under my shirt, he made me tell him everything."

Of course he did.

"Before we were through that day, he gave me a job cleaning up the picnic area after lunch. He didn't make me feel ashamed, and he always treated me with respect. Like a man." Santi glances at me. "Paid me more than a fair wage for what I did, and Elio, the cook, fed me and sent me home with food every day. I'd sneak it into the barn before my uncle got home from work, and my little brother and I would eat good. At the end of the harvest, my aunt and uncle moved away, and Nino and I went to live with Elio and his family. No one ever beat me again." He puts his foot down, and strides over to the thermos with a proud gait. "I would do anything for *Senhor* Antonio," he says, pouring himself more coffee.

Santi and his brother, and then Rafael. Maybe there are others. *Antonio Huntsman, protector of the lost boys.*

"I owe him my life, and my brother's. I doubt we'd still be alive if it weren't for him. I know my uncle wouldn't be."

Somehow I don't think your uncle's still roaming the earth.

"Antonio trusts you, Santi. That's why he assigned you to be Valentina's guard, and my shooting instructor."

"Do you trust me?" He studies me, carefully. It's an honest question and it deserves an honest answer.

"I was hesitant about you at first. You're a bit younger than the guards I'm used to." I foolishly equated youth with inexperience. "But being around you for the last few days has changed my mind."

"I'll protect Valentina with my life, *senhora*. No one will harm a hair on her head as long as I'm breathing."

It's a heartfelt response, and I have no doubt she'll be safe with him. "I have complete faith in you."

"Time to get back to work," he says, before I get too sappy for a tough guy like Santi.

I pick up the muffs and the gun, and trek over to the chalk mark on the ground. "Is this where Antonio's guards train?"

Santi smirks. "No, *senhora*. This is where wives train. Remember to keep your knee pointed in the direction of the target, weight slightly forward. A little more," he says, easing my lower back forward.

Boom! Even with the muffs on, I know the sound came from behind us.

Before I can react, Santi takes the gun out of my hands and steps in front of me.

49

DANIELA

*A**ntonio.*
Santi lowers the pistol immediately, and steps back. My heart is racing.

Antonio tucks the gun into his waistband and takes long strides toward us. There must be a hundred yards of ground to cover, so it takes a bit of time for him to reach us.

"What's going on?" I mutter. But Santi doesn't say a word as Antonio approaches.

"Since when did teaching my wife to handle a gun involve your hands on her body?" he snarls.

You have got to be kidding me.

Santi pales. "Boss, I apologize. I didn't mean anything. I was just trying to help *Senhora* Daniela find her stance. I would never disrespect you. Either of you."

"Antonio," I plead, hoping he'll stop. I don't think he'd actually hurt Santi, but he is not happy with him.

"Leave us," he tells Santi, who hands me back the pistol, then wastes no time getting the hell away from the crazy man.

"What if he'd turned around and shot you?" I ask, after Santi is out of hearing range.

"Santi's experienced enough to know that it was a warning shot fired in the air."

"Was that really necessary? He wasn't doing anything untoward—and neither was I."

Antonio peers into my eyes. "I know. But his hand was too close to your ass. I want to make sure he knows not to even think about it while he's teaching you to shoot."

This possessive Antonio. I've seen glimpses before, but never like this. "You fired a warning shot? You're out of control."

He shrugs. "Only where you're concerned, *Princesa*."

I ignore the buttery tone. "Did you come here to spy on us?"

"I don't need to make a trip out here for that. There's surveillance all over the grounds. I came to tell you I'll be in London tomorrow. Just for the day." He pauses for a beat. "I'm going to tell my mother and Rafael about Valentina. We're on borrowed time, Daniela."

My heart plops into my stomach, but I don't argue, because he's right. Rafael lives here, and he could show up at any time without calling. "I want to be there when you tell them."

"No."

Here we go. "Why not? I can help them understand better than you can."

"It's going to be hard enough on them. Before they have to face you, I want them to have some time to come to grips with what my family did to you and your mother."

"They're not responsible for what happened. Your mother and Rafael were their victims too. Besides, this is no longer *your* family and *my* family. It's *our* family. One family. We need to do this together. I'm going with you."

"Can't you ever just do as I ask? Why does everything have to involve a protracted discussion?"

"I could ask you the same question."

He glowers at me. "Have you learned to shoot that thing?"

Nice pivot. But I won't forget about London.

"Why don't you go stand over there?" I point to the target. "And we'll see."

50

DANIELA

Antonio and I are having coffee in the living room at his mother's apartment. Rafael's with us too.

As much as Lydia loves that we're here, she keeps eyeing her son, who's wearing the burden of delivering the crushing news like a heavy weight. I suspect the only reason she hasn't called him on it is because Rafael and I are here.

It took some prodding, but in the end, Antonio decided it made sense to tell his mother and Rafael together. He also decided that it might be helpful for me to be there.

I'm a bit edgy too. Antonio arranged for a meeting at St. Philomena's, and we're having dinner with Will and Samantha before we leave. It's the first time I've left Valentina for a full day and most of the evening. She's at home, in Mia and Santi's care, and under Victor's watchful eye, but it's still hard. I can't imagine what it's going to be like for me when she goes to camp.

"I'm tired of watching you fiddle with your shoelaces," Lydia says, focusing a sharp gaze on Antonio. "What brings you here?"

My chest tightens, as the weight of the moment comes to

bear. I prepared myself to tell the story again, but no amount of preparation will ever make it easy.

All eyes are on Antonio, and for a long, torturous moment, he says nothing. But there's sorrow in his expression. His mother and mine were best friends—like sisters. They became even closer after Vera disappeared. The news of what her husband did is going to shake her to the core. Antonio knows it.

"Hugo murdered Maria Rosa, Daniela's mother."

Lydia drops her cup, and coffee splashes all over her and the rug. She doesn't move. Not even when I grab a cloth napkin and blot the liquid off her slacks.

I know he didn't want to see her like this. *Why did he have to be so blunt?*

Because he's Antonio. He didn't even try to soften the blow or work his way to the hot center from the edges. He dove right into the storm, headfirst—it's what he knows.

"Did it burn your leg?" I ask, trying to distance myself from the story he's about to tell.

Lydia's head moves from right to left, almost of its own volition. I'm not sure she even knows if she's burned herself. She's that shaken.

Rafael is quiet, his eyes trained on his feet. And Antonio is stoic, all emotion tucked away, because he knows the worst is yet to come.

"Are you sure?" Lydia whispers, grasping my hand.

Antonio nods. "Daniela was there."

She looks up at me, with so much despair in her expression that it almost levels me. I would give anything to make it go away—for her—for all of us.

"Because they protected me," she murmurs.

"We don't know that," I say, before Antonio can reply, because the urge to comfort her is overwhelming. "My mother might have stumbled onto something that put her in peril."

She nods, but I'm not sure she believes me.

"There's more," Antonio says, his voice low and tight.

I want to scream, *No more! No more! She can't take anymore right now.* But now that he's started, he won't stop. He wants it done. And despite Lydia's pallor, part of me wants it over, too. Revisiting this at another time isn't going to make it any easier.

Lydia draws a ragged breath.

I pull up a chair beside her and take her hand.

"Hugo didn't go alone," Antonio continues, like a robot, but his clenched fists betray him. "Abel and Tomas were with him."

Rafael lists forward, elbows on his knees, and buries his face in his hands.

I hear the words too, but they don't touch me. I'm grateful that Antonio insisted that he should be the one to tell them. I don't think I could have done it. There's so much turmoil in the room it's staggering. At this point, I'm nothing more than a bystander looking in at the events as they unfold.

"Tomas raped Daniela, and she became pregnant as a result. Her daughter's name is Valentina."

Rafael storms out of the room like it's engulfed in flames.

I glance at Antonio, who is motionless, a stone statue. I want nothing more than to wrap my arms around him and hold tight until he recovers from the pain he unleashed on his mother and Rafael. But it'll have to wait. "Go to Rafael. I'll stay here."

He blinks a few times and nods, leaving without a cursory glance at his mother or me.

I get on my knees near Lydia. For the first time, I let go of the propriety of my pain. It belongs to me, but there are others who feel it acutely—maybe no one more than Lydia. I don't have to apologize, but I can share the pain.

"I'm so sorry, my love," she says between sobs. "So very sorry."

"Don't apologize for them," I murmur, through my own

tears. "As awful as it was, as bleak as I felt in the following weeks, Valentina gave me a reason to live."

"You were twelve. A little girl. Monsters—even beyond what I imagined."

I don't say anything, because there's nothing to say. It's true.

51

ANTONIO

As I go out to the porch where Rafael is trying to cope, I'm grateful I brought Daniela. My mother and Rafa need light and goodness after what I just dropped on them. They need empathy. Compassion. But a vicious rage is pumping through my veins right now, and all I can offer at this moment is darkness.

My father is dead, and Abel is reduced to little more than a shell, but Tomas? Before I'm finished with him, Tomas is going to beg for death.

Rafael's at the window, looking over the city, shoulders hunched, dissecting his life, looking for damning clues, and wondering if he's a monster too. I ask myself that same question nearly every day. But I won't let him go down that path. I won't let it eat away at him.

"You are not them. Just like I'm not them. We carry the same name, the same genes, but not the same heart. Don't ever forget it."

"How long have you known?" he asks, still staring out the window. His voice is hollow, but I hear the pain—the self-loathing.

"I learned about it the morning after the wedding."

He nods. "What are we going to do about it?"

"We're not going to do anything. This is mine to handle."

He swivels to face me, anger sparking in his eyes. "No way. Don't you dare leave me out of this. I'm a man. And what *my* father, and *my* brother, and *my* uncle did was reprehensible."

He might be a man, but some part of him will always be a boy to me. "Yes, you are a man. And yes, what they did was beyond reprehensible. But the kind of vengeance you want stains souls. I won't allow it to stain yours." *I won't.* He had a rough beginning, but I'll be damned before he's burdened with that kind of guilt.

"And what am I supposed to do now? Sit on my hands and let God sort it out?"

There will be a reckoning long before it gets to God. "I have a job for you."

He lengthens his spine and peers directly into my eyes. "Anything. What do you need?"

"Things are about to become unpredictable in Porto. I'm concerned that my mother will be at some risk, even here. Will and Samantha have agreed to take her in. She'll be safe there. But she won't stay without some incentive. You're that incentive. I need you there too."

"Antonio. No." He shakes his head vigorously. "I'm not hiding. I'm done hiding from them."

"I'm not asking you to hide. I'm giving you an important job. The responsibility for my mother's safety. No one is going to be able to get her to stay there—I need to give her a reason to stay. You are that reason."

He clasps his hands at the base of his neck and tips his head back. I've put him in a difficult position. As much as he seeks bloodshed, he knows my mother's safety is not something I take lightly. Neither does he.

"I trust you more than anyone to get in touch with me if it

seems like she's even beginning to think about leaving. I have a lot on my plate, and this is something you can take off it. I can't lose her to this, Rafael."

He nods and meets my gaze. "You won't."

I plan on telling my mother something similar. It's manipulative, but I won't lose either of them to this.

"Am I still welcome at the house?"

"What house?"

"Your house in the valley. She's your wife, and my brother—she was a little girl—I remember her. How could Tomas have possibly done something so vile?"

It's worse than you know. "It was on my father's order. I don't think there's any doubt about it." I pause for a moment. What I say next will leave a lasting impression, and I don't want to make a mistake. "The house in the valley is your home. Does Daniela seem like the type of woman who would forbid you from going home?"

"She'd have every right to."

She would.

"She's not like that. And even if she was, I'd never allow it."

He nods, as the words sink in.

"When should I plan on taking your mother to Samantha and Will's?"

"I'll let you know."

52

DANIELA

"Can I get you anything?" the flight attendant asks once Antonio and I are seated on the plane, returning to Porto.

He glances at me from the other end of the sofa, and I shake my head. "Just some privacy," he says, crisply, shooing her away.

"What a day." I slip off my shoes and sprawl out. "But it's over."

"Not quite." Antonio slides closer to me and stretches out his long legs on the coffee table. "You still need to talk to Valentina."

I can't think about it, and I certainly don't have the energy to argue with him. "Do we really need to discuss this right now?"

"No." He reaches for my bare foot, massaging the arch expertly. "We could go back to the bedroom, and I could lick your pussy until you beg me to stop."

"You have a filthy mouth."

"You like it."

"I do. I've come around to all your dirty ways." I inch my foot closer to his cock, but he holds my ankle steady so that I land short of my destination.

His jaw is tight and the cords in his neck rigid.

"I should have been the man who helped you ease into sex, after those bastards terrorized you. If I hadn't sent you away after your father died, I would have been that man."

This isn't about Josh—that's behind us. This is about Antonio's guilt over letting me leave Porto and go to a life that was more difficult than it needed to be. When I first arrived, he taunted me about cleaning toilets and frugal shopping. But in truth, that life helped make me a woman who believes she can do anything—including stand up to him when necessary.

"First of all, you didn't send me away. You just didn't stop me from leaving."

He shrugs. "Semantics."

"I wasn't ready for you," I murmur. "You sensed it. You just didn't know why."

I pause, deciding whether to open up to him, or if sharing details about my experiences with Josh is worth infuriating him. He needs to hear it, but I need to orchestrate carefully, or I'll make things worse.

"Before I could experience you," I divulge cautiously, "without being scared to death, I needed someone who would let me have control so that I could feel safe. More than anything, I needed to feel safe. I needed to experience intimacy with a partner that didn't leave me recoiling in fear."

His fingers dig into my foot in a way that's no longer pleasant, and I pull away. His head snaps toward me. "You're hurting me," I say softly.

Antonio swallows and takes hold of my foot again, resting it on his lap, but he doesn't continue the massage.

"Is that what you feel inside, when we're having sex?" He's raw and exposed. "Does some part of you recoil in fear?"

He's as vulnerable as I've ever seen him. *He wants to know if he's a monster.* That's what he's really asking. Even my fingernails ache for him.

No. You're not a monster. It would be so easy to say. But he'd never believe it.

"I don't know what it's like for other survivors," I explain, "but there were two parts I had to conquer when it came to sex. The first was being able to have physical intimacy without fear."

Josh was gentle, and even though he didn't know my history, he let me set the pace—always. I don't share this with Antonio. It would haunt him. It's not something he could ever do—or even what I want from him.

"The second hurdle was exploring and accepting what I enjoy without guilt or shame. You helped me learn what I like. What I need. You push me to expand my boundaries, and you don't judge any of it."

"You haven't answered my question," he says, quietly, the lines on his brow carved deep. "Do you recoil in fear?"

Recoil isn't the right word. "Am I sometimes afraid?" I nod. "Yes."

I feel him stiffen and begin to pull away, not physically, but emotionally.

"Let me finish before you retreat."

He doesn't so much as glance at me.

"Sex with you is like being on the ocean in a raging storm. I'm pulled under by giant waves, over and over, and I'm not sure I'll survive. But each time, just when it seems like I'll be fully consumed by the dark sea, the tide ebbs and I surface, gasping for breath. When it's over, after the tempest's final roar, my body drifts onto shore, beaten and battered. Spent. But with a sense of peace that only comes after a spirited storm." I reach for his hand and squeeze. "I don't recoil. I welcome it."

His thumb makes careful circles on my palm. "You awaken something primal inside me. You have since that day in your father's office. Even when the storm isn't rampant, its intensity never wanes. I would be lying if I told you it will ever be anything else."

"I would be lying if I told you I wanted anything else."

After a few minutes of a comfortable silence, I swing my legs off the sofa and onto the floor.

He reaches out and hooks his arm around my leg. "Where do you think you're going?"

I smile sweetly, leaning over, until my mouth is near his ear. "To the bedroom, where you're going to lick my pussy until I beg you to stop."

53

DANIELA

Antonio doesn't follow me right away. He makes me wait, wondering if my cheeky attempt at seduction fell flat. Demanding him to pleasure me like that is a new frontier for us. Maybe it was too much too soon for a man who likes to be the one who makes the demands.

By the time the door opens, I'm not sure he's coming.

As soon as he enters, I know the waiting was his twisted brand of foreplay. His eyes are gleaming, and his cock is already hard.

I'm naked, and his eyes roam freely over my body.

Neither of us speaks, but I feel the energy spiraling between us, and my arousal grows.

He lowers himself to the edge of the bed, and with two fingers, he beckons me over. My body sings as he pulls me between his legs.

"You're wet for me," he purrs, in that seductive tenor. "I don't even need to check, *Princesa*. I smell your sweet musky scent from here."

I stand perfectly still, while my cheeks burn, not with shame, but with passion for the dirty game he's playing.

Antonio unbuckles his belt and makes haste of the zipper, before sliding his trousers over his hips and kicking them aside. His eyes don't leave mine. "Do you want my cock, *Princesa*? Does your tight little pussy ache for it?"

The long, thick shaft juts straight out, below the trail of dark hair that begins on his rippled abdomen. It twitches under my gaze, and my mouth waters as it leaks a milky bead.

He pulls me onto his lap, and I straddle him, supported by his thighs. There are no words, just the promise of what's to come.

He reaches for the nape of my neck and drags me closer, my nipples hardening against his solid chest as he takes my mouth roughly. I surrender fully, my eager pussy grinding against his cock.

After he's had his fill, Antonio slides his fingers into my hair and tugs my head back, exposing my throat. I cling to his shoulders while his mouth assaults the tender skin.

The relentless throb between my legs. The sting of my scalp. His teeth and lips owning me with every delicious nip. The sensation is too much, but I don't want him to stop.

When we're at the edge of control, he lifts my hips and impales me on his thick cock.

My cry is lost in his neck.

He moves me roughly, because even though I'm on top, Antonio's in control. *Always.*

"The price for being at my side is high, *Princesa*. I'll take everything you have and more. I'll leave you trembling as I steal your soul."

"Take it. Take it all," I murmur into his damp skin. "It's yours."

Without stopping the punishing thrusts, he slides a hand between us, fingering my clit until my body tightens and mind is blank. "I can't," he mutters. "Too close." His ragged breaths are quick and shallow. "Let go. Now," my dark prince demands.

We find our pleasure together. The orgasms tear through us as we cling to each other.

It's only when I collapse against him, counting his heartbeats, that I'm filled with an unexplained sense of dread. *Tomorrow is promised to no one,* a small voice inside me whispers.

I wrap myself tighter around him and savor everything about the moment. Because I know it's true. *Tomorrow is promised to no one.*

54

ANTONIO

I'm in the car on my way back from a meeting when the phone rings.

A blocked number.

I hesitate for a few seconds, before answering, but it could be one of Will's men. "Yes?"

"The boy wonder," a curt voice replies from the other end of the line. "Dimitri Fedorov here."

The *Pakhan* placing his own calls. *Interesting.* We've spoken on occasion, but it's rare. The extent of my communication with the Bratva leader normally involves a nod from across a crowded room at a social function.

"I'm hardly a boy."

"Hardly. And I see you've amassed the confidence of a man. If I had called you the boy wonder ten years ago, you would have told me that you're no man's second-in-command."

"What do you want?"

"*Ah*, still impatient, Huntsman," he clucks. "There's a storm brewing. I'm getting whiffs of it all the way up here. My house is so secluded, I normally don't hear a damn thing when I'm home. It's disturbing my orange trees. They prefer warm, predictable weather."

"I'm short on time, Dimitri, and I hate riddles. What can I do for you?"

"Pity about the riddles. I'm a fan myself. But I think we have something we can do for each other."

"And what would that be?"

"If you want the details, I'll be at the Majestic Café at 11:30, enjoying a custard tart. Come alone."

Alone? So one of your goons can shoot me in the back? It's so preposterous I almost laugh. "And you'll be alone?"

"Don't be ridiculous," he says, before ending the call.

What exactly does he want? And maybe more importantly, what does he know?

I haven't shared the details of how Tomas will be delivered with either Lucas or Cristiano. Not because I don't trust them. There's no way either of them is leaking information to my enemies. But I don't have many details about the transfer, and I assured Will I'd keep his name out of it. Although they know the day is coming.

We're operating with a lot of unknowns right now. Including who will run Premier after Tomas is dead. Fedorov senses something in the wind. Maybe he wants Premier? *Not a fucking chance.*

I punch a number into my phone. "Are you both in the villa?" I ask when Cristiano answers.

"Yeah. Everything okay?"

"Put me on speaker."

"Done."

"I just received a call from Dimitri Fedorov."

"What did he want?" Lucas asks, with all the suspicion I would expect under the circumstances.

"A favor for a favor. He wants me to meet him at the Majestic tonight after closing. Alone."

"Alone? Fuck that," Lucas mutters.

"He picked the Majestic because he knows you'd never do anything to destroy it," Cristiano says carefully.

The Majestic Café, with its baroque architecture, is frequented by tourists as well as locals. But when it first opened, it was a meeting place for the city's elite—writers, politicians, artists, and others gathered to cement Porto's future. It's an irreplaceable landmark, much like Santa Ana's church.

"But he wouldn't hesitate," Cristiano adds. "That gives him a huge advantage."

"I agree."

"What's your plan?"

"I'm going. I don't hide."

"Alone?" Lucas asks, like I'm insane.

"Not a chance."

55

ANTONIO

I stare out the tinted SUV window, wondering what Fedorov has in store for me. But even my mortality isn't enough to keep my mind off Daniela. She was going to talk to Valentina about camp this morning and then call me. I haven't heard a peep from her. Not sure what it means. *Only one way to find out.*

"*Bom dia*," I say when she answers. "What's all that racket?"

"I'm in the kitchen." She sounds frazzled.

"Slaughtering chickens?"

"Very funny. Making *arroz doce*. But Victor's going to be back soon, and I need to be out so he can prepare a midday meal for the workers."

"You're making *arroz doce*?"

"Yes. It was Isabel's favorite dessert and it's her birthday tomorrow. I thought we would have it for her *alma*."

Unlike me, Isabel doesn't need offerings for her soul. But this sort of thing, steeped in tradition, is something Daniela would never ignore. "Have you talked to Valentina about camp?"

"Yes. She's excited. Maybe a little nervous too, but mostly

excited. Everyone's doing their best to keep her busy, but I think it's been hard for her without friends. I'm going to miss her."

"Don't sound so wistful. It's two weeks." Although it could be more, but there's no reason to share this yet.

"It's not just about that. When I asked her to help me make the *arroz doce*, she balked. And then she said she's behind in her reading, and she's not sure she'll be able to make tomorrow night's dinner."

I can feel Daniela's anxiety from here.

"What did you say?"

"Nothing," she admits, with some sadness. "Dr. Lima told me I have to give Valentina opportunities to remember Isabel, and that I should talk about her often, but she cautioned me to let her deal with Isabel's death on her own terms."

I don't like the unhappiness in her voice, or the worry. *Not one bit.* "You're the adult. You're permitted to set rules, even for a child in mourning. Coming down for dinner isn't an unreasonable expectation, especially when it's an occasion. The more you let her get away with, the less safe she's going to feel."

"She wasn't disrespectful, but she clearly isn't ready to deal with it. Dr. Lima said it was normal."

Childhood is filled with normal reactions to life, and children should be permitted to have those reactions, but that doesn't mean that adults need to bless every fart. Kids can't be allowed to do whatever they want, whenever they want, without consequence. Dr. Lima once said that too.

———

WHEN I GET off with Daniela, I call Valentina. I don't have the same reservations about setting expectations.

"It's Antonio."

"Yes, I know. How are you?"

"I'm very well. How are you?"

"Very well too. Thank you."

I smile. Despite her respectful response, her tone is forced, and she's close to asking why I'm calling, but she's too polite—or maybe too afraid. "How's Demeter?"

"She's wonderful. Silvio says that we're bonding. He's going to take care of Demeter while I'm at camp. He promised she won't forget me."

"She won't. Do you have any questions about the camp at St. Philomena's?"

"No. Not really. I had a lot when I first heard about it, but Daniela answered everything and she showed me some pictures."

She sounds excited about camp, which doesn't really surprise me. Kids her age want to be around other kids. A mother's love isn't enough to sustain a budding teenager.

"She said your niece, Alexis, goes to school there, and that I'll meet her before camp starts."

"You will. If you think of anything else you want to know, we can talk about it at dinner tomorrow."

"Dinner? Are you coming to the valley?"

"Of course. It would have been Isabel's birthday. Daniela is making *arroz doce,* and we'll eat it together, for her *alma.*" There's not a sound coming from the other end of the line. I'm not even sure she's breathing. "It's important to Daniela that we remember her friend. She does so much for us and asks so little. Of course, I'll be there for Daniela, just like you'll be there."

I don't threaten or warn. I simply lay out the expectation and assume she'll rise to the occasion. I've done it dozens of times with Rafael. Sometimes it works, and sometimes it bites me in the ass.

Dr. Lima is an expert. But psychology is not an exact

science. Sometimes adults need to set expectations. In the end, I don't know whether Valentina will come to dinner, but I've reframed the issue and given her something to chew on.

I suspect she'll come around. Although I'll apply more pressure, if necessary.

56

ANTONIO

We arrive at the Majestic Café neighborhood shortly before eleven. Cristiano and Santi are with me, and Thiago is driving. We park several blocks away while Lucas feeds us the lay of the land, in real time, as he watches it unfold on the monitors in the villa.

Fedorov sent a couple of men to sweep the place after it closed, and he showed up with a handful of guards at 11:30. Two are inside with him, and the others are spanned across the outside perimeter of the cafe.

My men are currently circling his, and I'm flanked by Cristiano and Santi when I enter the building. Alvarez stayed at the house in case this is a diversion—although I don't think so. He apparently wasn't happy about being left behind, but that's too damn bad. I take no chances when it comes to Daniela—or Valentina.

"Dimitri," I say, sliding into the seat across from him.

The edge of his mouth curls when he glances at Cristiano and Santi. He didn't expect me to come alone, but I'm sure he's somewhat amused that I matched him man for man.

After I'm seated, he nudges the plate of pastries toward me. "The pastry chef here never disappoints."

"I'm all set."

"They're quite delicious." He's nearly seventy, with weathered skin, and what's left of his hair is snow white. But despite the outward signs of aging, and all the talk of pastries, he's not a doddering fool and I'd be a moron to think it.

"Why are we here?"

He wipes a crumb from the corner of his mouth. "I have a shipment arriving in ten days. I don't give a fuck what you're up to, but that shipment will move through this city without a hiccup."

Only if I allow it, you bastard. "Women?"

"Not my game, Huntsman. You should know that by now."

"What's coming through my city?"

"Arms. Same as always. Not that it's any of your business. I leave the drugs to the cartels, and the flesh trade to those without daughters and granddaughters."

I couldn't care less about guns and ammunition passing through the city. I have more pressing concerns. "Does Tomas help you distribute those arms, or just move them?"

He narrows his eyes. "Your cousin?"

I nod.

"Don't confuse me with an idiot. I don't do business with him."

"That's not what I heard."

"Don't believe every little thing you hear." He takes a drink of coffee. "Tomas contacted me shortly after you paid his father a visit at the hospital."

I have eyes everywhere, but so does Fedorov.

"I listened, because I always listen, but he has nothing I want."

That, I don't believe. "He can give you the kind of access that an outsider will never have."

"Why would I want that?"

"It would give you a foothold in the region. Legitimacy. This is a good spot on the Atlantic, where you can ship your toys in and out without hassle, and play a little game of chicken with the Americans. Isn't that what the big boys in Moscow want?"

He peers at me from across the table, his jaw clenched. But he doesn't respond.

"Isn't that why you planted a bomb at Santa Ana's to stop my wedding?"

"For someone who claims not to be a boy, you have a wild imagination. Do you have a pen?"

"I'm not a secretary."

"Bring me a pen," he calls to one of his men. Fedorov opens a napkin, then balls it up and tosses it aside. "Paper too."

The guard brings a pen and a small pad of paper from near the cash register. Dimitri pulls back some pages and begins to write.

"What are you doing?"

"Giving you a civics lesson that outsiders normally don't get. I suggest you pay attention."

He draws two *X*s in the center of the page. "These represent the two oligarchs in Porto. Nikitin and Chernov. They want a foothold, and they take their cues from Moscow. They're like siblings fighting for Papa's attention." Above the *X*s, he puts a triangle representing Moscow.

At the very top, he draws a sun with rays emitting from the center. "This is the Bratva—they take their orders from me." He places a dot in the center of the sun as he says the word *me*. "I take my orders from no one."

"Why are you telling me all this?"

"Because Nikitin and Chernov are not just thorns in your side, but in mine too. While I don't take direction from Moscow, I'm not foolish enough to spit in the president's face."

"So you want me to do your dirty work for you?"

"I want to arm you with information so that when you do your dirty work, you clean up *all* the trash."

I want all the information he's willing to give, but I'm not foolish enough to take him at his word. This could be a trap. "I'm supposed to just believe everything you say?"

"I've watched your ascension to power. You're smart, albeit somewhat arrogant for a man who is still so young. Believe what you want. But if you choose to ignore my lesson, you do so at your own peril."

He drops the pad of paper in front of me.

"I'm not interested in footholds, and certainly not in grapes. Port is a lucrative business, but not anywhere near as lucrative as arms. You have fire in your belly about it because these are your people, and this is your calling. I have no sons or grandsons to step into my shoes when I die. While it's a shame, it also brings clarity of purpose.

"At this stage, all I want in life is for my shipments to come and go, so the money continues to flow into my pockets, allowing me to live out the rest of my days on the hillside, tending my citrus groves with my beautiful Raisa at my side."

"While wielding the kind of power that makes your enemies quake."

He shrugs. "A man has to have something to keep himself busy. Caring for orange trees doesn't take up a lot of time." He holds my gaze. "My shipment will come and go without a blip. That's all I want from you. Don't fuck it up."

"What do I get in return?"

"You get your mole. I'll send him to you on a silver platter."

"What mole?"

"Don't insult me. Porto might be your city, but nothing happens here that I don't know about."

In large part, that's true.

"Your shipment will enter and exit the country without issue."

He nods, and I stand and head toward the door.

"Antonio."

I stop several feet from the table.

"I'm from St. Petersburg. Have you ever been there?"

I turn around to face him. "Years ago."

"Then you know it's a beautiful city filled with palatial structures and rich history. Although you never got to see some of the most historic buildings. They were destroyed by the time you visited. When I was a boy, my father and grandfather told stories of the horror and mass destruction they witnessed when the Axis Army marched in and seized the city during the Second World War. They wept as they described the lost history of Leningrad." He pauses briefly. "I don't destroy iconic churches."

57

DANIELA

Not only is Antonio here for Isabel's dinner, but Rafael showed up about an hour ago too.

He came not for Isabel, but I suspect his curiosity about Valentina got the best of him. Either that, or he wanted to see if he still had a place in our home.

Rafael hasn't met Valentina, but he assured me before we left London that he wouldn't breathe a word about anything. I have no reason to believe he'd say anything to hurt her.

While I'm thrilled to have them both here, it's Valentina's coming into the dining room as I fuss with the flowers that makes my heart swell. She's wearing a dress—*a dress*—and not just any dress, but the one Isabel helped her pick out for her confirmation. She never got a chance to wear it, but Isabel gushed endlessly about how gorgeous it was on her.

"You're beautiful, *meu amor*. So grown up." I wrap my arms around her and hold her close. When we pull away, her eyes are glazed with unshed tears. I don't have a chance to tell her it's okay to cry—I cry for Isabel sometimes too—because Rafael Huntsman waltzes in before I can say a word. He's full of mischief and good humor. It's the mask he wears.

"Did you know Daniela stalked Antonio when she was a girl?" he whispers to a wide-eyed Valentina not thirty seconds after he meets her. He leans closer to a giggling Valentina. "I saw it myself."

A casual observer would think he had already come to terms with Valentina being part of the family, but I catch him, a few times, studying her during dinner when he thinks no one is looking. As for Valentina, she's quite taken with his easy charm.

After dessert, Antonio excuses himself to make a call, and Valentina goes upstairs to change. Rafael promised to watch some ridiculous movie with her.

"I'm so happy you're here, Rafael, but I didn't expect you. Otherwise, I would have freshened your room. Do you have everything you need?"

He nods, gnawing on the corner of his bottom lip. "I wanted to see her. To meet her."

I'm sure he did. We dropped a bomb on him, and on Lydia too. But she's better emotionally equipped to handle the blows. "What do you think? Remind you of me when I was a young girl—you know, annoying?"

"She's great," he says quietly, with a faraway look. He doesn't even smirk at my joke. "If I hadn't seen her with my own eyes, I would have never believed how much she looks like my mom when she was a girl."

Rafael gazes across the table at me, with a resolve I can't quite place. "I've been thinking a lot about my mother since that day at Aunt Lydia's." He lifts his chin and straightens his shoulders. "She would expect me to do right by you and Valentina. That begins with an apology for what my father and brother did to you and your mother."

My protective instincts kick in, and I want to throw my arms around him and tell him it's going to be okay. That none of it was his fault. But I don't, because he's not a boy. He's a man.

Rafael is a Huntsman through and through. There's

nothing of him that resembles his father or brother. But he has so much of the man who raised him inside. Antonio is a big believer, not in apologies, but in doing right by people.

"You don't need to apologize for things that had nothing to do with you." I pause for a few seconds. I want him to understand that I don't harbor any ill will toward him. "You're not obligated in any way, but I'd love for you to be a big part of Valentina's life—and mine too."

He swallows hard, and we sit in silence for a long moment before he comes around the table and takes the chair next to mine. "I have something for Valentina. I know she doesn't know about any of this. But maybe you can hold it for her, until the time is right." He takes a velvet pouch out of his pocket and hands it to me.

"Can I peek?"

"Of course."

Inside is a delicate gold necklace, with a charm dangling from a dainty lobster clasp. The charm is the letter *V* in a cursive font. It's not a new piece of jewelry.

My heart.

"This belonged to your mother."

He nods, soberly. "She wore it often. It was an eighteenth birthday present from her parents. My grandparents—Antonio's grandparents too."

The emotion whirls in my chest. Most of it's joyful, but the anxiety that comes with the prospect of telling Valentina the truth dims some of the joy.

I hold the necklace in my palm before returning it to the pouch. *He should give this to her after she knows the truth.* I press the velvet sack into Rafael's hand. "I want you to keep this. You can give it to her when the time is right. It should be you. You're her uncle. Valentina has so little family—I want her to know about the good people. About you, and your mother. You're the best person to tell her about her grandmother."

"I'm ready for the movie," a cheery voice calls seconds before Valentina saunters into the room.

Rafael quickly dons his cheerful mask, sliding the necklace back into his pocket. "Then let's get to it."

As they leave the room together, chatting about horses, I almost forget there's turmoil brewing in Porto, formidable enough to etch black circles under Antonio's eyes.

58

DANIELA

Antonio and Will are huddled in a corner. They appear totally engrossed in conversation, but their eyes continuously scan St. Philomena's ballroom for any sign of danger. After spending a few days in London with Samantha and Will, I've concluded that Antonio and Will are like two peas in a pod. I'm not sure it's a good thing. One force of nature seems like plenty.

We arrived in the UK early, to take in the sights and do a little shopping, and so Valentina and Alexis could get to know one another before we left them at camp. Of course, we didn't sightsee like normal tourists. Will arranged for us to visit the attractions when they were closed to the public. *Like I said, two peas in a pod.*

"You're so quiet. Are you okay?" Samantha asks, touching my elbow.

St. Philomena's is hosting a small reception for families before we say goodbye to our campers. I'm in the center of a lovely room with a few dozen girls, and many more adults milling around. But in some ways, I feel alone.

I smile. "I'm fine. This is all new to me."

"The first time you leave them is the hardest. After that, each time gets easier."

"It's just this one time," I say quickly. *I hope.* Although I'm not foolish enough to believe that two weeks' time is enough to wage war and bring the peace.

She nods sympathetically. Samantha is older than me, closer in age to Antonio, but we've become fast friends, bonding over our formidable husbands. I wish she lived closer.

I watch as Valentina and Alexis break free from a small group of girls and make their way over. They formed an easy friendship too. As hard as this is on me, it's the right decision, not just for safety reasons, but because Valentina needs to be around girls her age. *It's vital to her development*, Dr. Lima explained, when I sought her advice.

"The headmistress told us to come say goodbye to our parents," Alexis chirps.

Our parents. I wonder how that makes Valentina feel. As far as she knows, she's parentless. But it doesn't seem to faze her. She's bursting with energy. Some of it's nerves, but she's excited. There's no denying it.

While Samantha relays last-minute instructions to her daughter, I hug Valentina tight, clinging longer than I should.

"Santi and Mia will be here the entire time. We'll be able to video chat after the first week, but if you need anything before that, they'll help you." I stop myself, because I sound more intense than Antonio, and I don't want her to think there's danger lurking. I will myself to relax and force a smile. "You're going to have a wonderful time. I can't wait to hear all about it."

"Make sure you sign up for sailing lessons," a deep voice behind me says. "We can always use another competent crew member on our boat."

Sailing lessons? She's not a strong swimmer. But I don't say anything because I want her to have opportunities. I don't want her to be afraid of everything. And I know from our original visit, and from everything Samantha has told me, that they take no risks here.

"On the Huntsman boat? For the regatta?" she asks, beaming at Antonio like he hangs the stars.

"Why not? If you meet all the requirements."

I'm taken aback, and I have to remind myself to close my mouth. He's very matter-of-fact, and it will be years before Valentina meets the requirements—but as of now, the crews consist only of men. Not just on the Huntsman boat, but on all the boats. *Antonio could change that, though. He just has to decide it's the right thing to do and set an example.*

"Will you check on Demeter?" she asks. "I'm going to miss her so much."

What about me? Will you miss me? I'm embarrassed to admit that those thoughts really did cross my mind, although they didn't stay long. I don't want her to miss me. I really don't. I want her to have fun.

"I'll not only check on her, but I'll even take her for a little ride, if that's okay with you."

She smiles, her head bobbing up and down. "Make sure you rub her down when you're through."

"Valentina," Alexis calls.

I give her one more quick hug. "Go," I tell her. "Make lots of friends and wonderful memories."

She peers up at Antonio. "Take care of her," she tells him. "She's going to miss me."

He embraces her and whispers something that I can't hear, but Valentina nods.

As I watch her disappear through the double doors with the other girls, he places a strong hand on my back. "There's nothing to worry about. She deserves a chance to be a girl."

He's absolutely right.

59

DANIELA

"You've got two weeks to yourself," Antonio says, engaging the privacy screen between the front and back seats. We're in the car on our way to the airport and back to Porto. "Have you thought about what you're going to do with your free time?"

Hopefully something more interesting than writing thank-you notes and sorting mail.

"I haven't given it much thought. You'll be busy during the day, but we could spend the evenings together. At least some of them. And the nights." I wriggle my brow.

He leans over, kisses me, then touches his forehead to mine. "I'd like nothing more than that, but no promises. It'll be hard to break away most nights to go to the valley."

Disappointment is a bitter pill, and I'm having trouble swallowing the damn thing.

It won't be hard to break away if I'm upstairs in the apartment at the lodge. But that's going to take some finesse.

When he pulls back to gaze into my eyes, I run my fingers through his hair. "I don't want to be alone at the house while

Valentina's at camp and you're waging war. Let me stay with you at the apartment."

He takes my hand and presses a kiss to the knuckles, before sitting up.

"No." He tilts his head back and closes his eyes.

"That's it? No?"

He doesn't reply.

"You need me there."

When he doesn't respond, I climb onto his lap, straddling him. His eyes bolt open.

"You need me there. By your side. That's where I belong. I'm strong enough to withstand any storm, and more than capable of holding my own on the choppy seas."

Less is always more when dealing with him. I've made my best case. Now I wait.

He studies me, his hands resting on my hips. I watch his mind turning, weighing the pros and cons, analyzing the safety issues. When the gold flecks in his eyes shimmer, I know I've won.

"You're more than capable, *meu amor*. But there will be a high price to pay for your demands."

Bring it on.

I glance at the privacy screen, before sliding off his lap and easing my knees to the floor.

"What are you doing, *Princesa*?" From the gravelly sound of his voice, he knows exactly what I'm doing.

I gaze up at him through my lashes. "Paying the piper."

60

ANTONIO

When my phone vibrates on the nightstand, I untangle my limbs from Daniela's soft, warm body before reaching for it.

We have the package. Are you prepared to take delivery as planned?

Yes, I text back.

I immediately notify Cristiano and Lucas, who have been camped out downstairs for days, waiting for just this moment.

It's certainly not a surprise, but still, I lie here for a few minutes, coming to terms with what I've set in motion. Am I having second thoughts about killing Tomas? Not a single one. Although his disappearance will not go unnoticed.

With my uncle incapacitated, Tomas runs one of the oldest and most successful Port companies in the world. Premier might not have earned as many accolades as the Huntsman label, but it's not inconsequential. The disruption will likely hinder productivity this year, which will be felt by everyone. I've done everything I can to prepare for this inevitability, but it won't be enough.

As much as I hate that innocents will suffer, it can't be

helped. If the oligarchs are the ones helping Tomas and we don't sever the connection, there will be more than just small suffering in the region.

Reluctantly, I climb out of bed and get dressed, leaving the woman who has become my lover, my conscience, my hope for a life I never dreamed possible. Men like me either end up alone, or with a woman we never fully embrace. At best, we find a lovely adornment who makes a good mother for our children.

I don't know exactly what Daniela and I have, or what it will become once the gravest danger to her is eliminated. But I'm not giving her up. That I do know.

On my way out of the bathroom, I stop to watch my *Princesa* sleep. While I wasn't keen on it at first, I'm glad Daniela insisted on staying with me at the lodge. It's been like the honeymoon we never had, except I've had to sneak out at all hours to get some work done while she slept.

I kneel beside the bed and gently brush the hair off her gorgeous face, letting the silky strands caress my fingertips as they fall. While I've wanted to satisfy my vengeance for a long time, I'm sorry we didn't have more time alone before the ground rumbled.

"I need to go, *querida*."

"What time is it?" she asks, blinking.

"Time for you to go back to sleep."

"When will you be home?"

"I don't know."

"It's happening," she says, white-knuckling the sheet. "Whatever it is, it's happening."

"Nothing's happening that you need to worry about." I stand and press my lips to her forehead. *Your nightmare is almost over.* "Sweet dreams, *Princesa*. Only sweet dreams."

"Antonio," she cries, before I reach the door. "Promise you'll come back to me. Not in a body bag, but with your heart beating strongly."

I go back to sit beside her on the bed. The sheet is somewhere at her waist, exposing her creamy tits. Her dark hair is curling around her taut nipples. I take a ringlet between my fingers.

"Don't let your imagination get away from you. It's not what you think. I'm in no danger." I let the lock of hair slip from my fingers. "We're stretched thin today. Behave. Don't give Alvarez heartburn. I'll be home before you know it, and then I'm going to own this gorgeous body all day and all night, on every surface in this place, until Valentina gets back, when I'll have to own it more discreetly."

Her eyes dance at the promise of lust-filled days and nights, where she'll revel in my darkness, while I bask in her light. I allow myself one last look, my gaze lingering on her round breasts, before it reaches her eyes. She trembles—not in fear, but in anticipation. *Her angels play so nicely with my demons.*

Given what I'm about to do, I'm surprised to feel the tug at the corners of my mouth. But there's no denying it.

"*Te amo,*" she murmurs, cradling my jaw.

Te amo. Words I never expected to hear from her.

An unfamiliar swell of emotion knocks, but I don't let it in. "I'm not deserving of such a gift, but I'll take it." *Like I've taken everything else.*

I press a rough kiss to her mouth, tamping down the desire to crawl back into bed and bury myself inside her one last time, before our world turns upside down.

61

ANTONIO

When I get to the dungeon, Tomas is chained to a folding chair in the center of the room. I don't know how Will's men lured the rat out of his hole, but he doesn't appear to have a scratch on him.

I grab a chair and straddle the back about five feet away from him. I don't say anything. I just wait. There's a rhythm to these types of interrogations.

This is the fun part. The part where the initial adrenaline fades, and he begins to think somewhat clearly about his situation. Plotting a way out. It doesn't take long before a sheen forms on his neck. The question is, will he begin by begging for my mercy, or will he lash out?

"You left your *puta* to come to see me. How nice."

I want to wring his neck, but I don't flinch. This is as personal as it gets, but I can be a disciplined motherfucker when warranted, and I will interrogate him like any other traitor.

"I hope every time you're inside her used-up pussy, you think of me. I was there first. While it was pure and tight."

Control, Antonio. You have all the power.

Interesting. Most men in his situation wouldn't begin to lay out the facts like this. They'd hold onto this type of information, so they'd have something to barter with later when things begin to get really bad.

But Tomas is a coward. He's goading me because he knows I'm going to kill him, and he wants it to be quick. *Not a fucking chance.* He'll suffer, and he's going to tell me plenty before I let him take that last breath.

"Huh? Do you think about me when you fuck her? I know she thinks about me." The sheen on his neck is thicker.

"Actually, Tomas, I don't think of you at all when I'm with my wife. And she doesn't think of you either. No one who has access to my dick would ever give your tiny pecker a second thought."

Outwardly, I'm a man in control, but inside I'm craven and the devil has taken over. "I heard the day you raped her, you got in two pumps before you blew your load like a chump." I sneer, but the thought of him on Daniela—inside her innocent body—claws at me, like nothing else has.

"My knife." I hold out my hand to Cristiano. "This is my favorite knife. Pity it's going to get all dirty when I plunge it into your belly." I stare straight into his eyes. "Did you take a shit this morning, or are your bowels full?" I run my fingers along the edge of the blade before I set it on my thigh. "If you want the end to come quick, you'll answer my questions truthfully. If not, I've cleared my schedule for the week. I'm prepared to wait a *long* time."

He turns his head away from me. "I'm not telling you a damn thing."

You will tell me everything before this is over. Without a word, I get up and walk over to him. I stand perfectly still for several long moments, before bringing the knifepoint to his throat.

"Do it," he spits out.

"Oh, I will, but not yet." I slash his exposed forearm, twice.

He whimpers like a baby. It takes everything I have not to sink the knife into his gut, but he'll bleed out too quickly.

"Who are you working with?" I ask.

"Nobody," he replies, but with much less bravado.

I step back and hand Cristiano the knife. "String him up and bring in the vat. I'll be back after I've had my breakfast."

"Don't bother," he mutters. "I'm not telling you a fucking thing."

I turn around and smirk. "We'll see."

62

ANTONIO

I take the elevator up to the apartment. It won't be long before whoever Tomas is working with realizes he's disappeared. I want to double-check the security leading to Daniela myself. With any luck, she'll be fast asleep.

I pass armed guards all along my route, nodding at each man who I expect to protect Daniela with their very life, if it comes to it.

When I unlock the door, Alvarez is there, gun drawn, and I begin to relax.

"*Senhor* Antonio. I wasn't expecting you." He holsters his weapon.

That was the point. Only Cristiano and Lucas know Tomas is here. He was shuttled into the building in a shipping container, much the same way he'll go out. My men are trustworthy, but this requires a level of trust only my two childhood friends have earned.

There's a noise from the kitchen. "Is my wife up?"

"No, *senhor*. Alma is here."

"It's four a.m."

He shrugs. "She arrived shortly after you left the apartment."

Some days she gets here at an ungodly hour, but this is insane, even by her standards.

"Why?" I bark. Alvarez opens his mouth to say something, but I wave him off. I'll ask her myself. I almost half expect her to tell me she had a premonition of some kind. For as long as I've known her, God, or the angels, or some dead person has been sending her messages.

"*Bom dia*," I say, entering the kitchen that looks like it's set up to feed an army.

"*Bom dia*," she replies, not surprised to see me. Alma knows I don't keep banker's hours. "I tried to be quiet so I wouldn't wake you and *Senhora* Daniela."

"You do realize it's four o'clock?"

"I went to bed early, and I don't need much sleep anymore." *God help me.*

"We're only two people, and even if I take food down to Cristiano and Lucas—that's only four."

"I'm making meals for the freezer so that there will be good food for you to eat while I'm gone. Even newlyweds have to eat."

While I'm gone? What's that about? She never goes anywhere, except to visit my mother, and my mother is at Samantha and Will's. *At least she better be.* "Where are you going?"

"Cristiano didn't tell you?"

I would have remembered if he told me. "No."

"I'm going to visit the US. I've always wanted to go. Cristiano is sending me, and his sisters, and the children. We're all going."

I study her for a minute, my gut sending up a small flare. I'm surprised Cristiano never mentioned the trip. *It's not like him.* Although we've had so much on our plates, and every free moment I've been able to steal, I've been with Daniela.

"When are you leaving?"

"Saturday. I did mention it to Daniela in passing yesterday, but I thought Cristiano had already cleared it with you. We'll be gone for three weeks. I hope this is fine with you. Up until the last few days, you've been spending a lot of time in the valley. I didn't think you'd mind."

"Alma, you're entitled to a vacation. You don't take enough time off. We've been very busy, and it must have slipped Cristiano's mind." *But I will ask him about it as soon as that asshole in my dungeon is dead.*

"Do you want breakfast?" she asks, reaching for an onion.

"No. Just coffee. I'll get it. You keep chopping so we don't starve."

"While I'm in charge of the kitchen, no one is starving. The trip is a dream come true, although I hate to miss the rebelo boat race," she says wistfully.

I'd almost forgotten about the regatta. Huntsman Port participates every year, on June twenty-fourth, the Feast of St. John. Although this year it's late because of some burgeoning pandemic concerns that never amounted to anything.

"I haven't missed one yet."

"Don't worry. You already know how it ends."

She wags a finger at me. "Be humble, Antonio. One day you might get a big surprise."

I've known this woman all my life. She and my mother are very close, still. Alma sat with her the day my father almost killed her—the day he died. I put an arm around her shoulders. "You know how much I hate surprises."

"I do. Now go find your pretty wife, and let an old woman finish her work."

"Don't go overboard with those onions," I tell her on my way out of the kitchen. Not that she's likely to listen to anything I have to say about cooking.

I pass Alvarez standing watch, on my way to the bedroom.

When I get there, I stop outside the door. I shouldn't go in, not even for a few seconds to check on her. If she wakes, she's going to ask questions that I can't answer, and I don't want to lie to her.

Before I leave, I press my hand to the bedroom door. *It's almost over. I'll have my vengeance, and you'll never have to worry about him abducting your daughter.*

63

ANTONIO

When I get back, they've taken Tomas's clothes and chained him to a hook attached to the ceiling. The same way an animal is hung after slaughter. It's fitting.

My prisoner is on tiptoe, and I lower the chain so that he can stand on his feet. They were rough with him, but they didn't beat him—that pleasure is mine.

Tomas is docile now.

There are stages a man goes through as he approaches death by torture. Not every man spends time in every stage, but he experiences all of them, even for a fleeting moment. It's the interrogator's responsibility to know what implement to use, at any given time, for the best result.

I take a bullwhip from where it's hanging on the wall.

"Who are you working with?"

"Fuck you." There's no steam behind it, as it lands with a plop at my feet.

The whip hisses before it makes contact with his back. There's a small delay, a nanosecond, before the first scream bounces off the walls. That's how it always is. He'll feel my wrath the same way any other prisoner would, but he's not *any* prisoner, and his scream gives me a rush I don't normally get.

"I hate to repeat myself. But I will, as many times as need be. Who are you working with?"

Tomas takes only six lashes before he spits out, "Sergei Chernov."

The Russian oligarch. I picture him as an *X* on Fedorov's drawing.

"What's the end game?" I sink my knife into his left thigh.

"Fucker!" he yells.

I hold up the knife, ready to plunge it into the right leg.

"Wait. I'll tell you."

I pause with the knife in the air to keep the pressure on him to talk.

"Chernov wants to be part of the decision-making in the valley." He grimaces. "Feels he can bring a fresh perspective that will benefit us."

What a stupid fuck. "And you were going to hand him the keys? Just like that? He's a fucking oligarch. He doesn't care about the valley."

"He's not looking for control. Just input."

"You are dumber than I thought. Chernov set off the explosion at Santa Ana's, didn't he?"

"Not supposed to happen like that."

I stick the knife into his side, instantly drawing blood. "How was it supposed to happen?"

"No more!" he cries.

"Then keep talking."

"He had information about the girl," Tomas mutters through clenched teeth. "She's my kid. I was going to take custody of her once that *puta* was dead."

He knows everything, and so do others. Although without him, the Russians have no easy way forward. *Just bloody ones.* "You mean take custody of Quinta Rosa do Vale."

He nods.

I already owned it, but he could have dragged the betrothal contract through the courts. He wouldn't have gotten anywhere, certainly not with the judges in Porto, but he would have made my life unpleasant.

I slide the knife point across his belly until it reaches his balls. "That puta you speak of is my wife. She was twelve when you raped her. Her name is *Senhora* Daniela. Say it." When he doesn't, I nick his balls with the blade while he writhes in pain, twisting and turning on his chains.

"Say it."

"*Senhora* Daniela."

I lay the bloody knife on the chair and leave before I end his misery much too soon.

The problem with torture is that at some point every man will tell you whatever it is they think you want to hear. This is especially true when they sense the angel of death hovering. At that point, they know there's no going back, and they just want it over.

Tomas surrendered early, not simply because he's a coward with no allegiance to anyone but himself, although he is that. But he talked early because when I walked into the dungeon, the angel of death was perched on my shoulder, ready to harvest his black soul. He knew the most he could hope for was a quick death.

Tomas didn't give me anything that Fedorov didn't hint at, or that we didn't already suspect. He just provided confirmation.

With the mothership behind him, Chernov is a much more formidable enemy than Tomas.

64

DANIELA

It's been two days since I've heard anything from Antonio. I'm feeling boxed in, ready to scream.

Alvarez hasn't left the apartment once, and he hasn't said a word to me about what's going on outside these walls. Not that he's ever very chatty. Alma, who knows less, has given me more.

"Something's going on," she whispered to me this morning. "Something big. For two days, the security has been tighter than normal around the building. And there are a dozen soldiers stationed outside the apartment door."

I'm sure she's worried about her son. I'm worried too. "I don't know what's going on, Alma. But I agree, it's big."

A dozen soldiers. I texted Antonio for tenth time, after she told me: ***I need to know you're alive. Please.***

There was no response. *Nothing.* So I texted Cristiano, then Lucas, and then Cristiano again. It was hours later when Cristiano decided to show some mercy: ***If something happens to Antonio, you'll be the first to know.***

After Lucas and you. It wasn't much, but I took it to mean that Antonio was still breathing. I held the hope close, until the sun set over Porto.

Now, the hope has become wispy shreds of nothing, disappearing like snowflakes in the warm air. I can't catch a single one to hold onto. Even a sky teeming with brilliant stars can't sustain my faith.

Alvarez knows something. *He must.*

I go to the kitchen and make him a generous plate from the platter of food Alma left.

"Thank you, *senhora*," he says politely, when I try to hand him the plate, "but I had my meal before Alma went home."

So much for that idea. "I'll cover it and save it for you. If you get hungry, help yourself."

He nods.

I had hoped to bribe him into telling me something, or to at least distract him enough with a tasty dinner that he might slip. But since subterfuge is not happening, I'll be direct. Although I'm sure it won't get me anything more than the last time I asked. "Have you heard from Antonio?"

"No, *senhora*. He's been gone two days. You have not heard from your husband?"

His tone makes me bristle. *No, I have not heard from my husband who has been gone two days. Thanks for rubbing it in.*

"I understand that there's heightened security in the building and outside the apartment. Under these circumstances, I think there's a better chance that you'll have heard something from Antonio than that I would have."

He shrugs. "I know nothing about what's going on outside the apartment. I'm wearing the same blinders as you." His mouth twists into an ugly snarl.

He's telling the truth. He's disgusted, almost insulted. I'm sure for a man like Alvarez, who is a top lieutenant, being kept in the dark, *like a woman*, is hard to swallow. This isn't the first bitter pill that Alvarez has had to swallow recently, either. He was grumpier than usual when Antonio had Santi teach me how to use a gun. I have no idea whether he wanted to be the one to show me the ropes, but he wasn't happy.

These small slights are not uncommon. My father never coddled his guards either. But I do feel a bit of empathy for this man, who risks his life to protect me.

"Antonio has tremendous confidence in you. Otherwise, he would have never assigned you to my protection."

"You are his most precious possession. That is true."

"I like to think of myself as a wife, not a possession. But you wouldn't be here if you didn't have his trust."

"But it will never be the same kind of confidence he has in Cristiano and Lucas."

If that's your standard, you'll be sorely disappointed. "He's known Cristiano and Lucas since they were boys, playing war games in the vineyards. If it makes you feel any better, I doubt he'll ever trust me as much as he trusts them."

He glances warily at me. Alvarez thinks that women shouldn't be trusted, certainly not in the way a man would trust his soldiers. He's smart enough not to say it, but I have no doubt it's what he's thinking.

"If you hear anything, please let me know."

He nods curtly. "Perhaps you'll do the same." His brow is knit tightly, and he doesn't look directly at me while he speaks. It cost him to say it—to even think I might have some news before him.

"Of course," I say softly. "Good night."

65

ANTONIO

After more than two full days of delivering calculated pain, I've heard enough from Tomas. I'm out of patience. His father, along with mine, murdered Vera. Tomas overheard them planning. *And he did nothing to warn her.* I almost ended him then. The bastard doesn't know why they killed his mother, or what they did with her body. After so many years, it almost doesn't matter. While it won't bring much solace, it will give Rafael and my mother a bit of closure.

I have only one question remaining unanswered: *who's leaking information to my enemies?* If Tomas knows, he's not telling. But I don't think he knows. He's squealed about everything else. Why wouldn't he just tell me?

I'm going to gut my cousin, like I promised him at the Camelia Ball. But I have to work fast, because I want him fully conscious when I dip him in the acid bath. Of course, it's not really acid. That's for gangster movies.

What I have for him is a vat of corrosive chemicals that will burn his body from the inside out, dissolve everything, including his teeth, within a matter of days. But he'll be at the bottom of the Atlantic before that happens.

Cristiano wheels the sealed vat closer to Tomas before I send him away. "I'm doing this alone."

"Antonio," he pleads, quietly. "Something could go wrong."

"Nothing will go wrong." I've planned carefully, and I can taste my revenge. Cristiano opens his mouth to say something. He's clearly not done trying to persuade me to let him stay, but I won't allow it. "Get out."

"Lucas," I call, facing one of the cameras, and signal for him to cut the feed.

Together, we've done some things that will never be forgiven. But their souls won't be tarnished with this, and their nightmares won't be tainted by the screams that I'm about to elicit from this pig.

I hold the blade to his stomach.

"You can kill me," he whimpers, his voice weak and hoarse, "but you have no idea what's waiting for you."

I slice into his abdomen, and the warm blood squirts everywhere, droplets raining on my skin like salvation.

While he cries, I go to the wall, and engage the lever to raise his body higher off the ground. When I'm satisfied, I roll the vat under him, and carefully slide off the protective cover.

There is no regret, no sense of guilt as I lower his body, inch by inch, into the chemical bath.

While he struggles and screams, I remember my aunt, who I adored. I remember Maria Rosa with her big heart that embraced the poorest of souls. I remember my mother's pain, and Rafael's. But mostly I remember the little girl with a sparkle in her eyes. I think about how he raped her, then forced her to watch while they slit her mother's throat. I think of her curled around her dead mother for hours in the meadow. And I think about the pregnant twelve-year-old banished to a convent, hidden away, like she'd done something wrong.

Every memory feeds my vengeance, and every scream frees my soul.

The suffering he caused will linger long after he's erased from existence, but his days of inflicting harm are over.

When the bubbling ceases, and he's totally submerged, I secure the top and test the padlock before I go.

On my way out, I pause in the doorway and peer over my shoulder. "When you get to hell, say hello to my father."

I flip off the light switch and walk away, knowing that while the danger hasn't been entirely eliminated, Daniela—and Valentina—are safer now.

66

ANTONIO

I shower before leaving the villa and put on fresh clothes. But when I get to the apartment, I take another look for any spattered blood I might have missed. Slaughtering a pig is messy business, and I don't want to bring any of it with me into the home I share with her.

After drawing a breath, I rap quietly on the door to get Alvarez's attention. *I don't want to be shot now.* "Antonio," I say from outside the door.

The lock snicks, and the door opens. "*Senhor*," Alvarez says, eyeing my wet hair. "Trouble?"

I glare at him, because he's overstepped. He doesn't have the right to question me—he's not that high on the food chain. Right now, he's damn lucky I'm bone-tired.

"You're done for tonight. I won't need you here in the morning. Call Cristiano. He'll have something to keep you busy."

"Good night," he says, head down. He knows he fucked up.

I text Alma and tell her to stay home. I want tomorrow, at least some of it, with my wife. I'll need to deal with oligarchs and arrange for a shipment to be dropped at sea. But first, I want to spend long hours worshipping my *Princesa*.

I check the door and shed my clothes on the way to the bedroom, where I find my wife fast asleep.

A good man would let her sleep. A decent man would wake her with tender kisses. But I am neither good nor decent. I am her dark prince, and the devil inside me is wide awake, craven, no longer lusting for revenge, but lusting for the kind of satiety only she can provide.

I climb into bed and crawl on top of her luscious body, like a feral animal during mating season. She cries out, startled as I pin her under me. Her cry sends a bolt of lightning straight to my cock.

"Antonio. You're here. Are you okay?"

She examines me through a knitted brow, gliding her soft hands over my shoulders and down my back. I ache for her touch—for her sweetness. And it's heaven.

While her warm hands run freely over my skin, I close my eyes and breathe her in, until the putrid coppery stench of fresh blood is replaced by orange blossom and goodness.

"Where have you been?"

"Keeping you safe, *meu amor*. You'll always be tempting to my enemies, but no one will ever hurt you to get to Valentina."

"He's dead," she whispers into the dark. "Tomas is dead." There's no elation, but there's no regret from her either.

Nor should there be.

"Tomas got the end he deserved."

"I suppose it makes me a horrible human being, but I'm not sad about it. I'm relieved," she says so quietly I barely hear it. "But I wish you hadn't dirtied your soul for me."

Oh, Princesa, it's too late to worry about my soul. It's not salvageable.

"My soul is already filthy," I reply, sucking a dusky nipple into my mouth.

"What about the valley? What happens now?"

I lift my head and meet her eyes. Her selflessness incites the beast in me. "I'm not your father. No man or woman who even thinks about hurting you will go unpunished. Not as long as I have a single breath left in me."

I slide off the bed and drag her body to the edge of the mattress. With my feet on the floor and the demons dancing inside, I tear the nightgown from her body.

Her eyes are wide, but she doesn't protest. *She's going to let me have this.*

I take my rock-hard cock in hand and pump savagely while she watches from her back. Eyes burning with passion. Long legs spread, arms at her side, submitting fully to my whims. "You. Are. Mine." While I'll never deserve her, I deserve her more now that I've punished two of the three bastards. The other is in his own special hell.

"I. Am. Yours," she says, her breath shallow and rough. "And you. Are. Mine."

A tormented growl escapes from my chest, as I spray my *Princesa* with thick ropes of cum, letting my seed fall on her belly, her cunt, and tits. Marking her. Owning every inch of her mind, body, and soul.

She slides her fingers through the milky ribbons and brings them to her mouth, sucking like they're coated in nectar. Her sultry gaze never wavers from mine.

I can barely breathe as I drink her in.

"Te amo." The world stops for a blistering moment while I whisper the unfamiliar words. *"Te amo."*

Her eyes sparkle, and my chest explodes. But it's not enough. My demons are still awake and dancing.

I tremble as I flip her over and sink my teeth into her flesh. Leaving mark after mark on her skin, until my dick is aching again.

Without a single qualm, I bury myself in her drenched

pussy, along with every remnant of the past, like relics in a time capsule left for historians to decipher.

We only move forward now.

67

ANTONIO

By the time I get to downstairs, it's noon. Not because I slept late, but because I feasted on my wife until she was a blubbering mess, and then dirtied her again in the shower.

For hours and hours, while she laid in my arms, all was right in the world. It killed me to leave our cocoon.

Now I have to deal with the aftermath of the last few days. Although it can't be too bad because neither Cristiano or Lucas tried to reach me.

"Anyone looking for our friend?"

We covered our tracks, but there will be questions. They'll never recover a body, but no one will believe Tomas just got up one day and decided to live off the grid. The police will have questions, but I'm not worried about them. The owners of the other Port lodges are a different matter.

They'll have plenty of questions, and they'll expect answers. Not that they give a goddamn about Tomas. They'll be worried about themselves. *Am I next?* That's all they'll care about. As president of the Douro Port Wine Foundation, I'm going to be doing a lot of hand-holding and giving out reassurances like condoms in a whorehouse. Everyone's going to need at least one.

"Nobody's asking questions yet," Lucas replies. "Although there's a lot of activity happening at your uncle's house."

Not a surprise. "What kind of activity?"

"More cell phone chatter than normal. I've been tracing the pings that are ricocheting around the world, to throw us off, but so far I've only come up with dead ends."

That type of diversion is not uncommon, but it takes a certain kind of skill to make it happen. With a little time and luck, Lucas will figure it out. I'm confident.

"What's going on with Fedorov's shipment?"

"It was delayed leaving Columbia, but it's on the way. If there are no issues, we're looking at an ETA of four days. Could be five."

Good. Because the minute his shipment exits the country, I want a name. Operating with a traitor in our midst poses all sorts of risks.

The biggest unknown regarding Tomas's death is Chernov. There's no telling how the Russian will respond. We don't know how long he's been working with Tomas, or how many resources he's poured into the scheme. I know what Tomas told me, but my guess is Chernov was working the angle long before he approached Tomas. That's how they operate. While I don't trust Fedorov, the oligarchs, with their direct connection to Moscow, are a bigger problem.

"Hey." I glance at Cristiano. "How come you never told me your mother was going on vacation?"

He pauses briefly, as if surprised by the question. "To be honest, I almost forgot myself until she called me this morning. Her boss gave her the day off to pack. What a guy."

I snicker. Cristiano forgetting isn't quite like Lucas forgetting, but it's unusual enough to keep me probing. "I'm surprised you picked now to send them, right before the Feast of St. John."

Cristiano knows the boat and the moods of the river better than anyone. I'm the captain, but he is as skilled a second mate as anyone could hope for, and certainly a better sailor than I am. We would never win the regatta, year after year, without him. "Your mother loves to take a picture of you on the winning stand."

Lucas chuckles. "She'll have to wait until next year. I can live with it."

He doesn't want to talk about the trip, which makes me want to talk about it more.

"You didn't answer my question. Why now?"

"I'm not sure," he says, looking me straight in the eye. "I'm not sure."

"What the fuck does that mean?" Lucas taunts.

If Cristiano tells me he got a message from God, or some dead relative came to him in the night, I'm going to smack him. It's one thing to listen to that shit from Alma, but it's quite another from my right-hand man.

"I don't know if it's all the stuff that's come to light in the last month, but—" He shakes his head. "I just want them out of Porto for a little while."

His unease awakens something in my gut, but it doesn't churn.

It's been a fucked-up time that's lasted too long. It's always a shitstorm, but this has been extra, no question. Cristiano has sisters, and the sisters who have children have girls. All this with my father, and uncle, and Tomas has got to have made his blood run cold. He grew up with me. Those men touched his life—if not every day, often.

"Whoa, whoa, whoa," Lucas cries, his eyes glued to both monitors on his desk. "Sergei Chernov has been called home."

"He's dead?" Because as much as I'd like that, dead creates a whole other set of concerns.

"Called back to Russia. But what does it mean?" he adds quietly, engrossed in what's on his screen.

Called back to Russia isn't all that much less complicated than dead. "Too soon to tell."

"Maybe Moscow knows about Tomas," Cristiano says, "and they're pissed Chernov fucked up. They could be calling him back to rap his knuckles."

"It's plausible, but it's just as likely a ploy of some kind to lull us into a false sense of comfort. Either way, it will make the feast more peaceful. They won't act so quickly." I glance at Cristiano. "We should take the boat out once or twice before the race."

"Tomorrow after work?"

"Only if we can do it early. Daniela's leaving for London the next morning to pick up Valentina from camp. I promised to be home for dinner before the sun sets." The moment I say it, my two friends side-eye each other, trying to hide their smirks. I walked right into it—and I don't even care.

"Camp's over already?"

"Not until Friday, but she wants to allow herself plenty of time in case there's a weather front—" I hold up my hand to shush them. "They're predicting sunny Mediterranean weather for weeks. I know."

"Is she staying with Samantha and Will?" Cristiano asks.

I shake my head. "With my mother."

Although, even with all the security, I hate having them together at my mother's apartment. One small lapse in security, that's all it would take for someone to send my world crashing down.

68

DANIELA

I board the plane with my entourage, right behind Valentina and Alexis, whose parents reluctantly agreed to allow her to come home with us to celebrate the Feast of St. John. It took much pleading and begging and promising from both girls.

Samantha was all for it even without the preteen theatrics, but I'm still waiting for Will to show up and drag his daughter off the plane.

We're also joined by Santi, Mia, Alvarez, Duarte, another guard Antonio sent with me, and all four—*four*—of Alexis's guards. At the last minute, Rafael decided to tag along, with yet more guards. We might have more soldiers on this plane than the Portuguese had when the Moors invaded.

"Girls," I tell the preteen conspirators, "you need to keep your seat belts on until we get an all clear signal from the pilot."

"Can we watch a movie?" Valentina asks. "Please?"

She seems to have matured in the last two weeks. Part of me wishes that we were coming back alone, just me and her, where she could fill me in on camp, and all the other details I'm dying to know.

I have an insatiable desire to make up for the lost past. Even though it's ridiculous, because I didn't miss out on anything, really. Thanks to Isabel—and even to Jorge—I was there for all of it.

"It's not a long flight, but of course you can watch a movie. We'll also have lunch, but not until we're airborne."

I strap on my seat belt and gaze at Rafael with his nose in an iPad. His entire nuclear family is essentially gone. *Like mine.* His father isn't dead, but he can't communicate. Any hope for Rafael to forge any kind of relationship with him, *or Tomas,* is gone.

I don't think he knows about his brother yet. I suspect Antonio will tell him soon, before he hears it from someone else. Lydia didn't know either. She might have been entirely preoccupied with all things Valentina, but she wouldn't have forgotten to mention her nephew's disappearance.

I've had a few days to think about Tomas's death. Given the state Antonio was in when he came home, I'm sure Tomas didn't have an easy passing. I haven't felt an ounce of sympathy for him. I haven't even been able to pretend. I'm beyond grateful he's off this earth.

Maybe some of Antonio's darkness has snaked its way into my heart. *"My greedy Princesa. That's what happens to angels who lay with the devil."* That's what he whispered into my damp skin the night before I left, while I begged for his cock.

———

WHILE THE GIRLS are busy watching a movie and Rafael's napping, I sneak into the conference room to call my devil.

"Princesa." He uses that seductive tenor that beckons. The one that dares me to come closer.

"My dark prince. You know, it's interesting. Most days, reaching you directly is no longer the problem it once was when I arrived in Porto. Did you have your phone fixed?"

He laughs. It happens so infrequently that when it does, my heart sings.

"As it turns out, the phone just needs to be stroked with a light touch. But I think you've figured that out."

Not entirely, but I'm getting there. "I have quite the entourage with me."

"Yes, I heard you boarded with some unexpected cock-blockers. I'm surprised you didn't call to check with me."

It's so Antonio, always needing control, but there's no menace in his voice.

"I'm surprised that you're surprised."

"*Ahhh*, that mouth."

My cheeks hurt from the stupid grin I've been wearing since the moment I heard his voice.

"I hope you don't think the extra people in the house will stop me. I'm hungry for you. Starving."

"I was gone two nights." But I'm starving for him, too.

"Two nights too many."

"Alexis is only here by a small miracle."

"I'm aware. Her father already called. I'm glad he let her come. It'll be good for Valentina to have someone her age to hang around with at the feast."

"It will be." I remember how my friends and I stalked Antonio at every feast. But even so, I wouldn't mind palling around alone with her for a bit tomorrow while Antonio is getting ready for the regatta.

"Maybe Lara can stay with the girls tonight while you and I sneak over to the early festivities," he suggests. "If you're good, I'll even buy you a slice of St. John's cake."

"Lara isn't at work. She has some kind of flu."

"Flu? In the middle of the summer?"

"I don't know. Why do you always question everything everyone says?"

"Because people are liars."

I roll my eyes. "For such a beautiful man, you have such a suspicious nature."

"It's why I'm still breathing."

His words send a shiver up my spine. "Maybe Rafael will babysit."

"Not a chance. Rafael is going barhopping with the crew tonight. I guarantee he'll be taking full advantage of his status."

This is Rafael's first year as part of the crew. He meets all the requirements. He's old enough, and he'll be working for Antonio this fall. Rafael is doing an internship at Huntsman Port as part of his school curriculum. He'll be looking at ways Huntsman can better position itself in the market. In other words, he'll be critiquing Antonio's business decisions. *What I wouldn't give to be a fly on the wall during that debriefing.*

"Why aren't you going out with the crew?"

"They'll be chasing women all night. And I have a beautiful young bride and far better ways to spend my evening."

69

ANTONIO

While I'm on the phone with Carvallo, one of the members of the Douro Port Wine Foundation, Lucas passes me a note. *Fedorov's shipment just entered Spanish waters.*

"Any problems?" I ask Lucas, after I finish telling Carvallo that I have no idea where Tomas is, and I highly doubt it's anything nefarious.

"Not in Portugal."

I send Fedorov a text. *The shipment went through with no problems. Time to pay up.*

Fedorov: *I'll send him to you on a silver platter. Give me twenty-four hours.*

Me: *Not a fucking second more.*

Fedorov: *Best of luck tomorrow.*

Best of luck. Fuck you. I toss my phone on the desk.

It's dangerous to do business with a traitor lurking, and I want him bad. But there's something warning me to be careful what I wish for. Not to mention that Fedorov is a shrewd sonofabitch, not to be underestimated.

70

ANTONIO

Blue skies, calm waters, and just enough wind to guide the sails. It's a perfect day for a regatta.

With Chernov out of the country, I'm breathing a bit easier. The Russians are likely to let us stew awhile before they strike, and their brand of terrorism doesn't normally involve wholesale terrorist attacks in the middle of a holy feast. *Although they've done it.*

Lucas approaches the dock with a sour look on his face. "What's up?"

"Cristiano's not coming."

"What?"

"He's got some type of flu. He can't get out of bed."

I pause for a second. *The flu?* Maybe Daniela's right. Maybe I'm too damn suspicious. Not going to change now. "The flu?"

He shrugs. "Fuck if I know."

I've never known Cristiano to take a sick day. *Ever.* "He must be really sick."

"Said he can't lift his head off the pillow."

"Was he with you guys last night?"

He shakes his head. "He was a no-show. He must have already been feeling bad."

If Cristiano isn't here, he's on death's door. "Did you talk to him by phone or text?"

"Text."

His family's away, and he'd die before he'd call us for something right before the race. "Send someone over to check on him."

Lucas raises his brow. "We're spread pretty thin today, especially now with our best man down."

"One of them," I tell Lucas. "You're still here."

He ignores me because he hates any kind of praise.

Lucas is right about being spread thin. "Let's hold off until after the race," I mutter.

"You shouldn't get on that boat without him, you know."

"Why not? I've been sailing for as long as he has."

"Your talents are on the track. We both know it. Besides, it's more than that."

It's a safety issue. He doesn't have to say it. We've taken extra precautions, but most of those are on and around the dock, where Daniela and the girls will watch the race.

"You need to change. I want you on the boat with me."

"Me? I'm not a sailor."

"Not a good one. But I'm a crew member down, and there's not enough time to find a suitable replacement. I don't want to pull a man from the security on the ground. Rafael's on the boat. I don't want to add anyone to the crew who hasn't been fully vetted."

"What about the feeds?"

"You have men working under you who are more than capable of that kind of surveillance and of getting the boat a message if necessary."

Lucas slides his hands into his pockets and scans the area. "This is a bad idea."

"Maybe. But I still have my balls. The day I hide because I'm scared, I might as well hand them over. With Tomas *missing,* it's especially important for the others to see that I'm on that boat. If Huntsman Port pulls out, or if I don't get on that boat, they all bail. What do you think the news reports will look like? We won't be able to control all of it."

71

ANTONIO

"That went well," I mutter to Lucas, who is definitely not a sailor. We came in second place, and that was a stroke of luck.

I shake each crew member's hand. "Good job, guys. We'll be back next year to kick a little ass."

"Have you heard anything from Cristiano?" I ask Lucas before disembarking.

He checks his phone. "Nothing."

I try calling Cristiano, but the call goes directly to voicemail. Something doesn't feel right. "Send someone," I tell Lucas. "We'll manage until he gets back."

Daniela's at the edge of the pier, waving at me, and there are two gangly girls running my way, flanked by a small platoon of guards. I promised Valentina and Alexis they could board the boat at the end of the race.

"Congratulations!" they cry in unison, but only the girl with the violet-blue eyes gives me a big hug.

"Thank you. But we didn't win."

"But you came in second," Valentina gushes. "You still get a trophy."

"That's true."

"Can we go on the boat?"

"Yes, but be careful. The water's shallow at this part of the river, but the boat's not a toy. You can get hurt." I send Santi a pointed look. He nods to let me know he's on top of it.

I turn around for a second and watch them climb aboard before making my way up the ramp. My stunning wife meets me partway down.

"Congratulations," she says as I brush my mouth against hers.

"What is it with you and Valentina? The congratulations go to the winner."

"I saw that trophy. I have a much better prize for you," she says, wrapping her arms around my neck.

Someone behind Daniela is clearing his throat to get my attention. *Fuck that.* When he does it again, I pull my mouth from hers, and glare over her shoulder.

Alvarez is red, clearly embarrassed to interrupt us. *If I were him, I'd be more worried than embarrassed.* He's carrying a silver tray with an envelope on it. "I'm sorry, *senhor*, but the man said it was urgent. He said you were expecting this."

"What man?" I ask, taking the tray. I keep my voice even because I don't want to alarm Daniela.

"A tall man, with red hair." Alvarez searches the crowd behind him. "I don't see him."

The package has a return address of St. Petersburg, but no postmark. *Fedorov.*

"A letter on a tray? Who do you think it's from?" Daniela asks.

"A business associate who promised to send me something on a silver platter."

"Well, open it," she urges.

There's no way I'm opening it anywhere near her. Those fuckers love ricin.

"Go back and wait for me on the pier," I tell her. "I won't be long."

"Are the girls okay?"

"They're safer on the boat than in that crowd." I turn to Alvarez. "Don't let her out of your sight." I shove the silver platter at him. "Take this with you."

"Antonio," she says, with a hand on her hip. "Is that letter something we need to be worried about?"

"The only people who need to be worried is Alvarez, if he doesn't get you off this ramp, and you, if you don't get moving."

She lifts her chin, but wisely doesn't defy me.

I lean against the rail, partway down the ramp, and carefully open the package. There's a folded piece of paper inside. I pull it out cautiously.

Check your email.

That's all it says.

I take out my phone and pull up my inbox. There's a message from someone I don't recognize. The subject line says *St. Petersburg*.

The message contains an attachment. *A recording.* I press play and hold the phone to my ear.

72

ANTONIO

The conversation is fuzzy at first—but after several seconds, I can make out Cristiano's voice and that of another man.

"Tell me why you've agreed to help," a man with a Russian accent demands.

"I've been looking for the right opportunity to bring him down, for a long time. At first, I wasn't sure this was it, but I think it just might be."

What the hell? My heart is hammering.

"You still haven't told me *why* you want to bring him down."

"He's a selfish sonofabitch. Only cares about himself. I've worked for him for years—my mother for her whole life. When the explosion happened at Santa Ana's, my mother was there—the bastard never asked about her. Not once."

Is that true? No. I saw her on my way to the back of the church. I stopped. Alma was unhurt. *I told Cristiano that, didn't I?*

"We're not sending you back. I don't trust you not to play both sides. You can help us from here."

"I don't want to go back. When we're done, I want to go to

the US, and I want the money I was promised. But more than anything, I want to see that bastard on his knees, in ruin."

The Russian snickers. "It's always about money. Doesn't matter what a man says about principles. It always comes down to money. Huntsman doesn't pay you?"

"Not anywhere near what I'm worth."

"What do you think he'd do if he knew you were here—working with us?"

"He would be enraged, and ultimately the betrayal would destroy him."

The man laughs.

The blood is pounding in my ears. I can barely think. There isn't anything Cristiano doesn't know about me or my business. He could bring me down in no time or bleed me to death slowly.

"I've known Antonio my whole life," the man who I would have laid down my life for says. "As boys, we played soldiers in the vineyards along the river. Even when we were surrounded by the imaginary enemy, he would save himself first."

Is that how he remembers it?

"When your back's against the well, you know who your friends are."

The tape gets fuzzy again, and then it ends.

Cristiano is working with the Russians. My closest friend, *my brother*, is a traitor. *No chance.* It's not possible.

Don't let emotion cloud your judgment. The facts are the facts. Traitors come in many forms.

I lower myself to my haunches, my back against a post, and play the recording again. This time listening for clues.

Cristiano doesn't sound under duress. We have precautions in place. But he doesn't use a single code word to let us know he's been abducted. Not one. *I'm fucked.*

I scan the crowd behind Daniela for Lucas, replaying the recording over and over inside my head, every word tattooed on my brain. My legs are like rubber as I make my way up the ramp to Daniela. The day is not going to end as we planned. She's not going to like it, but she needs to go to the house with the girls, right away. *And stay there.*

When your back's against the well, you know who your friends are. When your back's against the well, you know who your friends are.

Against the well.

I pull out my phone and listen one more time. *"When your back's against the well..."*

"Get her out of here," I shout at the guards surrounding Daniela. "Now!" I roar over my shoulder as I race toward the boat, barking orders the entire way.

73

DANIELA

"Get your hands off me," I shriek, throwing a world-class tantrum, with an unsuspecting crowd behind me. "I'm not going anywhere without Valentina and Alexis."

"*Senhora*, I have orders," Alvarez chides, like I'm a four-year-old.

"I don't care about your orders."

Even as I argue, my eyes are glued to the waterfront. *Something's wrong. Very wrong.*

Antonio disappears onto the boat. Within seconds, everyone's jumping overboard into the river.

Panic ensues, and I cling to the railing, kicking and spitting at the guards who are trying to pull me to safety. It buys me a few minutes, because they have to be cautious. I'm Antonio's wife and they won't risk his wrath by manhandling me.

"Valentina!" I scream. "Valentina!"

I'm losing my struggle with the guards when the boom knocks me off my feet.

There's shouting from all directions. The crowd disperses in terror, tripping over one another. It's bedlam, even before the bloodcurdling screams.

I turn toward the river.

Black smoke obscures everything along the bank. I can't see anything but fiery embers flying through the dense fog.

All the air leaves my lungs.

The boat!

Where is it?

I don't see the boat. *I don't see anyone.*

The boat is gone.

No!

"Antonio! Valentina! No! No!" I screech, breaking free from Alvarez and running toward the river.

THANK YOU FOR READING **LUST**! Find the conclusion of Daniela and Antonio's story in **ENVY HERE**

JOIN me in my FB group, JD'S CLOSET, for all sorts of shenanigans **HERE**

ABOUT THE AUTHOR

After being a confirmed city-girl for most of her life, Eva moved to beautiful Western Massachusetts in 2014. She found herself living in the woods, with no job, no friends (unless you count the turkey, deer, and coyote roaming the backyard), and no children underfoot, wondering what on earth she'd been thinking. But as it turned out, it was the perfect setting to take all those yarns spinning in her head and weave them into sexy stories.

When she's not writing, trying to squeeze information out of her tight-lipped sons, or playing with the two cutest dogs you've ever seen, Eva's creating chapters in her own love story.

Sign-up for my monthly newsletter for special treats and all the Eva news!
Eva's VIP Reader Newsletter

I'd love to hear from you!
eva@evacharles.com

MORE STEAMY ROMANTIC SUSPENSE BY EVA CHARLES

A SINFUL EMPIRE TRILOGY

Greed

Lust

Envy

THE DEVIL'S DUE (SERIES COMPLETE)

Depraved

Delivered

Bound

Decadent

CONTEMPORARY ROMANCE

THE NEW AMERICAN ROYALS

Sheltered Heart

Noble Pursuit

Double Play

Unforgettable

Loyal Subjects